'Where are you taking me?'

Simon stared at her. 'To England, of course… where else?'

'And when do we start?'

'As soon as possible, Miss Lynton, unless our departure is delayed by the need to answer useless questions…'

Emma was not a violent person, but she was strongly tempted to slap his face. Instead, she made a valiant effort to control her temper.

'I'm sure that you will need every moment to work out a plan which might have some hope of success,' she said sweetly. 'It will be difficult for you. I do appreciate that fact…'

She turned away then, but not before she had seen an appreciative grin on the faces of his companions. Clearly it was not often that Simon was given such a set-down.

After living in southern Spain for many years, **Meg Alexander** now lives in East Sussex—although, having been born in Lancashire, she feels that her roots are in the north of England. Meg's career has encompassed a wide variety of roles, from professional cook to assistant director of a conference centre. She has always been a voracious reader, and loves to write. Other loves include history, cats, gardening, cooking and travel. She has a son and two grandchildren.

Recent titles by the same author:

THE MATCHMAKER'S MARRIAGE
THE REBELLIOUS DEBUTANTE

HER GENTLEMAN PROTECTOR

Meg Alexander

MILLS & BOON®

All the characters in this book have no existence outside the imagination of the author, and have no relation whatsoever to anyone bearing the same name or names. They are not even distantly inspired by any individual known or unknown to the author, and all the incidents are pure invention.

First published in Great Britain 2005
Harlequin Mills & Boon Limited,
Eton House, 18-24 Paradise Road, Richmond, Surrey TW9 1SR

© Meg Alexander 2005

ISBN 0 263 84363 7

Set in Times Roman 10½ on 12 pt.
04-0405-81006

Printed and bound in Spain
by Litografía Rosés S.A., Barcelona

HER GENTLEMAN PROTECTOR

Chapter One

1793

Emma shuddered as a series of explosions rocked the port. She clutched at her father's sleeve.

'The guns are so close,' she whispered. 'Will the royalists hold the town?'

'Toulon is lost, my dear.' Frederick Lynton sighed as he closed his book and slipped it into his pocket. The *Meditations of Marcus Aurelius* was proving of little comfort in his present situation. Now his words were intended for Emma's ears alone as he drew her apart from the rest of her family.

'That was not the sound of gunfire,' he said in a low voice. 'The defenders are blowing up the last of the ammunition dumps. They must not fall into enemy hands. You must be brave, my love. We should not distress your mother or the children further…'

Emma nodded. She was tired, hungry, thirsty and very frightened, but she knew that he was right. She slipped an affectionate arm about her mother's shoulders and hugged the older woman close.

'Not long now!' she comforted. 'Then we shall be aboard a British ship and on our way to England…'

Mrs Lynton did not reply, and Emma gave her an anxious look. Her mother was unrecognisable as the calm, efficient person who had run her household with such ease. The fair skin, so characteristic in her family, now had an unbecoming pallor, and beads of sweat were standing upon her upper lip. The long hours of waiting on the quayside had taken their toll, but it was the increasing danger to her family that had sapped her courage.

The threat was all too real. For days the British fleet had ferried thousands of refugees out to the waiting warships, but the numbers did not seem to lessen as crowds streamed from the narrow streets of the old town towards the sea and safety.

The sudden surge proved disastrous. Some of those closest to the harbour wall lost their footing and fell into the water. No attempt was made to save them. The few who could swim managed to regain the jetty. Others tried to climb aboard the already overladen boats, but they were beaten off without mercy.

Emma turned her back upon the scene as she attempted to shield the children from the dreadful sight, but she could not prevent the screams reaching their ears. The twins began to cry, but Julia, her younger sister, was too shocked for tears. Emma glanced at her father in despair, but his attention was elsewhere.

She followed his gaze to see a detachment of Sicilian troops being marched towards a waiting transport. The sight of the ship caused panic in the ranks and a sudden charge towards the gangways. A sharp volley of shots from the British pickets stopped the men in their tracks, forcing them to embark in a more orderly fashion.

Emma turned to her father in surprise. 'These are not wounded men,' she exclaimed. 'They still have their weapons. Could they not defend the town?'

'I'm afraid there is no hope of that, my dear.'

'None whatsoever!' An ironic voice behind them broke into their conversation. 'What hypocrites you are—you British! Do you not claim to rescue women and children first?'

Emma stared at the speaker. He was a well-dressed man, possibly in his late thirties. She was about to fly to the defence of her fellow countrymen when her father laid a restraining hand upon her arm.

'My dear sir, this is distressing for all of us,' he replied without the least trace of irritation. 'Unfortunately, the Allies will have need of every fighting man in the years to come. I expect that Admiral Hood is simply following orders—'

'And we are expendable?' the ironic voice continued.

'I hope not, sir. The evacuation is going well—'

'But will it continue?'

There was no time to reply. Another surge propelled the Lynton family towards the harbour wall. The sight of a waiting boat spurred Frederick into immediate action. Seizing his two young sons, he called to Emma, her sister and his wife to follow him as he hurried down the slippery steps.

The vessel was already crowded, but eager hands took his children from him. The bo'sun frowned as Julia and Mrs Lynton were helped aboard, but he made no demur. Then, as Emma was about to take her place, she was thrust aside.

Three young men had broken from the crowd to jump aboard. The bo'sun took immediate action. 'Stand off!' he shouted to his men. Then he seized an oar and laid about him. The latecomers were beaten off to flounder in the widening gap between the ship's boat and the jetty.

Emma struggled to regain her footing on the steps. She was too close to the water's edge, but she ignored the danger as she waited for the bo'sun to order his men back. Close though he was, he shook his head.

'Durstn't risk it, miss. We're from HMS *Reculver*. Remember the name and take the next boat…' With that he ordered his crew to row away.

Emma gazed after them in horror. How could they leave her? She could see her father pleading with the bo'sun to return, but to no avail. She caught a last glimpse of her mother's anguished face and then the boat was gone.

She took a few deep breaths. Nothing would be gained by giving way to despair. The next vessel to reach the steps would take her off and this time she would be prepared. She fingered the small pistol in her muff. She'd never fired it, but the weapon might be enough to deter anyone else who tried to take her place.

Meanwhile she was too close to the water's edge. The lapping waves were already soaking her half-boots. If the crowd behind her pressed too close, she would be thrown into the sea and she had seen what happened to anyone pleading for help. Panic was rife. From now on it would be the survival of the fittest. Wearily she climbed back to the quay.

Her back was to the harbour, but she sensed at once that something was amiss. As cries of despair and anger filled the air, she saw that the refugees were staring out to sea.

She watched in disbelief as the warships raised anchor and began to disappear beyond the headland.

'Well, miss, was I wrong?' The man who had spoken to her earlier now smiled with fatalistic calm. 'After the blood bath in Marseilles we know exactly what awaits us here... The British have left us to our fate.'

'You are mistaken!' she cried fiercely. 'The ships will return for us.'

'I think not! In any case, it will be too late. Do you not hear it? The Red Terror has begun...' He listened for a moment to the triumphant chanting from the town behind them. 'May I beg you to stand aside, *mademoiselle*?'

Emma stared at him. Perhaps he too was afraid of being forced from the edge of the quay. Obediently she moved aside.

She was completely unprepared for his next action. It was only when she saw the flashing blade that she realised his intention. With a single stroke he severed the main artery in his wrist, apologising wryly as he did so.

Emma screamed as a bright stream of arterial blood gushed towards her, soaking the skirt of her redingote. She sank to her knees beside the fallen body. Then she was seized in a muscular grip.

'Stay on your feet!' a deep voice urged. 'Go down in this mob and they will trample you to death...'

Emma's senses were reeling. The stones of the cobbled quay appeared to be coming up to meet her and the voice of her companion seemed to be coming from a great distance. Speechless with shock, she found that her limbs were no longer under her control. There was a roaring in her ears and she began to sway.

The man beside her held her upright by main force. 'Come away,' he said roughly. 'This is no place for you.'

At last she found her voice. 'Please help him!' She

forced out the words through stiff lips. 'He will bleed to death.'

'It wouldn't be a kindness,' came the blunt reply. 'In any case, he is already beyond our help.'

'You can't be sure of that…' Emma struggled to free herself.

'I know a dying man when I see one. Now, Miss Lynton, will you come away? You can do no good by staying here—'

'No!' For the moment Emma did not notice that he had used her name. 'Let me alone! I must wait here…the ships will come back…'

'They will not do so, I assure you. The British navy is needed elsewhere. Admiral Hood has already exceeded his orders—'

'I don't believe you!' Emma pushed him away. 'The navy will not abandon us—'

'The navy has no choice, *mademoiselle*. However, if I can't persuade you…' He shrugged and turned away.

'Wait!' Emma realised that this man might be her last hope. 'You are English, are you not? How do you know my name?'

'Is it a secret, Miss Lynton?' A pair of hard grey eyes looked into her own.

'No, of course not…' Her head was beginning to clear as she studied her companion more closely. He was not much above the middle height and his clothing was unremarkable. He could have passed through the crowd unnoticed had he taken the trouble to hide an unmistakable air of authority. It was apparent in his carriage, the turn of his head, and his crisp way of speech.

Emma hesitated. If he was right and the ships did not return, she would be quite alone. She was torn between a strong desire to wait for rescue from the sea, which might or might not come, and a strange unwillingness to have this man abandon her.

He was English, he knew her name, and even on first acquaintance she guessed that he would handle himself well in an emergency. She decided to play for time.

'Have we met before?' she asked. 'I do not recall—'

'Good God, woman! This is no time for introductions. You may wish to make the acquaintance of Madame Guillotine, but I do not. My name is Avedon...Simon Avedon...though why it should be of interest to you now I can't imagine.' He turned away again.

Emma looked about her. If she had imagined that matters could not get worse, she was now disabused of that idea. Others beside her companion had realised that the British Fleet would not return. Screams of panic filled the air and men began to fall as shots rang out.

A wave of nausea threatened to overcome her. The man who had slashed his wrists was not the only suicide. Now the crowd began to thin as the refugees fled in all directions. Some made for the surrounding countryside, whilst others made their way back into the town, hoping to find sanctuary in one or other of the churches still standing in Toulon.

Emma came to a quick decision. 'Will you help me, sir?' she pleaded. 'I have money. Perhaps we might hire a boat?'

She heard an ironic laugh. 'Are you mad?' her companion said. 'Anything that will float was snapped up long ago. The merchants were the first to leave, in their own cargo vessels. Look about you, Miss Lynton! Would you trust your person to any of these craft?'

Emma followed his pointing finger. The harbour was a scene of chaos. Much that was unseaworthy had already sunk. Other boats had been manned by those who had never sailed or rowed before. Collisions were frequent, throwing their occupants into the water.

'I don't know what to do,' she said in a low voice.

'May I suggest that you start by keeping the fact that you have money to yourself? These people are desperate. They will do anything to survive, including robbing you.'

'I'm sorry…I did not think…'

'Then it is time that you began to do so. Will you come with me or not? There is no time to lose…'

From his tone she guessed that he was losing patience and, with a last despairing glance at the empty horizon, she turned to follow him.

'Where are you taking me?' she faltered.

'You'll soon see. Keep up, and pray stay close to me. If we are stopped, I beg that you do not speak. I will do the talking…'

Emma gasped. She was unaccustomed to such curt treatment. What an arrogant creature! Her dislike of Simon Avedon grew as she followed him back into the town.

Here too there was chaos, but the crowds were different. The stench of unwashed humanity rose like a miasma from the ragged mob. It was clear that the shops and the warehouses had been looted in search of wine, and drunkards littered the streets.

Others were still on their feet, arms linked with their womenfolk, who were in no better case. They formed a barrier across the street, preventing Emma's passage.

A huge man clutched at her sleeve. 'Here's a pretty one!' he growled. 'Keeping her all to yourself, citizen?'

'Nay, friend, she ain't for the likes of me. I'm taking her to the committee. Like as not she'll be another to lose her head tomorrow…'

Emma forgot the horror of those words in her astonishment. Simon had spoken the patois so fluently that he
might have been taken for a native of those parts. His
air of authority had disappeared, to be replaced by one
of friendly camaraderie.

'Pity! She's a prime bit o' goods!' A filthy paw
reached out to fondle Emma's breast, but somehow Simon Avedon was in the way.

'Do me a favour, citizen?' he pleaded. 'The biggest
warehouse in the town is just down yonder street. There
will be naught left by the time that I get back. Wilt save
me a flask or two?'

It was enough to divert the man's attention. With a
fervent promise that he had no intention of keeping, he
set off for the warehouse, taking his companions with
him.

Simon Avedon scanned the empty street. Then he
ducked into an alleyway, dragging Emma behind him.
He paused at a battered doorway and gave a series of
staccato knocks.

Emma flinched as the door opened, revealing a dark
interior, but Simon drew her forward.

'Upstairs!' he ordered. 'Take the first door to your
right.'

She could only obey him. Her life had taken on a
dreamlike quality. Was it truly Emma Lynton who had
stepped from a quiet and well-ordered life in the France
she loved to life as a hunted creature in the slums of
Toulon?

And this was most certainly a slum. It was little better
than a hovel. She had never entered such a place in her
entire existence, and the men who rose to greet her did
nothing to allay her fears.

For one frightful moment she thought that Simon

Avedon had deceived her. These creatures in their rough garments were indistinguishable from the men who had just accosted her. She shrank back in terror, only to be reassured by a bow of exquisite grace and a smile that seemed to light the room.

'Miss Lynton, is it not?' A tall man came towards her, holding out his hand. 'You must be very tired, *mademoiselle*. Will you not sit by the fire and rest? We can offer you refreshment…'

He snapped his fingers and within seconds a gigantic negro came towards her, bearing a tray of glasses and a bottle of what, she guessed correctly, was a bottle of Madeira wine.

'This is Joseph,' the tall man said. 'How we should live without him I have not the least idea…'

The man grinned his appreciation as he poured the wine, but Emma hesitated. Her thoughts were racing. These men seemed to know her, but how could that be? She ignored the proffered glass.

'Who are you?' she demanded. 'And how do you know my name?'

The man raised an eyebrow and looked at Simon, who shook his head.

'I didn't tell her,' he said brusquely. 'There was no time…'

'What went wrong? Are the others safe?'

'They are, but Miss Lynton here was thrust aside in the scramble for the boats. I could hardly leave her…'

'Of course not!' The speaker turned his attention to Emma once more. 'My dear young lady, you must be wondering at this strange turn of events. Believe me, we have not abducted you.'

Emma did not answer him, and after a swift look at

her face he picked up the glass of wine and offered it to her.

'Do pray drink this,' he begged. 'It will restore you...'

He bowed again and Emma didn't know whether to laugh or cry. She was on the verge of hysteria. Had it not been for his tattered clothing, this man would have been perfectly at home in the most exclusive drawing rooms in England.

She held on to the last remnants of her self-control. 'You have not answered my question, sir. I ask again, who are you?'

He frowned. 'I beg your pardon, ma'am. We had not expected... I mean, we hoped that at this present time you would be safe aboard a British warship...'

'Why should that concern you? I do not know you, sir. My safety can mean nothing to you...'

'On the contrary, Miss Lynton, it is of the highest importance. Allow me to introduce myself. I am Piers Fanshawe. Simon, you have already met, and Joseph too—'

'That tells me nothing.' Emma threw caution to the winds. These men did not appear to mean her harm, but she sensed some mystery in their reticence. She had nothing to lose. They were either for her or against her. Either way, there was little that she could do about it. 'You seem to know me. How can that be?'

She heard an exclamation of impatience from Simon Avedon. 'For God's sake, tell her, Piers. You'll have no peace until you do.'

Piers hesitated, but he realised that his explanation could not be long delayed. Emma was under appalling strain.

Smiling, he threw himself into a rickety chair beside her and took her hand in his. 'You may think us naught but a band of adventurers, but our mission is to rescue those who can be of most use to England in the coming struggle. Sadly, as far as your own family is concerned, we do not seem to have succeeded…'

'My parents have escaped, and the younger children too, no thanks to you—' She heard an exclamation of disgust.

'How did you travel here from Lyon, when there was not a coach to be had? It did not strike you as strange that you were able to hire a vehicle for the journey?' Simon Avedon glared at her.

'We had money,' Emma told him stiffly.

'Ah, yes, the money again…' Simon Avedon sneered at her. Then he turned to Piers. 'Miss Lynton believes that a few gold coins are the answer to the troubles of the world.'

'I'm sure she does not.' Piers gave her a warm smile. 'You must forgive our friend,' he said. 'Simon prefers his plans to proceed without mishap…'

'I see. And I am a mishap?'

'Not in the least, but you see our difficulty. We are responsible for your safety.'

'Not at all. Apparently you have succeeded in helping my father to escape. That was your object, was it not?'

'It was our main object, but we cannot allow you to fall into enemy hands. As a hostage you could be used to bargain with your father, and he is all important to us.'

'Why?' Emma stared at him.

'Think, woman, think!' Simon Avedon strode towards her. 'Was not your father in sympathy with the aims of the Revolution?'

'He was at first,' she admitted with some reluctance. 'It seemed to him that France was ripe for change. The burden of taxation fell upon the poorest, whilst the clergy and the aristocracy were not required to pay. The old order was rotten to the core. He welcomed the storming of the Bastille…' She fell silent.

'And then?' Piers Fanshawe prompted.

Emma looked up at him. 'Everything changed,' she said. 'The fanatics gained control. My father deplored the execution of the King and also of Marie Antoinette, but the leaders still took him into their confidence—'

'They would!' Simon's voice was harsh. 'An Englishman, regarded with awe by his contemporaries? What a trophy for them!'

'He broke away,' Emma said quietly. 'It saddened him to think that a worthy cause had descended into chaos and brutality.'

'But he is still in possession of their plans…' Piers began. Then he paused as the door burst open and a woman entered the room. She was accompanied by a young boy, barely into his teens, and a grizzled elderly man.

The woman threw back her hood and Emma gasped. The tattered clothing could not disguise the fact that this was an exotic creature, as vivid in colouring as a macaw. The blue-black hair fell almost to her waist, framing the perfect oval of her face. Now she hurried towards the men, a smile of triumph evident.

'I found him!' she announced in husky tones. 'Pierre will lead us over the border into Spain, but Marcel must come too. We cannot leave him here—' As she caught sight of Emma her expression changed.

'What's this?' she cried. 'Another of your lame ducks, *monsieur*? I thought I had made it clear that our party is already large enough….'

'Miss Lynton goes with us,' Simon announced in an indifferent tone.

'No, she does not!' The woman glanced away from him. 'I won't have it!'

'Mado, please… Won't you listen—?' Piers was about to attempt an explanation, but Simon stopped him with a look. Then he walked over to the angry girl.

'Madeleine, if that is your decision, we part company here. Before we go, you will allow us to thank you for your help—'

She spun round then, mortified by his cool tones and his refusal to beg her to change her mind. 'I did not say that,' she protested. 'I did not say that I would refuse to help you further—'

'Really? I beg your pardon, but that was my impression—'

'Oh!' she cried. 'You English…you are impossible!'

'Perhaps we should postpone discussion of that subject to another time…' Simon turned to the elderly man. 'Will you guide us, sir?' he asked.

The older man sized him up, and was satisfied with what he saw. 'You will get through, *monsieur*, I make no doubt, and possibly the men here, but the mountain passes are difficult at any time of year. The young lady will find the journey impossible. Consider the alternatives, *monsieur*! There may be a better solution to your problem…'

Simon turned to Piers. '*Is* there an alternative?' he asked.

Piers was silent for some time. 'I can't think of one,' he admitted at last. 'We can't get away by sea, and Italy is out of the question. It is already under threat from the French.'

'Then the land route is the only one…' Simon's face

cleared. He had made his decision. Miss Lynton would accompany them, but whether she survived or not would be up to her.

Meantime, Emma appeared to be dozing by the fire. She had not betrayed the fact that she understood the local patois in which her companions had been speaking. She'd used it since childhood, but if she pretended ignorance she might learn much about this curious band of people...much that they would not tell her if she asked them outright.

She glanced at the lovely Madeleine through lowered lids. Feminine instinct told her that Simon's good opinion was of far more importance to this girl than that of anyone else.

Emma herself was not well versed in the arts of courtship, but it was all too obvious that Madeleine was in love with him. Did he know it? Emma thought not. She doubted if he had ever given way to a human emotion in his life.

She looked at him as he stood in the middle of the room, square and solid and very much in command of himself. Not a handsome man—in fact, some might consider him ugly—but it was not an unpleasing face, and his freckles gave him an oddly boyish look. Then she recalled those hard grey eyes, as cold as pebbles washed by the winter seas. Her first assessment had not been wrong. This was a dangerous man, but she was not afraid of him. She would bide her time, probing for some weakness in his complex character.

There was something chilling about his matter-of-fact approach to any problem, and the way he cut through inessentials to the heart of the matter. She had not heard him raise his voice, nor had she heard him argue. His path through life was clear and straight and she longed to shake him out of his complacency.

Now, as she studied him more closely, she wondered what there was about him which made him so clearly the leader of their little band. Possibly a ruthless quality? A lack of sentiment and a total indifference to the opinions of others? Clearly there was something more. Though Emma was exhausted and still badly shocked, she knew in her heart that this was a man who would always inspire those about him.

Then Mado was standing over her. 'She stinks!' the girl announced. 'Has she been killing pigs?'

Emma glanced down at the skirt of her redingote. The blood from the unfortunate suicide had dried in the heat of the fire, and the fabric was now dark and stiff.

Simon walked over to her. 'Take off your coat!' he ordered. 'It will be washed and dried—'

'Not by me!' Mado announced.

'Did I suggest that you do so, Madeleine?' Simon's tone was curt. 'I am finding your tantrums wearisome. Either make yourself useful and bring some food, or leave us.'

She stared at him for a moment, and Emma detected the sparkle of unshed tears. Then, with a muffled sob, she fled the room.

Simon picked up the offending redingote and handed it to Joseph. 'Will you ask Marie to look to this?' he said. Then he looked down at Emma's feet. 'Your half-boots…are they made of fabric?' he asked.

Startled, Emma nodded.

'Then they too will wash. Take them off, Miss Lynton!'

Emma stiffened. She had a strong objection to being

ordered about, but she knew that he was right. In silence she removed her boots and handed them to him.

He turned away then and beckoned the other men to him, but Piers came over to Emma.

'You must be very tired,' he said gently. 'Will you eat first, or would you like to rest?'

Emma could cope with rudeness and hostility, but kindness was too much to bear. 'I…I could not eat…' she choked out. 'I can't stop thinking about that man who killed himself. I shall remember it all my life.'

'Let us pray that you won't see worse!' Simon had overheard her words. 'And you will eat, Miss Lynton. I won't have you faint from lack of food. We have a perilous journey ahead of us…not an expedition for weaklings!'

Emma felt a surge of indignation. Tired as she was, she struggled to her feet to confront him. Without her boots she reached barely to his shoulder, but she eyed him coldly.

'Don't worry about me, Mr Avedon!' she snapped. 'I shall give you no cause to doubt my courage, or my endurance.' At that moment she felt that she could have walked barefoot across the Pyrenees, if only to wipe the sneer from his face.

'I'm glad to hear it!' His tone made it clear that he did not believe her. Then he turned away to begin his discussion with the others.

Emma was blazing. He and Mado would make a splendid pair,' she thought to herself. They had such charm, such consideration for others. Well, at least they would not spoil another couple.

'One moment, Mr Avedon!' she called him back to her in a tone as icy as his own. 'I should like to know your plans. Where are you taking me?'

Simon stared at her. 'To England, of course...where else?'

'And when do we start?'

'As soon as possible, Miss Lynton, unless our departure is delayed by the need to answer useless questions.'

Emma was not a violent person, but she was strongly tempted to slap his face. Instead, she made a valiant effort to control her temper. 'I'm sure that you will need every moment to work out a plan that might have some hope of success,' she said sweetly. 'It will be difficult for you. I do appreciate that fact...'

She turned away then, but not before she had seen an appreciative grin on the faces of his companions. Clearly, it was not often that Simon was given such a set-down.

Emma sighed. She was a fool to make an enemy of him. He and his companions were her only hope of getting back to England, but the thought of spending weeks and possibly months in the company of this arrogant brute was hard to bear.

For the moment he had forgotten her. Deep in discussion with the others, he broke off his planning only when Mado returned. She was accompanied by an elderly woman and between them they carried a steaming cauldron.

'What's this?' Piers beamed at them as the appetising smell reached his nostrils.

'*Monsieur*, this is our traditional dish...*le pot-au-feu*.'

'My favourite!' Piers announced. 'Miss Lynton, will you take a little of this delicious broth? The meat comes later.'

Mindful of Simon's scathing remarks, Emma resolved to eat, even if every mouthful threatened to choke her.

It was the boy who brought the food to her. 'Don't

mind Mado, miss,' he said in a low voice. 'She's cross because she's frightened…'

'And you?'

'I'm frightened too, but Monsieur Avedon has promised that all will be well.'

'You believe him?'

'Oh, yes!' The child's face was radiant. 'He always does what he says he'll do.'

Emma smiled in spite of herself. The boy's devotion to this difficult man was close to idolatry. She hoped that he would not be subjected to their leader's sarcasm.

To her surprise, that did not happen. Simon lounged, perfectly at ease, with the boy at his feet, as they enjoyed their meal. Then he reached out a hand to tousle the child's dark curls.

'Get some rest!' he ordered. 'We must be away before dawn.' He looked across at Emma. 'I should advise you to do the same, Miss Lynton. Our accommodation here is primitive, but in the weeks to come you may think back upon it as the height of luxury… Marcel will show you to the upper chambers.'

Emma rose to her feet, but he stopped her before she reached the door. 'Pray do not use a room that looks across the square. The rooms at the back will be quieter.'

Surprised though she was by this apparent consideration for her comfort, Emma paid little attention to his words. It was not until much later that she understood their terrible meaning.

Aroused from a deep sleep by the sound of hammering and the trundle of machinery, she stole across the landing in the early hours to look across the square.

There was no mistaking the purpose of the wooden scaffold. The guillotine was already in place, and even at that early hour the ghouls who relished every spilt drop of blood were already taking their places.

Emma swayed. All the horrors of the previous day returned to haunt her, but somehow this was even worse. It was calculated savagery, visited, in many cases, upon the innocent.

A strong arm slid about her waist. 'Did I not warn you not to look across the square?' Simon said roughly.

'I heard the hammering… I did not know…' Emma was trembling, much to her own disgust.

'Perhaps in time you will learn to trust my judgement, Miss Lynton. Now, I suggest that you go back to your room. Put these matters from your mind. This is an ugly sight…the only purpose it can serve is to remind you of your own danger.' He looked down at her as she lay in the shelter of his arm with what she thought was a strange expression. 'Remember, we are to make an early start…' With that last reminder, he was gone.

Chapter Two

The dreadful sight in the square had banished all hope of further sleep from Emma's mind. She could imagine all too well what would happen in the days to come as helpless victims formed a human sacrifice for the angry mob.

What had happened to her beloved France? She loved this country almost as much as England. Knowing her to be spirited and intelligent, her father had treated her as a son, placing no limits upon her education, and encouraging her to discuss the problems of the day with him.

He'd done his best to counter the worst abuses of the *ancien régime*, speaking out boldly in favour of reform—which as a foreigner, might have led to deportation, or worse—but somehow his charm had taken the sting from his remarks and King Louis himself had been pleased to receive him.

When revolution came his name alone was something of a talisman. Here was this eminent man, renowned in his own field of science, who supported the downfall of the hated aristos and was all for the common man. Better still, he was an Englishman, the native of a country with a firm belief in freedom.

He didn't welcome his fame, but it gave him something of a lever in the first years of the revolution. Then his insistence upon moderation had been cast aside as the fanatics came to power. For a time he'd been admitted to their councils, learning much about their plans, but he had made powerful enemies. Invited at last to seek a quieter role, he had returned to his home in Lyon. Only at the last had he decided to seek sanctuary in the country of his birth.

Dear Papa! Emma's eyes filled with tears as she thought of him. He must be out of his mind with worry as to her fate. Then something of his own iron determination crept into her soul. She would survive, even in the face of hardship, danger and the open hostility of at least one of her companions. Mado, she knew, would lose no opportunity to injure her.

Then, in the stillness of the night, she heard the sound of a creaking door. That would be Pierre, going to fetch his mule cart, as they had arranged.

Their departure would not be long delayed. She rose at once and struggled into her half-boots. They had been washed free of the blood and set to dry by the fire. Now the fabric was stiff and uncomfortable. She tried to soften them a little by working them in her hands, but they would never return to their former glory. She pulled them on and began to pace the room, hoping to ease them with use.

Her redingote had not suffered quite so badly, though the ugly stains had not entirely disappeared. The garment was warm, and it was all she had, so she threw it over her arm and went downstairs to join the others.

She sensed at once that something had gone wrong.

'What is it?' she asked quickly.

'Pierre has not returned.' Simon's curt reply was flung in her face like a challenge.

'Should he have brought the cart so soon?'

'We allowed him ten minutes at the most... The stable is close at hand.'

'There could be a dozen reasons why he has been delayed,' she pointed out reasonably.

'Indeed! And all of them a cause for concern.'

Simon's sarcastic tone brought a flush to her cheek, but she turned away and ignored him.

'No brilliant ideas, Miss Lynton? I thought at least that you would have given us the benefit of your advice. Come now, pray let us enjoy your views...'

Emma spun round then and faced him squarely. 'If you will have it, sir, I have been wondering why you dislike my sex so much?'

For once she had him at a disadvantage.

'I...? I dislike women...?' He sounded astonished.

She stared him down, blue eyes locked with grey. 'Do you deny it, sir? You lose no opportunity to vent your spleen upon us.'

'Nonsense! You yourself have given me the best of reasons for any man to be wary...'

'I should like to hear it.'

'Well, then, you are touchy, argumentative and, given the least excuse, I make no doubt that you will burst into tears...'

'Don't count upon it!' she informed him grimly. 'I find you insulting, sir.'

'Your opinion is unlikely to keep me awake at night,' he said in an indifferent tone. 'We have other matters to consider.'

He called the others to him. Emma would have broken

in upon their counsels, but she had no wish to give away the fact that she understood the local dialect. She listened carefully as Simon outlined his plans.

'If Pierre does not return, I believe that we must leave in daylight, probably within the next hour or so. It may be no bad thing. We shall be less conspicuous without the mule cart, and the mob will be fully occupied to-day…' His face was grim.

Mado objected at once. 'We need Pierre,' she insisted. 'He knows the border country well. Without him it will be much more difficult for us to cross into Spain. Besides, the mule cart will be useful…' She cast a scornful look at Emma. 'I doubt if our fine lady here is much accustomed to walking.'

Simon ignored the gibe, but he looked thoughtful. 'You have a point,' he admitted. 'But the mule and the cart could prove an irresistible temptation to some of our revolutionary friends. It might draw unwelcome attention to our party, especially if we had kept to our original plan of stealing away in the hours of darkness.'

Emma guessed that he was attempting to keep up the spirits of his companions in their disappointment.

Mado would not be convinced. 'I still believe that we should wait,' she cried. 'An hour or two can make no difference. In any case, we are safe within these walls.'

'But for how long, my dear?' Always the peacemaker, Piers determined to use all his powers of persuasion to avoid a confrontation between his friends. 'To date we have escaped suspicion, but how long will that last?'

Mado cast a triumphant look at Emma. 'Not long, I fancy, with Miss Lynton here. Can you pretend that she is still your prisoner if you are taking her out of the town and away from the tribunal?'

Simon stared at her. Then he shifted his gaze to

Emma. 'You are right,' he said thoughtfully. 'These clothes must go. Mado, will you find her some coarser garb?'

'With pleasure!' The girl made as if to leave the room, but Simon stopped her.

'None of your tricks, my beauty! I shall examine the clothing. I have no wish to find it crawling with lice.'

Mado tossed her head and flounced out.

It was Piers who broke the silence. 'You are determined to leave in daylight?' he asked.

'I think we must go today. The back streets will be deserted since the mob will be baying for their entertainment in the main square. How long will that last? When the supply of victims runs low they will search for others. This is an opportunity not only to kill the aristos, but to settle old scores. A denunciation will serve. They won't be too nice in searching for proof of guilt or innocence.'

Piers nodded, but his face was sad. Then, before he could speak, the door opened and Pierre slipped into the room. He was a sorry sight, with his bloodied nose and a swollen eye.

'What happened?' Simon asked quickly.

'I lost the mule and cart, *monsieur*. It was seized in the name of the revolution.' He spat with disgust. 'It was nothing of the sort. Young Gavin saw a way of adding to his loot, and his friends were with him.' Pierre poured himself a glass of brandy and swallowed it at a gulp.

'It is no matter,' Simon told him. 'We have changed our plans. We shall do well enough without the cart. But we plan to leave in daylight.'

'*Monsieur…?*' Pierre was startled.

'Listen!' The kitchen was at the back of the house, but a rising tide of sound reached every ear.

Emma did not understand at first. The tumult was a curious mixture of excitement and exultation.

Then, quite suddenly, it stopped. There was a silence, heavy with expectation, and then an ugly thud. The shrieks of glee that followed were those of a mob insane with blood-lust.

'They have started!' Simon said quietly. 'It will go on…'

Emma understood him then. What she had just heard was the sound of an execution. Madame Guillotine would claim many more victims before the day was out. The colour left her cheeks and she swayed in her chair.

It was Piers who reached her first. 'Put your head between your knees,' he urged. 'The faintness will soon pass. Miss Lynton, I am so sorry…'

With an enormous effort Emma straightened. 'I don't mean to be so foolish, sir. Do pray forgive me! It is just that it is so difficult to understand how ordinary people can be so cruel. They are not all members of the Committee, are they?'

'No, *mademoiselle*, they are not. Some are the *sans-culottes*, those who have suffered deprivation all their lives, under the old regime, but there are others who should know better.'

Piers poured her a glass of brandy and held it to her lips.

Emma shook her head. 'I don't want it,' she protested. 'It tastes horrible.'

'Nevertheless, you will drink it.' Simon was standing over her. 'Best understand me now, Miss Lynton. I won't put up with missish ways. What is happening in the square is ugly, but we have no power to change it.

You will be lucky if you don't see worse before our journey ends.'

Emma seized the glass and swallowed the fiery liquid at a gulp. 'Best understand me also, Mr Avedon,' she snapped. 'You will treat me with respect. Perhaps you won't put up with missish ways. I will not put up with sneers and insults. If you can't accept my terms, I will find my own way back to England.'

She had expected taunts and further insults, but her words had silenced him. There was a curious little smile at the corners of his lips as he turned away from her.

It was Piers again who restored some semblance of peace to the little group.

'Come now!' he coaxed. 'Since we are to share each other's company, had we not better learn to agree? You know the old saying, ''if we do not hang together, we shall most certainly hang separately''.' He was smiling as he spoke, and suddenly Emma decided that she had found a friend.

'You are very good,' she said shyly. 'In the ordinary way I am not quite such a crosspatch.'

'You have been under a fearful strain,' he comforted. 'Inaction is the hardest thing to bear. Once we leave Toulon and strike out for Spain, you will feel much better, as shall we all.'

Suddenly Emma longed for comfort. 'Shall…shall we get through?' she whispered.

Piers laughed aloud. 'Can you doubt it?' he teased. 'Simon will have nothing less.'

Emma returned his smile. 'You think highly of him, don't you?' she said slowly.

'As you will come to do in time, Miss Lynton.'

'I doubt it!' she told him drily. 'Sadly, Mr Avedon is not the type of person I admire. Of course, I am grateful to him for coming to my rescue, but it was not entirely altruistic, was it? He had an ulterior motive. I mean he had no wish to see me used as a hostage for my father's good behaviour.'

'That is true, but—'

'No, pray don't try to gammon me. Had that not been the case, Mr Avedon would have left me on the quay-side, to take my chance with the others.'

'You are too hard on him. Simon can't save everyone, much as he would like to do so.'

'Would he? I have the impression that most of the human race is not of much interest to him unless he can find a use for their services.'

'You do him an injustice.'

'Do I? Tell me, sir, is Mr Avedon married?'

'No, why do you ask?'

'I wished to confirm my first impression of him. I should have been surprised indeed to learn that he had a wife.'

Piers shook his head at her. 'Don't be too hard on him, Miss Lynton. You think him a man of stone, I think, but he is not. He may yet surprise you.'

Emma was tempted to announce that she would not await that moment with bated breath, but clearly Piers was devoted to his friend. She contented herself with nodding slowly. Piers meant well, and clearly he and Simon Avedon understood each other. Together they had faced hardship and danger. Under those circumstances she could imagine that Simon had borne himself well. What Simon lacked was any understanding of the human heart.

Well, she would confound his opinion of her sex. If it choked her she would not complain, no matter what the hardships. Simon Avedon would find that he had met his match. Emma was not her father's daughter for nothing.

Now she looked up as Mado returned. The girl was carrying a bundle of clothing, which she threw at Emma's feet.

'Pick it up!' Simon ordered. 'Did I not tell you, Mado, that I wished to inspect what you might bring?'

Mado coloured, but did not reply. Instead, she snatched up the garments and thrust them into his hands.

'At least they are clean,' he announced. 'Miss Lynton, we have not much time. May I beg you to change without delay?'

In silence Emma took the garments from him and left the room. She was trembling violently. Childishly, she longed to put her fingers in her ears to shut out the frightful sounds still coming from the square. All she longed for now was to get away from these scenes of horror and brutality. Nothing could be worse than this, no matter what Simon had predicted.

With shaking fingers she unbuttoned her fine wool morning dress and stepped into a coarsely woven skirt. The blouse was of the same rough material and it scratched her skin, but she ignored the discomfort. Then she bundled up her discarded clothing. It would go with her. If, by some miracle, they succeeded in reaching England she had no intention of appearing before her family and friends in her present guise.

Then, against all reason, the humour of the situation struck her. She must be mad to be worrying about such trivia. What could it matter how she looked? The question might never arise if their plans went awry and she was captured.

The last item in the bundle was a dark red cloak. She threw it about her shoulders and went to join the others.

Simon inspected her coolly. 'That's better!' he said at last. 'Now, Miss Lynton, if we are challenged I beg that you will not speak. That would give the game away at once.'

'What about her hair?' Mado sneered. 'The peasant women hereabouts do not sport curls and chignons.'

Emma responded at once. 'You are right!' she answered swiftly. 'Will you cut it for me, Mado?'

Gleefully, Mado advanced upon her, brandishing a pair of scissors, but Piers took them out of her hand.

'Let me!' he said gently. 'You will not mind, Miss Lynton?'

'Not in the least!' Secretly Emma was relieved to be spared Mado's attentions. She had known all too well that the girl would shave her head if possible. The only defence against Mado would be to give her enough rope to hang herself. If her enmity became too apparent it would work in Emma's favour.

She submitted meekly as Piers removed her chignon, cutting away the blonde hair which, when released, reached almost to her waist. The curls that framed her face went too and Emma sighed. She must look a freak. Then Piers ran a hand over her head. 'There!' he said. 'Now you are in the height of fashion, *mademoiselle*. These new short cuts are all the rage.'

Emma returned his smile. 'That is all very well,' she said, 'but shall I pass muster as a revolutionary?'

Piers hesitated. 'I think so, Miss Lynton, but will you trust me? We need to add some dust and possibly, if I wet your hair, it would stand on end…'

'I think you do not need to wet it,' Emma said quietly. 'It will stand on end of its own accord.' She bent her head. The frightful sounds from the square had continued.

Mado inspected her closely. Then she sniffed and turned away.

'Aren't you satisfied, my dear?' Piers asked kindly. 'You'll admit to the change in Miss Lynton's appearance?'

'Look at her boots!' Mado's smile was malicious. 'When did you see a peasant girl in such as those?'

This time Emma lost her temper, but she hid her annoyance well. She smiled up at the sulky girl.

'Did you find others to fit me?' she asked. 'Do pray give them to me. I will put them on at once.'

'There was nothing to be had,' Mado admitted.

'Well, then, I cannot walk barefoot as far as Spain. These boots will have to serve.'

The logic of this statement was irrefutable and Mado knew it. 'Be it on your own head,' she said indifferently as she turned away.

'No doubt it will be...' Emma smiled again.

It was then that Simon intervened. 'I'll have an end to this squabbling,' he announced. 'God help us! Must we fight among ourselves? You are behaving like a couple of alley cats...the pair of you.' He bent his gaze on Emma. 'Do you see now, Miss Lynton, why I have certain reservations about your sex?'

'As I have about your own, Mr Avedon! They have not shone in the best of lights recently.'

She heard a short laugh. 'Take a look in the square if you will! The spectators at today's entertainment are almost evenly divided between the sexes. Indeed, I understand that the women fight for the places closest to the guillotine.'

It was enough to silence her. She paled and bent her head.

A small hand slipped into her own. 'He doesn't mean

to be unkind,' Marcel whispered. 'Really, he is very good.'

Emma gulped and nodded, but her dislike of Simon Avedon was increasing by the minute. How dared he humiliate her with such a dressing-down, especially as Mado never lost an opportunity to taunt her?

Then common sense returned. What were a few insults when she stood in danger of losing her life? The important thing was to get back safely to England. She must remember always that that was her objective. Any unpleasantness along the way must and would be tolerated.

She looked down at Marcel. 'Do you suppose that we are almost ready to leave?' she asked.

'Oh, yes! Joseph is packing up the food. We are to take cheeses and bread and cold fowls, but not too much. Simon says that we must not draw attention to ourselves…sacks of provisions might be stolen from us.'

'They would also be very heavy to carry,' Emma admitted with a smile.

'Yes, they would, but Joseph is making small packages, so that we can share them between us and hide them in our clothing.'

Emma looked down at the eager little face and felt a pang of pity for the child.

'How do you come to be here?' she asked. 'Do you intend to go to England too?'

'Oh, yes!' he told her proudly. 'Simon has promised. I want to see the Tower of London.'

'But where have you come from?' she persisted.

'From Marseilles… We came on a boat. Mado said that it wasn't safe to stay.'

'Do you know Mado well?'

'Pretty well...' The child laughed. 'Mado is my sister.'

'And Pierre?'

'Pierre is one of our uncles. That was why we came here. We had nowhere else to go.'

Emma did not dare to question him about his parents. There must be some reason why these two young people had been thrown upon their own resources. She suspected some tragedy and her fears were confirmed when Marcel left her and Piers took his place.

'Marcel seems to have found a friend in you,' he observed.

'He is a charming child,' she agreed. 'Why are he and Mado on their own?'

'Their parents were murdered in Marseilles.'

'But why? They are not aristocrats, I imagine.'

'No, you are right...' Piers was lost in thought for several minutes. 'Miss Lynton, your father was quite right in losing faith in the revolution. Noble ideals have given way to appalling excuses. Now the main object of denunciation seems to be to settle old scores. Marcel's parents were not wealthy, but they made a comfortable living as the owners of one or two small vessels fishing off Marseilles. Their success aroused some envy. It was enough.'

'You mean...you mean that they were sent to the guillotine?'

'I do. They were charged as Royalist sympathisers... The whole thing was a farce and the Tribunal knew it. It made no difference.'

'I did not know,' Emma said quietly. 'Now I see why Mado is so bitter.'

'It has scarred her,' Piers agreed. 'Be patient with her,

Miss Lynton. She feels great responsibility for her brother, and she will stop at nothing to keep him safe.'

'She is to be admired for that.' Emma looked up as Simon called the assembled party to him.

'We'll split up,' he announced. 'Small groups will be less conspicuous on the streets. Remember, we are striking out towards the west. Miss Lynton, you and Marcel will come with me. Mado will go with Joseph and Piers, whilst Pierre will lead the way.'

Emma saw the mutinous look on Mado's face, but after Simon's sharp set-down she did not dare to argue further, merely voicing a wish to stay with her brother.

'No!' Simon's voice was firm. 'I won't have you two ladies together. Trouble will follow you as surely as night follows day.'

'Then let Miss Lynton go with Piers,' Mado pleaded.

'No, Miss Lynton goes with me.'

'It cannot matter, surely,' Emma said quietly. 'We are all heading in the same direction. Why not let Marcel and Mado be together?'

Simon confronted her then. 'You will please to obey orders, Miss Lynton. If you wish to take charge of this expedition, please do so. I cannot promise to join you, but I shall wish you well in your attempt to reach the Spanish border.'

Emma glared at him. 'You will not even consider a suggestion,' she accused.

'Not at the moment,' he agreed. 'We have no time to lose.'

Pig-headed, arrogant brute! Emma could have struck him. She would have preferred to make the journey in the pleasant company of Piers and Joseph, and she suspected that Simon knew it. Why did he feel obliged to go against her wishes at every turn? This journey was about to become a battle of wills, but she would not give way. Once back in England she would make him pay for every insult. He seemed to take a positive pleasure in irritating her. It did not occur to her to wonder why.

Now she listened as he outlined his plans. 'We will leave by the front door,' he announced. 'Stick to the fringes of the crowd, but make your way towards the west of the town. And, Miss Lynton, pray do not glance towards the guillotine.'

Mado gave him a bitter smile. 'May I look?' she asked.

'Don't be a fool!' he told her roughly. 'Look to your own safety, Mado, and spare me your missish ways.'

'Missish ways?' Emma could contain her anger no longer. 'Look to yourself, Mr Avedon! It may be that we shall all surprise you…'

He bowed, but it was not as a compliment. 'I shall await that moment with bated breath,' he said. 'Now, Piers, will you lead your party out? You know our rendezvous, further along the coast. On foot, we should reach it before dusk.'

He opened the door and motioned to the others to leave.

Emma glanced at Marcel. The child looked pale and anxious as he bade farewell to his sister. The baying from the square sounded as if it issued from the throats of wild animals rather than from human beings. It was almost like a physical blow.

Simon closed the door upon the sounds. Then he turned, his hand resting lightly upon the child's shoulder.

'Trust me?' he asked.

Marcel swallowed and nodded.

'Good! From now on we must rely upon each other.

I'll be glad of your help if we are to take good care of Miss Lynton. Will you give me your hand on it?'

There was no trace of patronage or condescension in his tone. He spoke to Marcel as if he were addressing an adult and the child seemed to change before Emma's eyes. His head went up and his shoulders straightened as he took the proffered hand.

'I won't let you down,' he promised. His admiration for Simon was clear to see.

'I never doubted you.' Simon grinned at him and again Emma was astonished. That smile seemed to light the room. Perhaps there was some trace of humanity in this unpleasant creature after all.

She was given no time to ponder on the matter. Simon reached for the door again, but then his eye fell upon Emma's untidy bundle. His face darkened.

'What have you there, Miss Lynton?' he snapped.

'My own clothing, of course.'

'And doubtless your bonnet too?' he jeered. 'You will leave that useless baggage here—'

'No, I will not. If you suppose that I shall arrive in England looking like a scarecrow, you are mistaken.'

Out of all patience with her he swung round then and took her by the shoulders, shaking her none too gently.

'Have you no sense at all?' he snarled. 'Will you risk all our lives for the sake of your precious finery? Suppose you are stopped and asked to account for it?'

Emma glared back at him. 'I could have stolen it,' she said defiantly. 'After all, I am wearing my boots—'

'Which you will doubtless explain away in those cultured tones? I doubt if anyone will believe that you have come to some arrangement with the executioner.'

'I could have found the things in some deserted house.'

'How fortunate then that they have proved to be a perfect fit.'

Marcel tugged at his sleeve. '*Monsieur*, we have found things, you know—Mado did not buy Miss Lynton's skirt and cloak.'

Simon was losing patience, but he did not contradict the boy. 'Very well,' he said. 'Miss Lynton, I withdraw my objections, but you will carry that bundle yourself. I doubt if you will cling to it for longer than an hour. Every extra ounce will feel more like a ton before the day is out.'

'I could help,' Marcel said quickly.

'You will do so at the risk of my extreme displeasure.' Simon's voice was stern. '*Mademoiselle* is stubborn, but she must learn that any action has consequences. Now, shall we go?'

He opened the door again, ignoring the wall of sound that reached their ears. 'To your left,' he ordered. 'Skirt the fringes of the crowd, but do not glance towards the scaffold.'

His advice was unnecessary. Emma bent her head and began to walk towards the far corner of the square.

She could blot out the sight, but not the sounds, of the executions. Again and again she heard the roar of glee as another victim was led up to be sacrificed.

Her heart thumped so wildly that she imagined that it would be heard by those about her as a dreadful silence fell, to be followed by that sickening thud, and then those appalling cries of exultation as the severed heads were held up to the crowd.

She had almost gained the far corner of the square when a young man turned his head and glanced at her.

'Can't you see?' he asked. 'Come on, I'll make a place for you.' He reached out a hand to her, but suddenly she was in Simon's arms and he was nuzzling her neck.

He winked at the young man. 'We've other things on our minds.' He said, 'You understand…?'

The man replied with a cheerful obscenity. 'It can have that effect, citizen,' he agreed. 'I've noticed it myself.'

Emma was blushing furiously, but Simon did not release her until they had turned out of the square and were far from sight. Then she pulled away from him.

'How could you?' she cried furiously. 'He must have thought… I mean…you gave him the impression that we were lovers.'

'That was my intention,' he agreed. 'Of course, Miss Lynton, if you would prefer to have the young man find you a seat beside the scaffold, do please return to him.'

'Oh!' she cried. 'You are always so clever, aren't you?'

'I try not to behave like a greater fool than nature intended…' His contemptuous tone left her in no doubt that he would not claim the same for her.

Emma flushed at the implied criticism, but she did not deign to answer him. Instead she bent her head and followed him into the warren of streets that led to the outskirts of the town. Then she flinched as an icy gust of wind tore at her inadequate clothing. She might have been naked for all the protection it afforded her. Even so, she would have had her tongue torn out by the roots before she complained.

The worst of it was that she knew he was right. It had been folly indeed to insist on bringing a heavy bundle of clothing. She might not have insisted had he not been so…so obnoxious. She had been determined that he would not issue orders to her, no matter how the others obeyed him.

She tucked the bundle more firmly under her arm. She might never wear the things again, but she would not part with it at his behest.

The decision was taken from her. Intent upon following in his footsteps, she had not noticed that she was being watched. A sudden eruption from a narrow alley brought her face to face with a noisy crowd. Then the bundle was snatched from her grasp and cast upon the ground, spilling out its contents. Eager fingers examined the fine clothing.

'Keeping the spoils to yourself, citizeness?' A thick-set man barred her way, his elbows akimbo.

Emma did not answer him. Simon had warned her not to speak.

Then one of the women lifted her skirt. 'Look at her boots!' she cried. 'She's an aristo, trying to escape...'

Emma faced her squarely. Then, in language that would not have disgraced a sailor, she lapsed into the local patois, casting doubts upon the parentage of her accusers. It was some time before she paused for breath, but in the meantime the crowd had backed away.

'Fiery little wench, ain't she?' The burly man was laughing. 'Come on, comrades, leave her with her prizes. We are missing today's sport.' With an ironic salute he led his friends in the direction of the square.

Emma found that she was trembling as she gathered up her few possessions. She would get rid of them at the earliest possible moment. It galled her to admit it, but Simon had not lied when he'd said that they would only draw attention. Now she never wanted to see them again.

She did not dare to glance at him, expecting a well-deserved tirade about her folly. Now she looked about her for some hiding place. It was Marcel who sensed her intention. He held out his hand in silence and took the bundle from her. Then, with a glance to assure himself of her approval, he thrust it deep within a pile of debris.

'You can buy more when we get to England,' he comforted.

Simon had not spoken, but when she looked at him she saw that he was regarding her with astonishment.

'Well?' she challenged.

'Well indeed, Miss Lynton! I had not supposed you so conversant with the local dialect. It was something of a revelation! You have been deceiving us!'

Emma shrugged. 'I have lived in France since childhood.'

'You have made good use of your time here. I am beginning to suspect that we have underestimated you. It was a clever move…to pretend that you did not understand when we spoke in the native tongue. In future, we shall be more careful.'

Chapter Three

'Had we not best get on?' Emma replied coolly. She was enjoying her triumph. At last she had succeeded in proving to this overbearing creature that she was not altogether helpless. She and she alone had succeeded in outwitting her accusers.

Simon sensed her mood at once. 'Pray do not get too carried away, *mademoiselle*. You were lucky in this instance, but your luck may not last. Not everyone is so easily deterred—'

'You've made your point,' she snapped.

'So you admit that I was right?'

'Only in this instance.' Emma drew her hood more closely about her head and proceeded to ignore him. She would need all her strength for the journey ahead. She could not afford to waste her energy in fighting with Simon Avedon.

He seemed content with her decision. In the following hours he did not speak to her except to urge her to keep up with his long stride.

By the end of that day Emma was exhausted, but she would have died rather than admit it. It was Marcel who brought them to a halt. He was gasping for breath and clutching his side.

'Just a stitch!' he pleaded. 'Give me a moment and I shall be right again.'

Emma looked at Simon. 'Have we far to go now?' she asked anxiously.

'A half-hour only, *mademoiselle*.' For a brief moment Simon rested his hand on Marcel's dark curls. 'Can you make it?' he asked gently.

The child struggled to his feet. 'Lead on!' he cried. 'I won't delay you.'

Emma held out her hand to him. 'I am so tired,' she whispered. 'Perhaps we should help each other.'

It was enough to bring a smile to Marcel's face. He took her hand, began to march ahead, but clearly it was only with a tremendous effort.

Emma resolved to speak to Simon as soon as they reached their destination. There was no way this half-starved boy could cover the long miles into Spain on foot.

In the event he had decided the matter for himself. He waited until they reached the isolated farmhouse that was their destination for the night. The others were waiting for them, elated to have escaped from Toulon without detection, but Simon took them aside.

'Our progress is too slow and much too difficult,' he said quietly. 'We must have transport of one kind or another. Any hope of horses here, or even a mule cart?'

'I doubt it! Pierre's brother here has done his best for us, but he has so little…a pig…some hens… He cannot afford to keep a horse, or even a mule. Now he risks what possessions he has in order to help us.'

Simon summoned the man to him. 'You know the dangers of offering shelter to our party?' he asked.

'I do, *monsieur*, but I have lived here all my life. No one has the right to tell me who may come to visit me.'

'Good man!' Simon said warmly. 'We shall try not to be a trouble to you.'

'No trouble, sir. My good woman will feed you, but you must bed down in the barn—'

'That will suit us very well,' Emma said swiftly. 'We shall be always in your debt, *monsieur*.'

Simon studied the astonished faces of his companions. 'Oh, yes!' he said. 'Miss Lynton is not all she seems. She understands the local dialect perfectly. How fortunate that we found out so soon.'

Piers laughed when he had recovered from his surprise. 'Confess it, Simon! Would you not have done the same yourself?'

'I'll admit it! Still, it came as something of a surprise to discover that the lady was so devious.'

Emma glared at him. 'I fight fire with fire,' she said. 'I don't trust you, Mr Avedon. You have only yourself to blame.'

It was perhaps fortunate that at this point the farmer's wife called them to their supper. The tantalising smell of the traditional *pot-au-feu* was rising from the enormous cauldron suspended over the fire. Now she lifted out the meat and began to serve the broth, redolent with onions, herbs and winter vegetables. It was accompanied by round loaves of crusty bread.

Emma found that she was starving. She set to with a will and brought a smile to the housewife's face when she accepted a second helping.

Piers raised a glass of wine in salute. 'Well done, Miss

Lynton! It is a pleasure to see a young lady with such a hearty appetite.'

Emma blushed a little. Suddenly it occurred to her that perhaps she was taking advantage of these good people. The food that they were offering so readily might be all they had.

She turned to Piers. 'I have some money with me,' she said in a low voice. 'Shall I cause offence if I offer to pay?'

Piers smiled down at her. 'I think you know these farmers better than that,' he teased. 'No sensible man will ever refuse an offer of payment as long as it is done with grace.'

Emma touched the money-belt about her waist. Then, satisfied, she allowed the farmer's wife to help her to a generous portion of the tender meat. She would ensure that these good people did not lose by offering their hospitality.

Then, warmed by the food and wine, she allowed herself to be led to the adjacent barn. She had never been so tired in her life. Now all she longed for was to be allowed to sleep. Wearily, she climbed the ladder to the hayloft, wrapped her cloak about herself, and sank into oblivion.

It was the clatter of hooves in the stable-yard that aroused her on the following day. With every sense alert, she peered down from her vantage point in time to see a stripling fling himself from his horse and hurry into the farmhouse.

Something was amiss! She could not mistake the urgency. Hastily, she descended the ladder and followed him.

Grave faces greeted her.

'What is it?' she asked quickly.

It was Simon who answered her.

'The hunt is up, Miss Lynton. I should have known that there were spies upon the quayside in Toulon. Your father was known to have made his escape…but you were not so fortunate.'

'I see! And this young man…?' Emma looked at the mudstained rider.

'Has brought us news, Miss Lynton. Your description has been circulated…you are now a target with a price upon your head.'

Emma thought quickly. 'So now I am a danger to you all?' She turned to Piers. 'Would it be best if I were to surrender to the authorities?'

'Miss Lynton, you can't mean it!' Piers was shocked.

'Indeed I do! If I am as important as they seem to believe, they will not harm me. I shall be held as surety for my father's good behaviour—'

'Dear me! What an innocent it is! Miss Lynton, your charitable view of the human race can only do you credit, but I think you can have no idea of the type of men you are facing…' Simon turned to their unwelcome messenger. 'Who is leading the hunt for Miss Lynton? Do you know his name?'

'Chavasse…they call him Robert Chavasse…'

Emma smiled with relief. 'Then it is not so serious after all. Monsieur Chavasse is well known to me. He is a close friend of my father. He must have heard that I did not escape with my family. He would be concerned for my safety…'

There was a long silence as Emma's eyes searched the faces of those about her. 'Oh!' she cried impatiently. 'You see treachery behind every bush. Is it so strange that a family friend should wish to help me?'

Piers took her hand and led her to a seat. 'The matter is not so simple, Miss Lynton. Yves, will you explain?'

The young man coloured. Clearly, he was unused to being the centre of attention, but he spoke out to tell his story once again.

'You hadn't been gone above a half-hour, *mademoiselle*, before the house in Toulon was surrounded by French troops. I'd come to see Mado...' He glanced shyly at the girl, but she tossed her head and turned away.

The young man's flush deepened, but he cleared his throat and continued. 'I was worried. I thought that Mado might be in trouble, so I waited to see what happened. Then this Chavasse arrived. He wasn't on no errand of mercy, *mademoiselle*. He cursed fit to burn your ears off when he found that house was empty. Then he began his questioning...' His face grew pale. 'There's one man as won't walk again after such a beating.'

Simon turned to Emma. 'You say that Chavasse knew your father well!'

'Of course. He dined with us each month, at least until he and father began to differ about what Monsieur Chavasse called ''necessary measures''.'

'So he knows you too, and could recognise you at a glance?'

Emma looked at him uncertainly, but she nodded. It was impossible to believe that Robert Chavasse could wish her harm.

Clearly, Simon did not share that belief. 'Then he is the man who has been sent to capture you—'

Emma flared up. 'Even if he did so, he would not injure me. At worst he could only beg me to persuade my father to return to France.' She looked up into a pair of hard grey eyes as stony as the sea-washed pebbles on the beach.

'You believe that?' Simon looked at her in disbelief. 'Unless I'm much mistaken, your precious Chavasse is one of the men behind this present reign of terror. You surprise me, Miss Lynton. I had not thought that the blood bath now taking place was much to your taste...'

Emma shuddered. 'You know that it isn't, but I can't believe that Robert is involved.'

'He and his friends would snuff out your life without a second thought,' Simon assured her. 'Refuse to do their bidding and you would join the others on the scaffold.'

He did not trouble to argue with her further. He turned to Yves again. 'How did you find us?' he asked.

'Mado had told me of this place. We came here once when she was living in Marseilles...' The young man blushed again.

Emma felt for him. His innermost secrets were being exposed to view and his heart laid bare. From the way he looked at Mado, she guessed that the girl was his whole world, yet she had not offered him a civil word.

Simon continued with his questioning. 'You took a chance in coming here,' he said bluntly. 'Were you followed?'

'Of course not!' The young man's tone was indignant. 'Would I put Mado...I mean...all of you in danger?'

'Not willingly, I imagine.' Simon unbent a little and smiled. 'This questioning you mentioned...? Did Chavasse learn anything from his victims?'

Yves frowned in an intense effort of concentration. 'There was a woman...' he admitted. 'She'd seen a small fair girl with fancy boots walking with a boy and an older man, but the girl had cursed her like a fishwife, so she couldn't have been *mademoiselle* here.'

Simon laughed aloud and Emma was startled. She had not thought him capable of such unrestrained amusement.

'Miss Lynton has surprised us all,' he said smoothly. 'Pray do not let that prim exterior fool you, Yves. The lady has hidden depths.'

His remarks were not meant as a compliment and Emma knew it. Simon would not soon forgive her for her small deception. The knowledge pleased her. She had no need of his forgiveness. He would have done the same in similar circumstances. Why then should he take it amiss that she could think for herself?

Her lip curled in scorn. He thought himself invincible. Women, to him, were stupid creatures. Decorative, perhaps, although she doubted if that thought had crossed his mind. To Simon Avedon their place was in the home, providing comfort for that most superior of creatures, a man.

Well, he would learn that not all women were the same. She began to smile. Before they reached England she would make him pay for every insult he had offered her.

'Something amuses you, Miss Lynton?' Simon did not wait for her reply. 'You have a curious sense of humour, *mademoiselle*. Personally, I see nothing in the least entertaining at the thought of losing my head—'

'On the guillotine, *monsieur*? I can think of no other occasion on which you would be in danger of losing it.'

Her remark surprised him. For once he was at a loss, and the smiles on the faces of his companions did nothing to reassure him.

'Enough!' he said brusquely. 'You may wish to indulge in idle chatter, but I do not. We have plans to make…' He looked at Yves. 'Chavasse has sent out search parties?' he enquired.

'Indeed *monsieur*. Once the young lady's clothing was discovered, he sent men in all directions, but some of them towards Marseilles.'

Simon thought for a moment. 'The man is no fool,' he said slowly. 'He would know that we cannot escape by sea…nor would we be likely to travel into Italy. From now on we must leave no clues.' He glanced at Emma. 'Will you disagree with that, Miss Lynton?'

It was a clear reference to her determination to take her own clothing with her. In doing so, she had placed them all in danger.

'I was wrong,' she said quickly. 'I won't make the same mistake again.'

'Another such and you may not get the opportunity.' Mado was eyeing her with unconcealed dislike. 'You were warned. Don't you ever listen?'

'As much as you do, I suspect…' Emma's anger flared. She had been in the wrong, but she had admitted it. Was she now to be pilloried by this jealous girl?

Piers smiled down at her. 'We are none of us perfect,' he said gently. 'But from now on we must trust each other. Mado, do we have your word on that?'

Her answer was a sullen nod. Then Simon called everyone to attention.

'We have no choice but to go through Marseilles in our journey to the Spanish border. What are your thoughts on that?'

'Dangerous!' Piers told him without hesitation. 'Would it not be best to strike out into the hills and thus avoid the town by travelling to the north?'

'Possibly, but our party will be less conspicuous in the crowded city. If we stick to the outskirts…'

Emma became aware that Marcel was trembling. He had seated himself beside her with a friendly smile, but now his mood had changed.

'What is it?' she asked quickly.

'I can't…I can't go back to Marseilles. I'd rather they killed me here.'

'No one is going to kill you.' Emma took his hand in hers. 'Come, now, have you not told me how much you admire Monsieur Avedon? Is he likely to allow us to be killed?'

The boy looked up at her and his eyes were filled with tears. 'You don't know…' he whispered. 'You have not seen…'

'I can imagine,' Emma assured him. 'But we cannot change the past. All that we can hope for is to influence the future—' She stopped, conscious that such sentiments were of little use to the terrified boy beside her. She tried another approach.

'I am relying on you, Marcel,' she said quietly. 'I am quite alone, you know. I was hoping…I mean…well, I need someone like yourself beside me.'

The child straightened his shoulders. She had not patronised him. In fact, she had appealed for his protection. Suddenly he forgot his own fears as he reached for her hand. 'I'll try to look after you,' he promised. 'You and Mado…'

'I know you will. Now, let us hear what Monsieur Avedon has to say.'

'Then the city it is?' Simon looked round, but no one argued further. 'We'll wait until dusk and split up as we did before.'

'You said that we needed transport,' Piers reminded him.

'So we do...but we must wait until we are through Marseilles. Horses, mules or even a cart will make us a target. Best not to offer temptation.'

'I have my own horse,' Yves said proudly. 'Mado, at least, could ride.'

'What nonsense!' Flushed, the girl rounded on him. 'You are not coming with us. Our party is over-large already.'

'I'm coming to look after you!' The young man's face was set.

'And what will your mother and father have to say to that?' she sneered.

'It was not their decision. I told them what I meant to do and I shall do it.'

'How noble!' she began bitterly. 'That is all I need...a boy on a man's errand.'

Yves looked at her as if she had struck him. He turned away.

It was Simon who confronted the angry girl. 'Madeleine, you had best make up your mind. Either keep a still tongue in your head, or leave us. We have troubles enough without you adding to them. You have vented your spleen upon Miss Lynton and young Yves here. Do you not see that if we are at odds with each other we add to our present danger?'

It was enough to silence her, but he would not let it go. 'Well?' he demanded.

'I'm sorry!' she said in a low voice. 'I should have thought—'

'Indeed you should!' His tone was icy. 'Yves is welcome to join us if he wishes. I, for one, have no objec-

tion to the presence of an extra defender if we are attacked.'

'And he has a horse,' Marcel announced cheerfully.

'A passport for any man!' Simon's stern expression
softened and he smiled at the child. 'Marcel, will you
help Joseph? He is making up our provisions.'

'Should he not be resting?' Emma was worried about
Marcel.

'More arguments, Miss Lynton?' Simon scowled at
her. 'Your concern for the boy is touching, but he is
better occupied. At least it will take his mind off the
ordeal to come.'

Emma stared at him.

'Oh, yes!' he continued savagely. 'It will be an ordeal.
Have you not wondered at his terror? Marseilles has
sickening memories for him. He saw his parents killed
in the main square.'

'And must we enter the city?'

'A detour into the hills will take too long, as I have
explained, but we shall stick to the outskirts and the
alleyways. In any case, I do not plan to make the attempt
until dusk. Now, if you will excuse me, I have matters
to attend.'

Emma was silent. She knew he was right. Marcel must
not be allowed to dwell upon his memories. She looked
across the room and smiled. Joseph had engaged the
child in an arm-wrestling contest and Marcel was squeal-
ing with delight as he tried to force his friend's massive
forearm flat against the table.

Then Simon clapped his hands for silence. 'We have
some way to go before we reach the city,' he announced.
'We must set off within the hour.'

'In daylight?' Emma was startled.

'We have no choice,' he said abruptly. 'If this Chavasse lives up to his reputation, he will soon be on our trail.' He glanced at Marcel and smiled. 'Of course, we are well ahead of him, but we must keep our lead.'

'Must you frighten the boy still further?' Emma asked in a low voice. 'Whatever else about Robert, he would never harm a child.'

She heard an ugly laugh. 'You believe that? My dear Miss Lynton, your friend's reputation is well known to me. He would tear the boy's arms from their sockets to get the information he requires. He has much at stake, you see, including his own neck. His fellow-revolutionaries do not look kindly upon failure.'

Emma was silenced. She turned away as Simon continued to outline his plans.

'We shall split up as before,' he said. 'But with your permission, Yves, Joseph will ride your horse. No one is likely to mistake him for an aristocrat, or even a Frenchman, for that matter…' He grinned at the gigantic negro. 'Joseph, what do you say?'

The man looked up from his task of packing their provisions and returned his smile. 'No one will stop me,' he said with pride. 'I doubt if they will try.'

Emma did not doubt him. Possibly for the first time in his life, Joseph's colour might prove to be an advantage. Aside from anything else he was heavily armed, with a brace of pistols at his belt and a cutlass by his side. It would be a brave man who would tackle such a formidable opponent, even to steal his horse.

'Then set off now!' Simon ordered. 'You know our next meeting place beyond Marseilles. We'll push on whilst daylight holds, but we'll wait for full dark before we enter the city. We should be with you in the early hours…' He glanced across at Piers. 'You are in agreement?' he asked.

Piers gave him a mock-salute. 'Your plans can't be faulted, General! As I see it, our greatest danger is to be seen in isolation for these next few hours. We must lose ourselves among the crowds when we regain the main road to the city.'

'True!' Simon nodded. 'Though the refugees will be travelling away from Marseilles rather than towards it. We must try to mingle with the looters, intent upon their spoils, and those who find their daily entertainment beside the guillotine.'

He kept his voice low, so that only Piers and Emma heard him, but his tone was serious. He saw her stricken face.

'How good an actress are you, Miss Lynton?' he asked. 'We saw something of your talents yesterday when you were challenged about your clothing. Can you pretend to be a harridan, out for whatever you can find?'

'Without the slightest difficulty, Mr Avedon.' Emma drew herself to her full height, but still she did not reach his shoulder. 'How could you doubt it? After all, you think me capable of anything, do you not?'

Was it her imagination, or did she see a slight smile curve the corners of his lips? It vanished in an instant. 'I ask only that you do not delay us, and that you do not give way to stupid folly.' He strode over to the door and opened it, motioning Piers to lead his party out into the countryside. Then he called the farmer to him.

'*Monsieur*, we are in your debt,' he said. 'Conceal this or you may lose your head.' He handed over a small leathern sack, which clinked as the farmer took it. 'Remember, you know nothing. I have checked, and we have left no trace.'

'Nay, master, none will come here in search of you, else I should not have offered shelter.'

Simon clapped him on the shoulder. 'At least you are honest. I hope you may be right.' With that he signalled to Marcel and Emma and they ventured forth into the cold of a December morning.

There was a biting wind and Emma caught her breath. It was hard to believe that in the summer months this coast could bask in sunshine and high temperatures. She drew her cloak about her and hurried on in Simon's footsteps.

It took them some time to regain the road into Marseilles, but when they did so, Emma gasped. It was a solid mass of refugees. Transport of every kind had been pressed into service. Farm carts were piled high with pathetic articles of furniture and sorry-looking bundles tied in bedding. Saddest of all were the children, looking about them with frightened eyes, and the old, resigned to their fate, yet determined to protect those who would come after them.

'Mr Avedon, these people are going in the wrong direction,' she said quickly. 'Why are they making for Toulon?'

'They can't have heard that the town is lost,' he replied.

'But should we not warn them? They are travelling into danger.'

'Look at them, Miss Lynton! Panic has set in! They would take not the slightest notice of anything you might have to say...'

'But?'

'Let me beg you not to call attention to yourself. This is a tragic sight, but you can do nothing to change it.'

'You are heartless!' Emma could have wept.

'No...I am a realist. Rather than mourn this exodus

from Marseilles, I welcome it. The road to Toulon will be blocked for hours. If Chavasse has picked up our trail, he will make little headway towards us.'

Emma looked at him in disgust. 'Must you turn everything to your own advantage?' she asked.

'I'd be a fool not to do so. Your safety and that of Marcel is my main concern at present. I will use any means to achieve that object.'

'I believe you, sir. No doubt you have further orders for us?'

'I have indeed. Keep to the verges of the road, Miss Lynton. You, no less than Chavasse, will find it impossible to force your way through this mob.'

Emma did not answer him. She took Marcel's hand and began to walk along the grassy verge against the flow of the traffic on the road. A woman called to her to point out that Toulon was in the opposite direction and she found herself the target of several curious glances, but she ignored them. Then she slipped and fell. She had not noticed the ditch.

Strong hands gripped her own and drew her upright.

'I should have mentioned the ditch,' Simon told her drily. 'Perhaps if you were to look where you are going…?'

'I have not the least idea where I am going,' she snapped. 'But the more I am in your company, Mr Avedon, the less inviting the prospect.'

To her fury she noticed that his lips had begun to twitch.

'We can't have everything,' he told her smoothly. 'Shall we say that these things are sent to try us?'

'Spare me your clichés, sir!'

'Certainly, Miss Lynton! I have no wish to waste my

breath upon a fool who will not take advice.' He motioned her ahead of him.

Emma ignored the insult. This obnoxious creature was wrong about her, as he was wrong about so many other things. Uppermost in her mind were his warnings about Robert Chavasse.

It seemed impossible to believe that the charming guest who had dined so often at her father's table could behave in such a monstrous way. So many pleasant evenings came to mind. She had listened intently to the conversation, which had ranged from discussions on Greek philosophy to arguments on political economy. Much of it she didn't understand, but Robert had never patronised her, or treated her like an ignorant girl. With her father's encouragement she had asked questions of both men, appreciating the grave courtesy with which they replied.

And those evenings had not been entirely serious. When she was younger Robert had teased her as he did the other children, chasing them about in games of hide and seek, and settling down to a hand of spillikins when the games became too boisterous for her mother's liking.

It was in this last year or so that his attitude had changed. She had been flattered when he bowed and kissed her hand in the graceful manner with which he greeted her mother. It was a subtle compliment, indicating that he now regarded her as a woman grown.

And Robert was clever. He had risen quickly through the ranks of the revolutionaries. She knew him to be an important member of the Committee.

Her lip curled in contempt. That must have been it. Simon was suffering from plain, old-fashioned jealousy. He was so full of his own importance that he could not bear to acknowledge that a man of his own age had risen to such a position of power. His attitude was both mean and petty.

She thought at first that she had settled matters to her own satisfaction, but then she remembered Yves. Something must have brought him racing from Toulon to Mado's side.

Of course he was besotted with the girl. He had made that all too clear. Emma sighed. It wasn't surprising. Mado was a stunning creature. Perhaps Yves could not bear the thought of losing her, but he too had warned about Chavasse.

She tried to piece together the pieces of the puzzle. Chavasse could have no interest in Madeleine or Marcel, so why would he include them in his search for her? The answer came to her only very slowly. Simon Avedon was the key. Perhaps he had been recognised in Toulon. Known to be a friend of the girl and also implicated in rescuing intended victims of the Terror, he could be traced through his association with her.

Yet Yves too must be mistaken about Robert Chavasse. Perhaps he had been listening to gossip and rumour. Successful men were always a target for the envious, and nothing was easier than to blacken a name with unfounded accusations.

Her thoughts were rudely interrupted by a blow between her shoulders. Next moment she found herself in the ditch again with Simon Avedon on top of her.

'What do you think you are doing?' Emma kicked out wildly in an effort to free herself. Then she heard the horseman. As the galloping hooves came closer she raised her head to look and narrowly missed decapitation.

A strong hand forced her down again and Simon cursed beneath his breath. 'Be quiet!' he hissed. 'Lie still, *mademoiselle*, or I shall be forced to render you unconscious…'

His tone left Emma in no doubt that he meant what he said. She stopped struggling and lay inert until the sound of the hoof-beats died away. Then he allowed her to rise.

'Are you quite mad?' she demanded. 'We might well have moved aside without resorting to such drama.'

Simon paid no attention to her words. His eyes were upon the figures disappearing in the direction of Marseilles.

'Well?' she said again. 'I am waiting for an explanation of your extraordinary behaviour.'

His face was dark with anger as he looked at her, tousled, dishevelled and with mud upon her face. Then, to her utter fury, he began to laugh. 'Believe me, I am not in the habit of throwing young women into ditches, Miss Lynton. That was yet another attempt to save your life.'

'What nonsense! I was in no danger from the horse.'

'Perhaps not, but the horseman might be another matter.'

'What do you mean? Do you know him?'

'No, but if I am not much mistaken the man has been sent ahead to warn the authorities and give out our description.'

'You can't know that!'

'I suspect it. The horse is a magnificent beast, which tells me that the rider must be upon official business.'

'You are guessing.'

'Indeed, but I'm not prepared to take a chance.'

Chapter Four

Emma did not answer him. Being tumbled so unceremoniously into the ditch had shaken her more than she cared to admit. In putting out her hands to save herself she had fallen heavily upon her wrist, turning it as she did so. Beneath the mud her face was grazed, but her knees had taken the brunt of the fall.

She would have died rather than admit to any discomfort, but as the day wore on she began to flag. Again, it was Marcel who crumpled first.

Simon had pushed them hard, and she could understand his reasoning, but the boy began to look so pale and ill that she could stand it no longer. 'Have you no sense at all?' she demanded furiously. 'Perhaps you wish to carry Marcel for the rest of our journey? We have not eaten since first light, nor have we been allowed to rest.'

Simon stopped at once, but Marcel gave Emma a reproachful look. 'I can go on,' he insisted. 'It's just that my stomach is making funny noises.'

'So is mine,' Emma said with feeling. 'And you can't go on without food, no more than I can myself.' She turned to Simon. 'We brought provisions with us, did we not?' she said. 'I suggest that now is the time to make good use of them.'

To her annoyance he gave her a mock-salute. 'Certainly, General! Your orders shall be carried out without delay, although I would suggest that the wind is too keen to allow us to enjoy a picnic in the open. Where would the General care to dine?'

Emma ignored the sarcasm. 'There is a building some yards distant,' she said quickly. 'It looks derelict, but the walls would shelter us from the wind.'

'You have good eyesight, Miss Lynton. Very well, but we must approach the place with caution. We may not be alone in searching for shelter.'

He bade them stay back whilst he reconnoitred, and Emma seized the opportunity to look about her. To her surprise, the crowd of refugees had thinned considerably as they approached the outskirts of Marseilles.

Then she understood. Those pathetic travellers must have been on the road for days. However fierce their longing to escape the city, they could move only at the pace of the slowest members of their families. They must have laid up in the woods or even a barn before venturing another mile or two along the road to Toulon each day. The strongest might have travelled through the night, but even they would find little comfort when they reached the old port. All hope of escape from there was gone.

But now the sight of other travellers caught her eye. They were walking briskly towards the city rather than away from it. She could not class them as refugees. Their faces held nothing of the bleak despair that she had noted earlier. They too were pushing carts and wheelbarrows, but all were empty.

Emma could not account for her feeling of unease as

she watched them. Perhaps it was the rapacious expression on certain faces, or their curious air of suppressed excitement.

Then Marcel tugged at her sleeve.

'Monsieur Avedon is signalling to us,' he said in a low voice. 'He wishes us to join him.'

Emma looked up just as Avedon disappeared into the derelict building. 'It must be safe, Marcel. Now we shall be able to rest.'

'And eat our bread and cheese?'

'Of course. I must confess that I am starving. We shall feel so much better with something in our stomachs.'

The boy crossed the road ahead of Emma, but neither attracted any attention from their fellow travellers. Clearly we are thought not to be worth robbing, she surmised with some satisfaction. It was evident that those who were making for the city were a predatory mob, intent on looting. At least they would not be tempted to enter the old stone farmhouse, with the window shutters hanging drunkenly from their hinges, the door caved in, and blackened timbers indicating a recent fire.

As she and Marcel stumbled over the threshold and into the gloom of the interior, Simon called to them.

'Over here!' Simon had already unpacked their few provisions. 'Eat now, and then you may rest. At dusk we shall enter the city.'

'Will it be safe?' Emma felt a strange churning in her stomach.

'We must hope so, *mademoiselle*, as long as we do nothing foolish.' His ironic tone left her in no doubt that his advice was aimed at her. 'Nothing can be guaranteed, of course, but if you can bring yourself to obey my instructions…?'

'Oh, but we will, won't we, *mademoiselle*?' Marcel was gripping her hand with such intensity that she was forced to agree.

She was exhausted, and so cold that she could no longer feel any sensation in her hands and feet. As Simon handed her a quarter of a loaf, she dropped it on the dusty floor.

'Oh! I'm sorry!' she said mechanically. 'Is the bread quite spoiled?'

'Not in the least!' The sharp eyes were upon her face. 'A little dirt won't hurt us... For now, however, I believe we must have a fire. There is plenty of kindling about.' He signalled to Marcel and they began to pick up lengths of the shattered shutters.

Emma was almost too tired to think, but some sense of self-preservation persuaded her to question him.

'Will that not be too dangerous?' she said. 'The sight of a fire may lead to unwelcome attention.'

Simon took out his tinder box struck a flint and set the dry wood ablaze. 'Why should it?' he asked reasonably. 'To seek warmth in this bitter weather is a normal human activity.'

Emma did not argue with him. Instead she moved closer to the fire, stretching out her swollen hands to the comforting blaze.

He saw the grazes at once. 'You did not tell me that you had injured yourself, Miss Lynton.'

'It's nothing!' Emma tried to hide her painful wrist in the folds of her skirt.

'Show me, please!' Strong fingers closed about her arm and she was forced to allow him to examine her injury. He was none too gentle, and she bit back a cry of pain.

He sat back on his heels and looked at her. 'It is not

broken, *mademoiselle*, but by tomorrow it will be twice the size. Anything else?'

Emma shook her head. It was Marcel who betrayed her.

'*Mademoiselle* fell upon her knees,' he insisted. 'I heard her cry out.'

Simon's face was a mask of anger. Seizing the hem of her skirt, he tossed it back almost to her waist, revealing the muddy, bleeding injuries.

Emma heard the indrawn breath. Then he turned to Marcel. 'See if you can find some water,' he said. 'There may be a well or even a stream.' He began to peel off Emma's stockings.

Her face was scarlet with embarrassment. 'I can do that!' she said quickly. 'But really, there is no need. It is just a little mud…'

Simon lost his temper then. 'I despair of you,' he said coldly. 'Have you not heard of the danger of infection, or even gangrene?'

'You exaggerate!' Her voice was as cold as his.

'Believe me, I do not! It is impossible to exaggerate the effects of gangrene. I have watched men die in agony as their own flesh putrifies before their eyes.'

She was silent then.

'Why did you not tell me of these injuries?' he demanded.

Emma was close to tears. Once again, she seemed to be in the wrong, although she'd struggled on with the best of intentions.

'I didn't wish to delay you,' she whispered.

'So you have walked all day in this state? It is of no credit to you, *mademoiselle*. Should you be taken ill, you will endanger all of us. We cannot leave you here to be taken by Chavasse.'

'You might cut my throat before you leave.' Emma glared at him. 'Then I shall be of no further interest to you.'

'I wouldn't say that!' he retorted smoothly. 'Now, ma'am, if we might have an end to this discussion? Here is Marcel...' He motioned to the boy to kneel beside him, and took out his knife.

'What are you about?' Emma asked in alarm.

'I have no plans to amputate your legs, if that is what is worrying you, but these cuts must be washed and covered against dust and dirt. Unfortunately we have no fabric suitable for bandaging other than your chemise.'

'I won't take it off,' she cried.

'There is no need.' He grasped the hem of the garment and handed it to Marcel. 'Hold this taut!' he ordered. Then, before Emma could argue further, he slit through the fine linen a few inches from the hem, tearing away a long strip of the cloth. He folded it carefully and laid it on Emma's lap.

'This water—is it clean?'

'I got it from the stream,' Marcel replied.

'Then we'll take the risk.' He tore off another length of the chemise and moistened it.

'Don't touch me!' Emma attempted to rise from the wooden crate that was serving as a seat. 'I'll wash these cuts myself.' With her skirts thrown up above her knees and her naked legs exposed to view she felt acutely embarrassed.

'Be still!' She was pushed down again without ceremony. 'Please don't waste my time, Miss Lynton. There is nothing in your present appearance that is likely to rouse me to heights of uncontrollable passion.'

Emma could have struck him. She gave him a haughty

look, but she couldn't prevent the hot colour flooding her face.

'Nothing was further from my mind,' she retorted. 'I doubt, sir, if you have ever been seized with uncontrollable passion, or any passion at all, for that matter.' It was the wrong thing to say and she knew it at once, but the words could not be recalled.

When he looked up at her, she saw the amusement in his eyes.

'Oh, I have had my moments…' he assured her smoothly.

This did nothing to reassure her as he gripped her ankle firmly and began to dress her wounds. Surprisingly, his touch was light and gentle and completely impersonal. He finished the bandaging, quickly washed his hands and began to share out the bread and cheese.

Emma was so furious that she was tempted to refuse her portion, but common sense, combined with gnawing hunger, persuaded her to accept. She would not give this creature the satisfaction of knowing that his rude treatment of her person and his remarks about her appearance had shaken her.

It was ridiculous to feel so humiliated. In normal times no man would have dared to touch her, much less cut her shift to shreds and then have the gall to inform her that she was a dowd, too plain to invite advances from any man.

In this instance Simon Avedon's sneering dismissal was a good thing and Emma realised the vulnerability of her own position, even among her rescuers. She would keep them at arm's length.

Except for Marcel, of course. The boy had finished his meal and was sitting at her feet, gazing into the fire.

'Won't you try to sleep?' she asked gently. 'Mr Avedon says that we may stay here until dusk…'

'I can't! *Mademoiselle*, these people who are looking for us…? Will they find us, do you suppose?'

'My dear child, no one is looking for you—'

'But they are! Yves said that they came to the house in Toulon after we left. If they questioned people, they would know who lived there.'

'Marcel, what can they know?' Simon was stretched out at his ease, his feet towards the fire. 'Why do you think I split us into smaller groups with you and your sister separated? Miss Lynton, I feel sure. regarded it as further proof of my heartless behaviour. In fact, the family resemblance is strong and might give you away.'

Emma stared at him. 'But they are not searching for Marcel and Mado.'

'They are searching for anyone who will lead them to you, and that includes anyone seen in the house in Toulon. We must have been followed there.'

'So everyone is in danger…Piers Fanshawe, Joseph, Yves, Mado and Pierre?' Emma's heart sank.

'Pray don't distress yourself. Think of the thousands on the roads at this present time. Joseph might have been a danger, but now he is travelling on horseback and alone. The rest of us are somewhat nondescript, if you will forgive the remark. In your own case, for example, they will be searching for a small, slim, blue-eyed woman with blonde hair. How many such are travelling the country?'

'And what of you, Mr Avedon?' Emma was not best pleased to find herself described in such careless tones.

'Me?' For the first time in their acquaintance Simon Avedon looked surprised.

'Yes, you. How would you have been described to our pursuers?'

'Oh, I should always expect to pass unnoticed in the crowd.'

'Would you, indeed?' Emma was tempted to laugh in his face. Her companion might pass unnoticed in a crowd of blind men, but even then he would need to moderate his tone. Those who could see would look at his eyes and know him for what he was—a ruthless man who would let nothing and no one stand in his way.

'You don't believe me? Come now, Miss Lynton, did I not convince the gentleman who was so taken with you in Toulon that we were comrades-in-arms?'

'Yes, you did!' Emma gave him a thoughtful look. 'You are something of a chameleon, are you not?'

'In my profession, the ability to dissemble is essential.'

'And just what is your profession?'

'Oh, I make myself useful here and there.'

'To whom?'

'Why, to my employers, of course.' His tone did not invite further questioning, and as Emma looked at his impassive face she realised that he would provide her with no further information.

She shrugged. What did it matter? She had no interest in this man. He had promised to help her to escape to England; if he kept his word, that would be enough for her.

Emma leaned back and closed her eyes. She longed to rest. The journey on foot from Toulon had taken its toll. She had never walked so far in her life. Now the fact that she had eaten and the warmth of the fire were lulling her into a doze, but her hopes were premature. She was seized about the waist and moved aside.

'We need the crate for firewood,' Simon explained.

'I can't sit on this filthy floor,' she objected.

'No, *mademoiselle*, but the fallen roof timbers are too large to burn. They will make some kind of platform for you.'

Without apparent effort he picked up the massive beams and began to lay them parallel to the wall. Then, to her surprise, he threw his cloak over them.

'There,' he said, 'that will serve until we leave. Now, let me see your wrist.'

'There is no necessity—' she began.

'No, of course not! I see from your expression that it is perfectly comfortable, especially when I touch it.'

Emma yelped with pain as he raised her hand.

'Hmm! It is swelling rapidly. Here, soak it in this cold water! Then I'll bind it up and you shall wear a sling.'

'Made with what?' Emma backed away from him.

'Well, ma'am, we have only one solution and that is your shift. You'd be welcome to use my shirt, but it is sadly travel-stained, and Marcel, I fear, has not so much as a handkerchief to offer you.' He reached into his pocket and brought out a length of carefully folded fabric. 'There is enough here for a bandage, but not for a sling.'

'In that case I shall manage perfectly well without one.' Emma eyed him coldly.

'No, you will not! I won't have a fainting woman on my hands. Don't be a fool, Miss Lynton! It is not as if I am asking you to walk about in your drawers.'

Emma blushed. 'Oh!' she cried. 'You are no gentleman, to refer to such items of clothing as—'

'Drawers? You wear them, do you not?'

'Be quiet!' she snapped. 'You will embarrass the boy.'

'I doubt it. He is already asleep. In any case, he is

French. Thankfully, he has never been exposed to such euphemisms as ''unmentionables'' when referring to nether garments, or taught to refer to limbs, rather than legs, to avoid offending some notions of respectability. Now, may I have another length of your chemise?'

It was clear that he would take it, whatever her objections, so Emma lifted her coarse skirt in silence and allowed him to cut away at her shift. By now the drawers in question were revealed in all their lace-trimmed glory, but he made no comment. Instead he waited whilst she bathed her wrist, then he bound it up in silence and fashioned a rough sling.

'Now, get some rest!' He turned away and began to dismantle the wooden crate to feed the fire.

Emma sat down beside Marcel and closed her eyes once more. This time she might be allowed to sleep. The makeshift pallet was hard, in spite of the comfort of her companion's cloak, but she was too tired to care. As usual he'd been right, and the throbbing in her wrist soon eased. Within minutes she had drifted into a doze.

She wakened to find herself in Simon Avedon's arms. Her head was resting comfortably on his shoulder, and her face was only inches from his own. Deeply humiliated, she struggled to free herself, but the arm about her waist held her in an iron grip. Then he bent his head until his lips brushed her ear.

'Lie still!' he whispered. 'We are not alone!'

Emma glanced quickly about the room, but she could see no sign of movement. 'You are lying!' she hissed. 'Let me go at once—'

For answer his mouth came down on hers, cutting off whatever she had planned to say, and Emma jumped as if she had been stung. No man had ever offered her such insult.

Then she heard a low laugh. 'The wench don't seem over-pleased with you, *monsieur*. Carried her off from her friends, did you? Perhaps she'd prefer another cavalier…'

Simon stretched out his legs towards the fire, apparently at his ease. 'You've hit it right, comrade! My wife ain't fond of travelling as we have done. She intends to make me pay for her discomfort.'

'Oh, aye! These women are all the same, but you'll make it right when you get her into bed, I make no doubt.'

'I hope so!' Simon bent his head again and bestowed another lingering kiss upon his unwilling charge. Then he nuzzled her neck. 'Don't speak!' he warned. 'Let me do the talking. I don't know their numbers yet. Do you look to Marcel.'

Emma felt dazed. She was only half-attending to his words. Why had she ever supposed that this man had no experience of women? Those kisses seemed to have taken possession of her soul. Then a small hand stole into her own, and she realised that Marcel was trembling.

'Who is there?' he whispered. 'I can't see them.'

It was then that Simon intervened. 'The fire is getting low,' he said. 'Be a good lad and build it up! Our friends here will be glad to share it with us. 'Tis bitter weather for travelling…'

As the leaping flames began to light the room two men stepped forward from the shadows. Emma noticed at once that they were booted and spurred. These were not footsore refugees. They must have arrived on horseback.

They nodded to her politely, but their appearance did nothing to dispel her fears. The younger of the two was a burly fellow, heavily muscled and deeply tanned as if he were accustomed to an outdoor life. A part of his face was still in shadow, but when he turned she caught her breath. A black patch covered the socket of his left eye, but above it and below was the evidence of a recently healed sabre-cut. It had pulled the corner of his mouth upwards into a sinister grin.

His companion was no more prepossessing, although he appeared to be uninjured. His eyes were fixed upon Emma's face and something in their unwinking stare unnerved her. He reminded her of a weasel, intent upon a kill.

Simon shifted slightly and Emma felt the comforting weight of a pistol against her side.

Then the younger man spoke. 'Let me do that.' He took the kindling from Marcel, and added it to the blaze. 'You look tired, lad. Come far, have you?'

Marcel nodded. 'From Toulon, *monsieur*…'

Silence was heavy in the room as the child realised his mistake. Emma stiffened as Simon's hand closed more firmly upon his pistol. She reached forward and drew Marcel to her, out of the line of fire. Then she began to talk, careful, as always, to use the local dialect.

'We ain't the only ones to leave the city,' she said quickly. 'By now it must be naught but rubble since the guns began to fire. Of course, we are glad that it was taken by our own Republican Army, but there's no shelter left, even for honest citizens.'

The older man smiled at her. 'A terrible experience for you, citizeness, but necessary, alas! We must crush these aristocrats, these vermin… It is unfortunate that so many were taken off by the British Fleet, but we'll have a reckoning there too in the years to come.'

'And they didn't get away unscathed,' his companion said with satisfaction. 'Ship after ship burst into flames as the British tried to take off the French fleet with them as they left. What a sight, eh?'

'You were there?' Simon asked casually.

'No, no!' It was a quick disclaimer. 'But we heard that we'd given the British admiral a bloody nose. Our artillery was in command of the town and he hadn't enough troops to hold it. The devil wrecked the arsenal and set fire to nine French warships.' His expression was ugly. 'I'd like to get my hands on him.'

'You may get your chance,' Simon said quietly. 'Do you travel to join the army in Toulon?'

'That's our plan,' came the swift reply. 'And you, *monsieur*?'

'We heard that Marseilles is pacified,' Simon told him smoothly. 'It will be safer for my wife and her young cousin here. Her mother lives in the city, and naturally she has been worried…'

'A pity that you had to rest here when you were so close,' the older man observed. His eyes had never left Emma's face.

Simon shrugged. 'I would not have done so, but Gabrielle fell and almost broke her wrist.' He lifted Emma's arm to show the bandage. 'She needed rest, but now she is quite recovered, are you not, my dear? Let us press on. Your mother will not care to open her door if we arrive much later.'

Emma tensed. If, as she suspected, these men had been sent in search of her, this was the time when they would make their move. To her surprise they stepped aside for her and stretched out, apparently at their ease, beside the fire.

Simon raised her to her feet and slipped an arm about her waist, urging her from the room. 'Come, my love,' he said tenderly. 'We have not far to go. Within the hour you will be with your family again.'

He nodded briefly to the strangers, wishing them a safe journey to Toulon. Then he hurried her from the building and back towards the road.

Once outside Emma struggled to release herself, but he continued to hold her to his side.

'Must you continue with this play-acting?' she demanded. 'We no longer have an audience.'

'Don't be too sure!' he warned. 'If I'm not mistaken, they will follow us.'

'Then you feel that they did not believe our story?'

'Not a hope!' A grim smile touched his lips. 'They believed us no more than I believed them.'

'What do you mean? They didn't try to stop us.'

'I suspect that they have had their orders. Their task was to find us and to send on word ahead.'

'You can't be sure of that. You said yourself that there are many women just like me.'

'Did I say that, Miss Lynton? If I did, I was mistaken.'

'Oh, you speak in riddles,' she cried impatiently. 'How could they be certain of finding their quarry among these thousands of refugees?'

'They could not, but the slightest suspicion will be reported to your friend Chavasse. If they are right, they will be well rewarded.'

'It is all my fault. I should not have told them that we travelled from Toulon.' Marcel's face was a mask of misery. 'I have betrayed you…'

'It would have made not the slightest difference,'

Simon assured him. 'Those men have ridden from Toulon and not Marseilles, as they were quick to claim.'

Emma stared at him. 'How do you know?'

'Was it not obvious? They know too much about the siege.'

'But they said that they had heard about it.'

'From whom? We have made good time, and only a single rider passed us on the road. I doubt if the news is common knowledge in Marseilles as yet.'

'But I did not see them on the quayside,' Emma insisted.

'As I recall, you were somewhat preoccupied at the time, *mademoiselle*, and there was a great crush of people.'

Suddenly, and unbidden, the face of the one-eyed man sprang to Emma's mind. 'You are right,' she admitted. 'They were there.' There was no mistaking the unholy joy on that scarred face as he described the scenes of carnage in the harbour.

'Agreement, Miss Lynton? Great heavens, ma'am, you must try not to shock me in this way. My nerves will not stand it.'

Emma smiled in spite of herself. Her companion was trying to ease the tension, as much for the boy's sake as for her own. She tried to match his mood.

'Now you are making game of me,' she told him cheerfully. 'What now, *monsieur*?'

'Now we slip through Marseilles as quickly as may be. Your friend Chavasse is no fool. He will have considered all our options. You cannot leave the country by sea, nor will you strike north towards the Channel coast. Italy is out of the question, and you will not cross the Pyrenees in winter. Spain must be your destination and he knows it. We are travelling west along the only route and he must stop you before you reach the border.'

Emma was silent for a time. 'Even now, I cannot understand how those men were able to find us,' she said at last.

'An unhappy chance, I fear. Of course, we do not know what threats are made against them if they failed.'

'Well, they weren't very intelligent to give themselves away so easily.' Emma's voice was tart.

'I doubt if that will worry them at this moment. If I am not much mistaken one will follow us, whilst the other rides ahead.'

'What shall we do?' Marcel was trembling with fright.

'Let me explain!' Simon rested a gentle hand upon the child's shoulders. 'Listen carefully, because our lives may depend on you. If we are stopped, you run! Wait for my signal first. It may not be necessary to split up, but it will depend upon the numbers facing us. I can take out one or two, but there may be more. You will be quite safe. No one will think it worth the trouble to follow a boy.'

'But what shall I do then?'

Simon pointed ahead of him. They were approaching the outskirts of the city and in the distance a tall spire reached into the night sky. 'If we are separated, you shall meet us there at the church of the Holy Name. Piers will come for you if we are...er...delayed.'

'And if I am followed by these men?'

'You will claim sanctuary.'

Emma drew him aside. 'Will that serve?' she asked. 'Our enemies have given up the Christian faith. They may not abide by ancient practices.'

Simon smiled at her. 'In this case they will have no

option. They will remove the charges of the parish priest only over his dead body.'

'Then you are sure that Marcel will be safe?'

'Can you doubt it? The priest is an old friend of mine. In any case the boy cannot be held responsible for the actions of his so-called elders and betters.'

'May we not stay together?' Marcel pleaded. 'If you give me a pistol, I can fight…'

'You may be able to fight in a better way. You wish to protect Mado and Miss Lynton, do you not?'

The boy nodded.

'Well, then, there may be a chance for you to do so. There may be no trouble, but if we are seized, Miss Lynton and myself, you must get word to Monsieur Fanshawe and Joseph. That will be our only hope of rescue. Do you understand?'

'Very well.' Marcel agreed to follow his orders, but with some reluctance.

Emma guessed that the prospect of being separated from his idol filled him with terror. Strangely, she felt much the same herself. In these last few days she had grown dependent upon the man who strode along beside her. She might dislike him, but she could not doubt his courage or his judgment.

'Come, then!' he continued. 'We'll follow the streets to the docks. They should be deserted since there are few pickings there for the looters.'

He moved with caution into the first of the narrow alleyways. Then he stopped. 'Do you and Marcel go on,' he said in a low voice. 'Don't look back. I will rejoin you in a moment…'

'Where are you going?' Emma asked in alarm. 'You cannot leave us here.'

'I have no intention of leaving you, but, as I expected,

we are being followed. I hope to reduce the odds against us by one at least.'

Emma shuddered. 'You mean…you mean to kill the man?'

'I mean merely to discourage him, *mademoiselle*.'

'You will take care?' Impulsively Emma laid a hand upon his sleeve. To her astonishment he took it in his own and raised it to his lips. Once again the touch of that cool, firm mouth succeeded in throwing her into confusion. She snatched her hand away.

'Forgive me!' Simon drawled. 'Your touching concern for my safety quite overwhelmed me.'

'I am not in the least concerned for your safety,' Emma snapped. 'I am thinking of Marcel and myself.'

'Quite! Now, pray continue along this street.' With that he disappeared into the darkness.

Emma was filled with dread. Suppose he did not return? Their pursuers were both dangerous men. She was in no doubt of that. She guessed that they had killed before and would do so again, given the opportunity. Simon Avedon had insulted her, even treated her with contempt, but she could not face the thought of some passer-by finding his lifeless body lying in the street.

As she moved away, following his instructions, her legs felt like lead, yet all her senses were alert, listening for some sound behind her. The temptation to look back was strong, but she resisted it.

Then she heard a low cry and a thud. She stopped, scarcely daring to breathe. Had Simon halted their pursuer? Which man would walk towards her, out of the darkness? Just as she was about to disobey her orders, Marcel caught at her sleeve. He was gibbering with fright, unable to speak as he pointed ahead.

As Emma followed his gaze her heart misgave her.

Silhouetted against the skyline was the motionless figure of a single horseman.

'It's the man who passed us on the road!' Marcel's voice was high with panic. 'I recognise the horse. It has a white blaze on its face.'

Emma bent towards him. 'If he tries to seize us, you must run,' she whispered urgently. 'Remember what Monsieur Avedon told you—'

Then her words were drowned as men erupted from the side streets and raced towards them. She gave Marcel a sharp push and turned to run in the opposite direction. She had not taken more that a step or two when she stumbled on the uneven cobbles, but she kept her feet and ran for the safety of a darkened alley.

'The girl! Get the girl!' She heard the stentorian voice even above the mêlée. Then she was down, enveloped in the suffocating folds of a heavy cloak. She struggled to free herself, but it was useless as she was seized by a dozen hands, then thrown without ceremony over a brawny shoulder and borne away. She could see nothing and hear nothing, but as she raised her head she felt a violent blow upon her temple. Then all was darkness.

Chapter Five

Emma opened her eyes to find a familiar figure bending over her.

'Robert?' she whispered. 'What are you doing here?'

'Hush, my dear! Don't try to talk! The surgeon is here. I wish him to examine you...you have taken a nasty blow to the head.'

Emma closed her eyes and leaned back against the cushions of the *chaise longue*. She winced as the surgeon's fingers explored the contusion of her brow, but when he suggested bleeding she sat up sharply.

'I won't have it!' she announced. 'There is nothing wrong with me—'

'But, ma'am, with leeches you will feel but the slightest prick of pain and the bleeding will be of benefit to you.'

'No, it won't!' she said decidedly. 'Leeches? Ugh, filthy creatures! I won't have them crawling over me and feasting on my blood.'

'Then perhaps ''cupping''?'

'No, you shall not cut into my arm to draw off blood. I have had worse bumps when I fell out of my father's apple trees.'

The surgeon frowned at her. Then he turned to Robert. 'I can be of no use to this young woman,' he announced. 'She is too self-willed to take my advice. I bid you good day, sir!' With that he stalked out of the room.

'Emma, are you sure?' Robert Chavasse was on his knees beside her. 'The man who injured you shall pay for this…I gave strict orders that you were not to be harmed.'

'No one struck me,' she insisted. 'I must have hit my head upon a door jamb or some such obstruction as they carried me away.' She looked about her for the first time. 'What is this place? It seems very fine.'

Certainly the wooden panelling in the room was of the highest quality. Rich tapestries hung upon the walls and the furniture was clearly the work of master craftsmen.

'This is my headquarters, Emma dear. You will be safe at last… What a struggle we have had to find you! I was beside myself with worry. Why did you not come to me for help?'

'I didn't know where to find you, Robert. Besides…'

'Ah, yes, your father disapproves of me. Such a pity! We were once good friends. I would have helped him, Emma, even to return to England, though I cannot understand it. He loves France. It was his second home.'

'You know his views. He could not tolerate the bloodshed.'

'There were reasons… Still, my dear, do not let us argue at this time. I am so thankful to see you safe. Whatever persuaded you to place your person in the care of that motley crew of adventurers and soldiers of fortune?'

Emma felt unreasonably annoyed by his contemptuous tone. 'They offered to help me,' she said coldly. 'And they were English.'

'Ah, yes…the English.' He smiled. 'Such gallant gentlemen! I was surprised to hear that you had been left to make your way at night through the city with just a child for company. Where were your friends?'

'I don't know,' she answered in a panic. 'But the boy? Did you find him?'

'Not as yet, but we shall do so. He cannot be left to wander into danger. He is a young relative, perhaps?'

'Why, no…! I mean, he is a distant cousin…'

The arm about her shoulders tightened briefly and in that moment Emma knew that Chavasse did not believe her.

'Well, then, I can understand your worries about him. Strange that I never met him at your father's home. However, possibly you had some rendezvous in mind in case you were separated?'

'No!' she said too quickly. 'Robert, I am very tired. Is there somewhere I can rest?' All her senses were alerted by his questioning, gentle though it was. Now she prayed that he would not find Marcel. It would be all too easy for him to trick the child into betraying their refuge at the church.

Something of her unease must have communicated itself to him. He put both arms about her, drew her to his chest and began to rock her as if she were a child herself.

'Dear Emma, I could have spared you so much anguish, but now I can look after you. If only your father had listened to me! Still, what's done is done!' He reached out and rang the bell beside him. 'From now on you are my honoured guest. My housekeeper will look after you. A bath, perhaps, and some more suitable clothing in place of these rags?' He fingered the coarse fabric of her skirt with unconcealed distaste. 'Later, when you have rested, we shall dine together. You will wish to make plans.'

'Oh, I do!' she cried eagerly. 'I must get back to England. Will you help me?'

'I'll do what I can,' he promised. 'But these are difficult times, my dear. You cannot travel alone. Give me time and I shall think of some way out of this dilemma.'

He looked up as an angular woman entered the room. 'Now here is Berthe,' he said in a cheerful tone. 'She will be happy to care for you. Go with her, Emma, and do pray ask for anything you need.'

Emma looked at the unprepossessing creature standing in the doorway. Happiness was not a word she would have associated with the woman. Dressed in unrelieved black bombazine, her only ornament was the bunch of keys attached to a set of short chains about her waist. It was a classic chatelaine, and an indication of her position in the household.

She bowed briefly and stood aside to allow Emma to precede her from the room. 'This way, miss. Your room is on the first floor.' Without waiting for a reply she began to mount the ornate staircase.

Emma was startled. *Her* room? Had Robert been so sure of finding her? Her thoughts returned to Marcel and Simon Avedon. Clearly the child had escaped his pursuers, but what of Simon? She had heard nothing since that dreadful cry and the thud of a falling body. Pray heaven it was not him!

She felt utterly confused. Robert had been kindness itself. Surely she should feel relieved to be safe in this luxurious house with a man who had been a close family friend? Yet a little worm of doubt had crept into her mind. Could she trust Chavasse? Tonight, as they dined, she would put him to the test. Any evasion or subterfuge upon his part would confirm her growing suspicion that she was not an honoured guest, but a prisoner in this house. His questioning had disturbed her. Clearly he was determined to capture her English friends.

Then all thought of him was banished as Berthe threw open the door to her apartment. It was magnificent. From the Aubusson carpet to the fine damask hangings on the four-poster bed, it was clear that no expense had been spared.

She looked at Berthe. 'Who owns this house?' she asked without preamble.

The woman was not disposed to talk, but she could not ignore the question. 'It was the home of Monsieur Diderot,' she said reluctantly.

'And where is *monsieur* now? Is he in residence?' Emma was astonished by the response to her question.

'He is in hell, where he belongs!' the woman announced triumphantly. 'He won't be grinding the faces of the poor no more.'

'But how did he do that?' Emma looked about her in wonder. 'He must have been a man of means. Did he not provide employment?'

'Aye, miss, a pittance! Him with his business in fine wines! He tried to get away on one of his own ships, but he was taken, thanks be to God, together with all his gold. Good riddance is what I say. I went to see him pay the price myself.'

Emma stared at her in horror. This woman must have stood beside the scaffold, rejoicing as yet another innocent victim met a cruel death. Perhaps she had betrayed him herself. Looking at the malicious gleam in the small, black eyes, Emma wouldn't have put it past her, though it was a shocking thought.

The woman held her gaze. 'Turns your stomach, miss, does it? Well, it don't turn mine.' She walked to the door and threw it back to admit two girls. They were straining under the weight of heavy pails of steaming water.

She motioned them towards a bathtub which stood before the fire. Then she turned to Emma and sniffed. 'You'll be wanting a maid to help you, I expect,' she said abruptly.

'Thank you, but no!' Emma's tone was as icy as her own. 'I need no help. I shall manage perfectly well alone.'

Perhaps it was a mistake, but she made no secret of her dislike for Berthe. It was returned in good measure. There would be no love lost between them.

'Master said as how you were not to be left alone,' the woman retorted.

Emma's smile did not reach her eyes. 'That was thoughtful of him,' she replied. Then she looked at the girls. One of them was eyeing her boldly whilst the other, who appeared to be much younger, stood shyly by the door, awaiting further instructions.

'What is your name?' Emma asked.

'It's Jeanne, *mademoiselle*.' The child had blushed to the roots of her hair.

'And will you help me, Jeanne?'

The girl nodded.

'Yon's a useless creature!' The housekeeper was quick to intervene. 'You'd do better with Brigitte here—'

'Perhaps so, but I have made my choice. Now, if you would be good enough to leave us, I should like to bathe whilst the water is still warm.' Emma opened the door herself, leaving Berthe no choice but to flounce away, taking the other girl with her.

Emma sighed with relief. It had been an unpleasant interview, but she did not doubt her own ability to deal with insolence. Shyness was something else. She smiled at the little maid. 'I'll be glad of your help,' she said. 'I wasn't telling the truth just now. I can't undo my bodice. It buttons down the back.'

She turned and waited whilst the clumsy fingers struggled with her fastenings. Then she heard a choking sob. 'What is it?' she exclaimed.

'I'm that slow, ma'am, but I ain't no ladies' maid, you see.'

'But I don't want a ladies' maid, my dear. I just need a friend to help me. Besides, we are in no hurry. Take your time and we shall go on very well.'

Thus reassured, Jeanne grew in confidence, and as Emma slipped out of the last of her coarse garments she turned away, her eyes modestly downcast, to arrange a pile of towels over a wooden rail, which she set before the fire.

Emma closed her eyes, soothed by the warming, scented water, but she did not linger over her bath much as she longed to do so. She needed to make plans, though it was difficult to decide which of her problems to handle first. The most immediate one was that of clothing. She could not bear the thought of dressing again in the soiled rags that she had worn for the past few days.

'Jeanne, would it be possible to have my garments washed?' she asked.

The girl stared at her. 'You don't mean these things, *mademoiselle*?' She looked at the unsavoury pile upon the floor.

'Why, yes, of course! I have nothing else to wear.'

'But master said— I mean, I thought you knew…' She stepped over to a closet set into the wall, and disappeared inside, returning with an armful of dresses. 'There's everything you need in here.'

'But where did they come from?' Emma was astonished. Robert might have hoped to find her, but surely he would not have gone to the lengths of ordering clothes for her.

To her dismay the girl's eyes filled with tears. 'They belonged to Mademoiselle Stephane. Poor young lady won't have any need for them now.'

Emma's blood seemed to freeze in her veins. 'Oh, Jeanne, you can't mean that she too has been killed?'

'Not yet, but she's on the list with her mother. They took her father first…' Jeanne's tears were flowing freely as she recalled the fate of her old master.

Pity turned to anger as Emma stepped out of the bath and wrapped a towel about her. 'We'll see about that!' she said decisively. 'Monsieur Chavasse is a force to be reckoned with in this city. His influence will be enough to save them, and I shall speak to him this evening.'

'It ain't for me to tell you, ma'am, but you'll be wasting your time—'

'I think not. When I am determined to have my way, I usually get it. Now, hand me one of those gowns! Under the circumstances I'm sure that your young mistress won't mind. There is underwear?'

In silence Jeanne brought her what she needed, but the racking sobs had ceased.

'You were fond of your old employers, were you not?' Emma spoke kindly to the girl and was rewarded with a watery smile.

'They were good to me and mine. Oh, ma'am, if you could find some way to help them?'

'I'll do my best. Now, you are not to worry. Hand me that comb. I must try to do something with my hair.'

She tugged at the short crop, but it was impossible to smooth the fair curls into submission. In the end she resigned herself to allowing them to tumble over her brow. After all, her appearance did not matter. She doubted if it would influence Robert in any way. He still saw her as a child—the daughter of his old friend.

He did not hear her enter the salon that evening and for a few moments she was able to observe him at her leisure. His dress was sober, as befitted a leading member of the Revolutionary Committee, but it was of the finest quality and it fitted him like a second skin.

She guessed him to be of an age with Simon Avedon, somewhere in his early thirties. Robert was lean and elegant and wore his clothing with an air that spoke of his French origins. Such style was unknown to Simon, but of the two men she knew which of them she would follow into danger. Her heart felt like lead within her breast. Where was Simon now? He could not be dead. Robert Chavasse would not have kept that news to himself, but he could be lying somewhere badly injured.

None of these worries showed on her face as she moved forward. Then Robert turned and saw her. He came to her with outstretched hands and a smile of pleasure on his lips.

'That's better!' he announced. 'Now I have my dearest Emma back again. How fine you look! You were always a pretty child, but now you are a beautiful woman!'

His voice was so warm that Emma decided to seize the moment.

'I am wearing borrowed plumage,' she confessed. 'The young owner of this gown is at present awaiting execution.'

Robert looked shocked. 'What can you mean?' he said. 'There must be some mistake… Where did you hear this story?'

'The staff here know about it, and there is no mistake. Monsieur Diderot is already dead. Berthe was happy to inform me that she attended the execution.'

Robert's face grew dark with anger, but Emma did not know if the gossiping had infuriated him or if the execution had taken place without his knowledge. Emma decided to give him the benefit of the doubt.

'You are a powerful man,' she pleaded. 'Won't you save his wife and daughter?'

'Of course, my dear. Just give me a moment…' He strode over to his desk and began to write. Then he tugged at the bell-pull before handing the note to Emma. 'Here, read it! Perhaps this will assure you of my good faith.' His orders were clear. Madame Diderot and her daughter were to be released from prison at first light on the following day.

Emma sighed with relief. Robert was not the monster people thought him. Now she felt she could trust him. On an impulse she took his hand and dropped a kiss upon it. 'How good you are!' she said warmly. 'I felt sure that you could not know of this injustice. After all, *madame* and her daughter can pose no possible threat to the Republic, can they?'

'Of course not!' He handed the note to his servant with instructions to deliver it at once. 'Satisfied, Emma?'

'I am delighted!' Her face was radiant as she looked up at him. 'I knew I had only to ask…'

'Well, then, now that we have set your mind at rest, shall we dine?' Taking her hand, he led her into the adjoining room.

It was as magnificent as the rest of the house, but Emma paid no attention to the paintings that hung upon the walls or to the fantastic workmanship displayed in every piece of furniture. She hung upon every word as Robert began to speak.

'I have been considering how to get you back to England, Emma. As I explained, it won't be easy. I can't accompany you myself, since I am needed here, and clearly you cannot travel alone with this country in such turmoil—'

'But I must rejoin my family,' she insisted. 'My parents will be out of their minds with worry…'

'I agree! Where are they now, do you suppose?'

'I don't know. It is some days since they sailed from Toulon. I believe that the British Fleet was making for Gibraltar. Perhaps they have taken ship from there…'

'In which case they will be in England soon.' Robert paused, idly twisting the stem of his wineglass. 'Emma, just suppose that I could get a courier through to Portsmouth to intercept your father as he lands—would he come for you if you sent a note explaining your predicament?'

His words sounded a warning in Emma's mind. 'He can't return to France, as well you know,' she argued. 'His life would not be worth a *sou* if he were taken.'

'He would be under my protection,' Robert told her smoothly. 'Have I not given you evidence this very evening that I don't hold with all this killing?'

'Yes, you have, but—'

'But still you do not trust me? I cannot blame you. You have seen too much horror in these past few days.'

'You can't imagine…' Emma said quietly. 'Those scenes upon the dockside will haunt me for the rest of my life. I would have done anything to get away.'

'I understand, but you took a terrible risk. These Englishmen…they did not offer you insult?'

She knew what he was asking and she coloured. 'They treated me with great respect, Robert.' Then a thought struck her. 'There may be a solution. If you were to offer them safe passage through France, I could travel with them back to England.'

'That is a possibility certainly,' he said smoothly. 'But we have no way of finding them. Perhaps you can recall some mention of a rendezvous…a safe house, perhaps?'

It was the second time he had asked the question and now her thoughts were in turmoil. Was she right to trust him? She would not put it to the test. 'I haven't the least idea,' she lied. 'I was a stranger to them. They did not make me party to their plans.'

Robert did not pursue the matter, except to mention once again his wish that she should write to her father.

'Then, Emma, it will be up to him. I have promised him safe conduct, but the decision whether or not to return to France must be his alone.'

Emma did not argue further. She addressed herself to the meal, but she did not comment upon the excellence of the food. It might have implied some criticism of the luxury in which Robert was living.

Liberty, Brotherhood and Equality might be the watchwords of the Revolution, but some, she realised with contempt, were more equal than others. She doubted if the ragged mob of *sans-culottes* were dining upon pâtés, truffles, and a vast array of meats and fowls.

Neither would they be given the opportunity to taste the vintage wines that Robert offered her with such pride.

Pleading exhaustion, she excused herself as soon as the meal was over.

'Of course, my dear!' Robert made no demur. 'For these next few days you must rest and try to regain your strength. I shall not see you in the morning as I must return to Toulon.'

'But I thought it was taken by the Revolutionary forces?'

'It's in our hands, that's true, but as you can imagine there is much to do. Tell me, did you hear anything of a young artillery officer—a Corsican by the name of Bonaparte?'

'I don't know the name...'

'Indeed, how could you, since you do not move in army circles? I suspect that you will hear it again. The man is a military genius, even at the age of twenty-one. It was his placing of the guns that gave us our victory. The place was thought to be impregnable, you know. Without his skill we might have faced a lengthy siege.'

'So it was he who razed the place to the ground?'

'Ah, Emma, you are speaking from a woman's point of view. You ladies are tender-hearted. Believe me, order will be restored quite soon, but I must meet this fellow. I want to know more of him.'

Emma could not rejoice in death and destruction. 'It seems to me that this country is descending into chaos,' she told him sharply. 'Law and order has broken down and the mobs are looting at will.'

'That will end,' he promised. 'For the moment the great unwashed are drunk with power...poor deluded fools!'

Emma did not pretend to misunderstand him. 'You will regain authority, Robert?'

'Naturally! We cannot allow this folly to continue, whatever the cost, but for the moment mob rule is unavoidable. It is for this reason that I ask you to stay indoors. I cannot guarantee your safety if you venture out.'

'Am I a prisoner here?'

He gave her a wounded look. 'Do I deserve such words from you? My dear, you are my guest here. Make yourself at home. There is a fine spinet in the salon, and a magnificent library, which is sure to please you...' He kissed her hand and led her to the door. 'Now, try to rest. You will see things in a different light tomorrow...' Then he paused. 'Whilst I am away, will you consider the question of a letter to your father? He may be your best hope of returning to England.'

Emma nodded, but the thought came to her mind unbidden that Robert was being more than generous with someone else's possessions, and why this insistence upon her father returning to France? There could only be one reason, but she didn't wish to believe it.

Once she had gained the safety of her room she removed her money-belt and took out several coins, which she wrapped in a handkerchief. Then she rang her bell to summon Jeanne.

'Madame Diderot and her daughter are to be released tomorrow,' she began without preamble. She was unprepared for the girl's reaction. Jeanne fell upon her knees and tried to kiss Emma's hands. Her tears were falling fast.

'No! This won't do!' Emma raised her to her feet. 'There are certain questions to consider. Where will *ma-*

dame go? Is there some place of safety now that her old home is lost to her?'

'There's nowhere, *mademoiselle*. All her friends were seized… Poor lady! What is she to do?'

'Jeanne, you told me that your mistress had been good to you and yours. Would your parents give her shelter?'

'They would, ma'am, and gladly, but a fisherman's cottage is no place for the likes of Madame Diderot.'

Emma sighed her impatience. 'Believe me, Jeanne, *madame* will not refuse a hand stretched out in friendship. She cannot live upon the streets. Now, can you get a message to your parents?'

'There's my brother, miss. He's the pot-boy in the kitchen.'

'Will you bring him to me?'

'He ain't allowed above stairs. Berthe would beat him black and blue.'

'Then I'll come down to him—' Emma was startled by the change in the girl's expression. Turning swiftly, she saw Berthe standing in the doorway. 'Berthe, have you not heard of the old custom of knocking at a door?' she asked sweetly.

A dark flush stained the sallow skin. 'I was only making sure,' the woman snapped.

'Making sure of what?'

'Why, *mademoiselle*, that you have everything you need. Monsieur Chavasse insisted on it.'

The insolent look of triumph infuriated Emma. 'Well, you have done your duty,' she replied. 'Jeanne will see to my wants from now on. You may retire. I have no further need of you this evening.'

She encountered a look of pure hatred, but the woman did not argue further. She turned on her heel and left.

Then Emma found that Jeanne was trembling. 'What is it?' she asked.

'Don't make an enemy of Berthe,' the girl pleaded. 'She's capable of anything.'

'Pray don't worry about her. I can deal with Berthe and a dozen like her. If her behaviour does not improve I shall report her to Monsieur Chavasse.'

Strangely, this threat did nothing to reassure the maid. She did not answer.

'Do you fear that she overheard us? That is of no account. We were speaking of your brother. Tell me, how does Berthe spend her evenings? Does she go out at night?'

'Not her! She goes to her room to gossip with Brigitte and drink the master's brandy.'

'Then let us hope that she will do the same tonight. Let us give her an hour. Then you shall return for me and take me to your brother.'

'But if someone should see you, *mademoiselle*?'

'I shall have the perfect excuse. I could not sleep and insisted upon exploring the rest of the house.'

Jeanne was unconvinced, but her affection for her former mistress overcame her fears. 'I'll do as you say,' she whispered. 'But, *mademoiselle*, you will take care?'

'Of course I will,' Emma cried gaily. 'Have you not heard? The English are an eccentric race…their strange behaviour is always a source of astonishment to others.'

With a laughing face she dismissed the girl, but when she was alone her expression grew sombre. She did not fear for herself. Even if Robert discovered her plan to help Madame Diderot, he would ascribe it to her tender heart.

What he would not forgive was her attempt to persuade his servants into deceiving him. Was she putting both Jeanne and her brother in danger? She thought not. For the moment Emma held the trump card. Robert needed her cooperation if he was to entice her father back to France.

The first suggestion of a plan began to form in her mind. She would outwit him yet. Even so, it was with some trepidation that she followed Jeanne an hour later. Moving cautiously, they descended the back stairs into the lower regions of the house.

Emma wasted no time. The boy was waiting for them. He was so small and thin that she hesitated, wondering if this wizened little creature could be made to understand his mission.

Jeanne understood at once. 'Don't worry, miss, Leon is sharp enough to cut himself. He's in and out of this place like an eel.'

'Through the back window,' the child boasted. His eyes were sparkling with excitement.

'This is important, Leon. Jeanne has explained that Madame Diderot is to be released?'

The boy nodded.

'Perhaps your father would meet her outside the prison at first light and take her to a place of safety.'

'He'll do that, *mademoiselle*.'

'Very well, then.' Emma felt in her pocket and brought out the knotted handkerchief. 'You are to give this to your father. It is for Madame Diderot. Take care of it. I am entrusting you with great responsibility. Can you reach your home without being seen?'

The child laughed aloud. 'I ain't been stopped yet,' he told her with satisfaction. 'No one troubles about boys. They ain't worth robbing.'

Emma accepted his words without comment, though she felt troubled. Leon was well worth robbing on this particular evening and she suspected that he knew it. Was she right to trust him? He would never have seen a golden louis in his life before. The contents of that handkerchief meant riches beyond the dreams of a poor fisherman.

Then Emma felt ashamed. Her suspicions were unworthy. This boy and his sister were risking dismissal, imprisonment and possibly even execution not only for themselves, but for their family, simply out of affection for their former mistress.

She held out her hand to Leon. 'You have great courage,' she said simply. 'I am proud to know you.'

The compliment reduced him to squirming embarrassment, but the look he gave her told of his delight.

'Best go, *mademoiselle*!' Jeanne warned. 'The guards change shift at midnight.'

'The guards?' Emma gave her a blank look. 'What guards?'

'Them in the house. Master takes no chances. Likely he feels no safer than the rest of us. I thought you knew.'

'No, I didn't! In that case, the sooner I regain my room the better.'

They met no one on the staircase, but as they reached the upper landing Jeanne heard voices. With a warning finger to her lips, she held Emma back. 'The guards are below,' she whispered.

The men were standing in the stairwell, out of sight, but not out of hearing.

'Back from the prison then, are you?'

'Aye! Can't think what's come over Citizen Chavasse. 'Tain't like him to sign a release.'

'Not when he went to so much trouble to get this place. I suppose it's down to the wench he's been so keen to get his hands on.'

'Can't say I blame him, friend.' His listener added a coarse remark that brought the colour rushing to Emma's cheeks.

'You may be right, but I doubt it. The master knows what he's doing. He don't make a move without it shows him a profit in some way.'

'True…and it won't be difficult to pick up the Diderot woman again if he should change his mind. They ain't likely to pass for peasants…' Both men laughed.

'I wouldn't mind a night with the young 'un,' one said to the other.

In her anger, Emma almost betrayed her presence. How could Robert Chavasse, a man she thought she knew, employ such creatures? She moved towards the head of the staircase with a sharp reprimand upon her lips, but Jeanne held her back.

'Come away, *mademoiselle*! It won't do no good to speak to them. They are beyond all pity, especially the one-eyed man.'

Emma knew that the girl was right, but it was with great reluctance that she slipped back to her room. She said little as Jeanne helped her to undress except to ask that she be told at once if Leon returned with news.

'Yes, miss, but won't you try to sleep? You look that tired.'

'I know it!' Emma caught a glimpse of her own face in the mirror. She was very pale and her eyes were shadowed, but her determination was unshaken. Robert would not use her to trick her father into coming back to France, nor would she lead him to her English friends.

She closed her eyes at last. So much had happened in the last few hours, but it was Simon Avedon who occupied her mind to the exclusion of all else.

She drifted into sleep with the memory of that cool, firm mouth upon her own, and a slight smile curved her lips. Simon was not dead. She felt it in her heart. He would save her yet.

Chapter Six

For the next few days Emma remained unshaken in that belief. Her spirits had lifted with the news that Madame Diderot and her daughter were safe.

'Madame has a sister in Perpignan,' Jeanne told her. 'My father hopes to take her there within the next few days. Mademoiselle Lynton, I am to tell you of her gratitude. It is a debt that she will never be able to repay…'

'Oh, Jeanne, you have done so much for her yourself. Will your father allow me to give him something at least for the expenses of the journey?'

'He won't take your money, miss, nor that of Madame Diderot. He didn't offer his help with any idea of gain.'

'I know that, my dear.' Emma felt humbled. These poor people were worth a dozen of their so-called betters. 'Perpignan is close to the Spanish border, is it not?'

'Yes, miss. It's easy enough to slip across to safety if need be.'

'Good!' Emma returned to her window-seat and gazed down into the street below. She had kept watch each day, hoping to see a familiar face, but those who passed were strangers.

Beside her Jeanne shifted uneasily. 'Don't show yourself!' she warned. 'The street is being watched. Should anyone give a signal, they will be seized at once.'

Emma froze. 'Upon whose orders?'

'The master's, of course. You ain't allowed out neither.'

'But Monsieur Chavasse explained that he was thinking of my safety.' She saw the look of disbelief on the girl's face.

'He wants your friends, miss. Your family ain't the only one they've helped to get away. Monsieur has seen his prizes slipping through his fingers.'

'Then thank heavens I have seen nothing of them. I should certainly have tried to drop a note.'

The girl hesitated. 'Must I take one for you?'

'No, you shall not! You have risked enough, my dear. I'll think of something…'

Emma spoke with more conviction than she felt. Even had she been willing to risk Jeanne's safety by accepting her help, the girl did not know her friends nor they her. Now she herself was virtually a prisoner in this house. She must find some way of getting out.

Even as she practised upon the spinet in the salon she considered the plan that had been forming in her mind. Nothing could be done until Robert returned from Toulon. His minions had had their orders and she suspected that even an offer of gold would not persuade them to disobey him. If they did so, they were dead men. She knew that now.

How could she ever have considered him a friend? As a child she had adored him, basking in his admiration, loving his wit and his unfailing good humour. What had happened to change him? She thought she knew. There had always been a touch of arrogance in his character. Handsome, elegant and sure of his own capabilities, he

had seemed like a god to Emma. Now she realised that
her idol had feet of clay. Power had corrupted him beyond redemption and he would use that power for his
own gain.

He would not use it with her help. Now that Emma
knew him for what he was anger strengthened her determination.

She spent many hours in Monsieur Diderot's library,
apparently lost in a book. In reality she was composing
a letter to her father. Just how good was Robert's command of the English language? To gain her own ends
she would have to take a chance on it. If she failed, she
could well be mounting the steps of the guillotine herself. Now she must deceive Robert with all the guile of
which she was capable.

When he returned to Marseilles later in the week she
greeted him with apparent pleasure, thanking him pret-
tily for the gifts which he presented to her.

'Perfumed gloves *and* sweetmeats?' she exclaimed.
'Robert, you are spoiling me!' Little did he know that
he had played into her hands.

'Who deserves it more, my dear? In my absence you
have not been bored?'

'A little, I must confess. I have not been used to spend
so much time indoors.'

'Ah, you English, with your extraordinary passion for
fresh air! I fear we shall never understand you, but,
Emma, do you not realise the reason why I counselled
you not to venture into the streets?'

'I know you are thinking of my safety, but now that
Marseilles is in your hands the danger must be less.'

'That is true to a certain extent, but I prefer to take

no chances. I should never forgive myself if you were injured.'

'You are very good,' she said sweetly. There, for the moment, she let the matter rest.

That evening she dressed carefully for the role she intended to play. Nothing too sophisticated, she decided. Robert must continue to see her as an innocent girl, incapable of devious behaviour. She settled upon a simple gown in a delicate shade of Madonna blue and with a modest neckline.

'Must I help with your hair, *mademoiselle*?' Jeanne advanced upon her bearing a pretty jewelled circlet.

'Not tonight, I think!' Emma looked at her reflection in the mirror and was tempted to smile. Even to her own eyes she looked about fifteen years old.

Jeanne was troubled. 'You aren't planning anything foolish, are you, ma'am?'

'Of course not, Jeanne! Do you imagine that I plan to knock Monsieur Chavasse upon the head and escape from the house?'

'No, but there is a look about you—I beg that you will take care…'

'You need have no fear. Now, hand me that pretty shawl! This is a draughty house and I have no wish to freeze to death.' With that she went to join Robert for supper.

He was all gallantry that evening, seating her with care, attentive to her every wish, and careful to avoid controversial topics in the course of conversation.

This suited Emma well. In her role as a curious schoolgirl, anxious to learn from an expert, she began to ask about the history of Marseilles. Robert beamed at

her. He was something of an authority upon the subject.
He told her of the changing fortunes of the city over
many centuries, each wave of invaders leaving their
mark.

'The Romans were here?' she asked, wide-eyed.

'Most certainly, and for many centuries, as were the
Phoenicians.'

'And the Greeks?'

'Of course. As you know, my dear, our own civili-
sation is based upon their teachings.'

Emma was tempted to inform him that in his case the
philosophy of the Greeks had fallen upon stony ground,
but she held her peace. Unknowingly, Robert had provided her with what she needed.

She waited until the meal was over and they had retired to the salon. There she sat down with a pensive
look, and gazed into the fire.

'What is it, Emma?' Robert appeared concerned.

'I have been thinking,' she told him quietly. 'I must
get back to England, but, as you say, I cannot go alone.
Are you sure that you can get a message to my father?'
She was aware at once of the look of triumph on his
face, although he tried to hide it.

'Nothing is more certain, Emma. Certain men move
freely between our two countries. Do you intend to write
to your father?'

'Only if you will guarantee his safe conduct through
France.'

'Did I not give you my word?' Robert looked indignant. 'A man's word is his bond, you know, although
perhaps you are a little young to understand these
things.'

'Perhaps I am,' she admitted humbly. 'But I want to be sure that he won't be harmed.'

He took her hands then and gazed deep into her eyes. 'Your father is one of my oldest friends,' he assured her. 'His safety means as much to me as does your own.'

Emma believed him. He would not hesitate to sacrifice the pair of them if it suited him. She gave him an artless smile. 'Shall I write now?' she asked. 'Perhaps we might compose the letter together?'

He fell in readily with her suggestion, although he disclaimed any wish to help her. He seated her at the desk, and found writing materials without delay.

Emma knew exactly what she planned to say. She had had three days to consider the content of this all-important letter. Now she paused, gazing into space as she pretended to be lost in thought.

At last she put pen to paper, writing carefully, and stopping at length between sentences. 'There, will this do?' She handed him the letter.

Robert seized it with ill-disguised eagerness. He scanned it quickly and hid a smile. What a child she was, to give her friends away so easily! Now he had the name of his enemy. Simon Avedon must be the man he'd sought for months. 'Emma, you are more than generous! Are you quite sure of this?'

'Of course. Let me read it aloud to you. Then you may correct anything with which you disagree.' She was taking a chance, but he had noticed nothing amiss.

'That might be best.' He settled into a chair and closed his eyes, prepared to listen to every word.

Emma began to read:

Dear Father,
Our old friend Robert Chavasse has promised

that this letter will reach you. He found me in Marseilles as I was attempting to return to England.

I am quite unharmed, though Robert believes that I took a dreadful risk in trusting certain Englishmen who promised to accompany me. He assures me that Simon Avedon and his friends must be adventurers and soldiers of fortune.

Robert has been kindness itself. I feel quite spoiled. He has showered me with gifts and we dine together each evening, discussing subjects that would interest you, such as the Romans, the Phoenicians and especially the Greeks.

For the moment I am not in danger, although Robert is worried about conditions in this country. He would bring me back himself, but he is needed here.

He is a man of great influence now and is able to promise you safe conduct through France if you will come to fetch me. Will you do this, please? I long to be with you again. My best love to you, Mama and the children.

Robert beamed at her. 'My dear Emma, it is perfect, although you overwhelm me with your praise. I have done so little for you. May I not do more?'

Emma hesitated. 'There is one thing. Will you sign the letter below my name, then Father will be assured of your good faith—?'

'Give me the pen!' He added his signature with a flourish. 'There, do you feel happier now?'

'I do indeed!' Emma spoke no more than the truth. She had taken a chance on naming Simon Avedon, believing correctly that Robert would regard this information as the most important item in her letter.

It wasn't. What he had overlooked completely was the warning to her father. Frederick Lynton, with his classical education, would pick up at once on certain references, such as the ancient warning to beware of Greeks bearing gifts. Surely now he would not attempt to return to France.

She sank into a chair, trembling with relief. She had named Simon with more than one purpose. It was not only to capture Robert's attention. Her father was sure to make enquiries about her mysterious rescuer. If reports were favourable, it might help to allay his fears about her safe return.

Emma gazed into the fire. Was she building castles in the air? She had heard nothing of her friends; for all she knew, they might be dead or captured. In naming Simon she could have added to their danger, but she thought not. Robert's look of triumph had assured her that their capture was still of prime importance to him. Now he was fidgeting in his chair, clearly anxious to leave her.

Emma excused herself at once. 'I shall sleep more easily tonight,' she told him. 'Robert, are you sure that my father will receive my letter?'

'I give you my word on it.' He laid a hand upon his heart. 'I am so pleased that you have taken my advice.' With that he dropped a gentle kiss upon her brow and left her.

Emma felt elated. So far her plan had worked. Clearly Robert thought her just a stupid girl. He believed he had tricked her into summoning her father back to France, and also into giving away the name of the man he sought above all others. Now he had only to wait and his enemies would fall into his hands like ripe plums.

He would discover his mistake, she promised herself fiercely. Meantime, there was still much to do. She had to find some way of getting out of this house, if only to give her friends a chance to speak to her.

The opportunity came on the following day. Robert did not appear until the evening, but when he joined her for their meal his manner was positively joyful.

'You have sent the letter?' she asked.

'Dear Emma, I made it the first task of the day.'

'How good you are!' she murmured as she waved the food away.

'What is it, my dear?' Robert was all concern.

'I fear I have the headache, Robert. I shall be so pleased when the streets are safe enough for me to walk abroad…I find this house so oppressive.'

'Of course you do.' He was surprisingly compliant. 'You have been indoors for far too long. I see no reason why you should not venture out this week, as long as you are guarded.'

Emma gave him a pathetic smile. 'Perhaps as far as a church? I have not performed my duties for so long. Besides, it is almost Christmas…'

'Emma, what is this? Your family is not Catholic. Your father is an agnostic, is he not?'

'He is, but he would never impose his beliefs upon us, and, as you know, I was convent-educated.'

'And the nuns converted you?' He looked his disbelief.

'They did,' she lied steadily. 'We all need something to believe in in this world, don't you agree?'

'I do, but hardly in myth and legend. However, I am being unfair. Your private beliefs are no concern of mine, much though I may deplore them.'

'Then you have no objection if I visit the church of the Holy Name on Sunday?'

'None whatever, my dear!' His eyes were intent upon her face. 'Berthe will be happy to go with you.'

'I doubt that,' Emma said swiftly. 'Berthe dislikes me. She has made her feelings all too clear.'

'Nonsense! Berthe is simply concerned about you. She feels that you are suffering from *crise des nerfs*. It would not be surprising, considering your recent terrible experiences.'

Emma was furious. How dared he discuss her with Berthe? 'Perhaps I have misjudged her,' she said sweetly. 'It's true! I have not been myself for these last few days. That is why I thought perhaps that a visit to a church might help lift my spirits.'

'You are right, my dear. Your religion will be a consolation to you at this worrying time. Berthe will be pleased, little though you may believe it.'

Emma smiled again. She had been about to ask that Jeanne might accompany her, but she decided against it. Robert must not suspect that she had a friend among the servants. It would mean certain danger for the girl.

And Robert had been altogether too complaisant. He had agreed at once to allow her to leave the house. Was he tired of waiting for her friends to try to get a message to her? Perhaps she was to be the bait with which he hoped to trap them.

Now he was all support. 'Shall we say this coming Sunday, then?' he asked. 'If you wish it, I will order the carriage for you, unless you prefer to walk. The church is not too far from here.'

Emma did not jump at the suggestion. Was he hoping that someone would try to rescue her if she went on foot? She must be very careful. 'You don't think it too dangerous?'

'Berthe will be with you and I have no intention of

leaving you without protection. One of my men will follow you.'

'Just as long as it isn't that hateful one-eyed creature,' she insisted. 'I don't like the way he looks at me.'

'Chabrol? Why, Emma, he is a Frenchman and overly susceptible to feminine beauty, I fear. Still, if he offends you, I will give you another guard.'

Emma felt relieved. Only the one-eyed Chabrol and his companion could identify both Marcel and Simon Avedon if they were in the congregation at the church of the Holy Name.

She hesitated. 'I don't mean to be unkind,' she said. 'The man cannot help the loss of an eye. Indeed, it is a tragedy for him, but…'

'But you are little more than a child and you don't yet know the ways of men. Emma, I do understand your misgivings.' At that moment he resolved to warn his most trusted henchman to be more careful. Once this charade was over, the man could have Emma to himself. In the meantime Robert needed her cooperation and she was giving it in full measure. Nothing must be done to cause her to withdraw it.

On Sunday her friends would be given every opportunity to attempt to seize her. Chabrol might not be visible in the street, but he would be there, together with a dozen others. Then, at last, these interfering Englishmen would get their just deserts.

As to the girl herself, it was unfortunate, but casualties had to be expected in this war of liberation. A wry smile curved his lips. Liberation for whom? Did these poor, deluded fools who screamed for the blood of the hated aristocrats imagine that they would be any better off under the Revolutionary Committee? Not if he had anything to do with it. He despised the ragged mob as heartily as he hated the nobles who had treated him with courtesy, at the same time making it clear that his ancestry did not match their own. He had been tolerated, even petted by some of the women, but he was an outsider and he knew it.

Well, he now had it in his power to make them pay for their disdain, and he would do so. In these next few months his name would become as familiar as that of the little upstart Corsican who had gained fame in Toulon.

If he could but have one triumph…one coup such as the capture of the Englishman, or assist in the return to France of the dangerous Frederick Lynton, his position would be assured.

And nothing would stop him, he vowed to himself. He'd worked too hard, abased himself before those he considered his inferiors, to turn back now.

Nothing of this showed in his face. He began to speak of happier times, when he had been a welcome visitor in the Lynton household. 'Those days will return,' he assured her tenderly. 'Once order is restored, conditions must improve for all the people of this country.'

Emma was tempted to remind him that too many of them would not live to enjoy that glorious future, but she held her tongue, nodding brightly at his outlined plans for the new Republic.

'But must you not secure your borders first?' she enquired in a bewildered tone.

Robert decided to humour her. The girl had always been outspoken, encouraged by a too-indulgent father. A man of her own would knock that nonsense out of her.

His eyes roved over her voluptuous figure. Emma was too short in stature to be compared favourably with the type of woman he admired, but she showed every sign of becoming a beauty. A susceptible man might drown in the gaze of those blue eyes and find it hard to resist the temptation to stroke that flawless creamy skin.

But he was not susceptible to her charms. He preferred a more sophisticated mate. Emma might believe herself to be intelligent, but he considered her a fool, with her stupid liberal ideas and a ridiculous urge to set the world to rights. She would never learn that the main business of life was the survival of oneself, no matter what the cost to others.

Now he considered her question with apparent care. 'You are thinking of Austria and Russia?'

'Why, yes! Their troops are massing on your borders, are they not? Doesn't it disturb you? After all, you are already at war with England.'

'A tragedy, my dear Emma, but in your own country the authorities were terrified that the British people might follow our example. They hope to crush us before that happens, but they won't succeed. As to the Austrians? Well, it was to be expected...the late queen was one of their own.'

'That was ill done of you,' Emma said quietly.

'Of me! My dear Emma, let me assure you that I played no part in voting for her execution. Surely you cannot believe me to be such a monster?'

Emma sensed that he was lying, but she pretended to accept his false assurance of innocence. She glanced at the clock.

'When I am with you I lose all sense of time, Robert, and I am unused to these late hours.'

He was on his feet at once, bowing over her hand with the utmost gallantry. 'Forgive me!' he pleaded. 'The fault is mine. I should not keep you from your rest.

I can only excuse myself by telling you of my pleasure in our conversations.'

Privately he considered them a bore, but he could afford such annoyance for the moment. With any luck he would have the Englishmen within his grasp before the week was out.

As Emma climbed the stairs she was lost in thought. Her plan was working, but was she putting her friends in danger by acting as Robert's tethered goat? Bait had but a single purpose: to assist in capture.

And she was the bait. She was in no doubt of it, but she could think of no alternative but to visit the church on Sunday. She could not be rescued from this house. It was too heavily guarded. Her only hope was to reach some public place where a message might be passed to her.

Her resolution wavered for only a moment. Was she placing too much faith in her English friends? For all she knew they might have decided to travel on without her, or, at worst, they might be dead or captured.

On reflection she dismissed that dreadful thought. Robert had been all too ready to fall in with her plans, and now she knew that he did nothing without a purpose favourable to himself. He was still in pursuit of Simon Avedon.

The knowledge should have worried her. Instead it raised her spirits. That difficult and complex creature would be more than a match for Robert Chavasse. Possibly even now he was planning a campaign to free her. Of course, it would not be because he had the least regard for Emma Lynton as a person. Simon's actions were determined only by his sense of duty. Even so, she longed to see him again.

She thought of her father's teasing test of a man's

character. 'Would you follow him through a jungle?' her father had asked. In Simon's case she could put her hand on her heart and agree to do so.

It was ridiculous. She hardly knew the man and their brief acquaintance had resulted for the most part in arguments and quarrelling. Yet when she compared him with Robert Chavasse she could be in no doubt as to which man she would trust.

Emma reached her room to find Jeanne waiting for her.

'You should have gone to bed,' she protested. 'I did not mean to be so late.'

'I was worried, *mademoiselle*. Is it true that you will go to church on Sunday?'

'It is. Monsieur Chavasse has no objection.'

'And Berthe is to accompany you? Oh, miss, why didn't you ask for me?'

'It wouldn't have been wise,' Emma told her. 'It might have been putting you in danger.'

'Oh, you ain't planning to run away? Chabrol has his orders. He will fetch you back.'

'I don't plan to run away,' Emma said steadily. 'Now, Jeanne, I shall need your help to look out the warmest clothing in the closet. The wind is bitter, so I understand.'

'But you'll be in the carriage, *mademoiselle*—'

'No, I shall not. I prefer to walk. I have been too long indoors and *monsieur* agrees with me…'

The girl's face was a picture of despair. 'He would! Oh, don't you see? He's trying to trap you.'

'Now you are allowing your imagination to run away with you. What harm can come to me with guardians such as Berthe and Chabrol? Come, Jeanne, help me with my gown.'

Try as she might, Emma found it impossible to raise the girl's spirits. There was nothing for it but to tell her the truth. 'I have no way of knowing,' she admitted, 'but my friends may try to get a message to me.'

'Oh, miss, you will be careful? That Chabrol—why, he thinks no more of snuffing out a life than he would of treading on an insect.'

'I know that, Jeanne, but I cannot remain a prisoner in this house.'

'Why not? We've all had our orders from the master. You are to have anything you want, and you are in no danger here.'

'Perhaps not, for the moment, and I am to be allowed anything but my freedom. Is that not so?'

Emma did not voice her main worry to the girl, but she had long realised her own importance to Robert Chavasse. Her father was his prime target, more so even than Simon Avedon. If he heeded her warning and did not come to France to fetch her, Robert would resort to another strategy and it did not take a genius to decide what that might be.

Robert would offer a life for a life. Her own in exchange for that of her father, and Frederick Lynton would not hesitate. He would save his daughter, and Emma would not be party to such a frightful bargain.

Beside her Jeanne was weeping softly. 'You could still take me with you to the church,' she sobbed. 'I always go to mass at Christmastide. Gilles would meet us there…'

'And who is Gilles, my dear?' Emma was happy to divert the girl's attention.

Jeanne blushed a little. 'Why, miss, he wants to marry me.'

'But that is wonderful! Do you love him, Jeanne?'

'I've loved him all my life, but it ain't no use.'

'Why ever not? If you marry, you could leave this house and you would have the protection of a husband.'

'It's his parents, *mademoiselle*. They have a young widow in mind for him. She was left well off, and they think her a better match.'

'But Gilles must have a mind of his own.'

'He has, it's me who won't accept him. They mean well, you see.'

'You are more than generous, Jeanne, but you must not distress yourself. All may turn out better than you expect. Now, listen to me carefully. I won't allow you to go with me because I may need you here. Suspicion must not fall upon you.'

'I don't understand you.'

'Well, let us suppose that I am mistaken in my friends. They may already have left Marseilles. On Sunday it may be that no one will approach me. Then I shall be a prisoner still with only you to help me.'

It was enough to satisfy the girl, but on the following Sunday she was unable to hide her misgivings.

'My dear, do try to smile,' Emma pleaded. 'Would you give me away?'

Jeanne shook her head and turned away as Emma took a small purse from her reticule.

'I want you to do something for me,' she insisted. 'Hold out your hand.'

When the girl obeyed, Emma shook out several gold coins into the work-roughened palm. 'This is your Christmas gift,' she said. 'It will serve you as a dowry.'

Jeanne stared at the coins in disbelief. She had never seen so much money in her life. It was more than she could earn in all her years of domestic service, but she coloured with anger and pushed the gift away.

'You said I was your friend,' she said in a low voice. 'Friends don't need money to give their help.'

'Jeanne, don't insult me, please! I had no thought of paying you for your help. Is it so wrong of me to want to give you a present?'

'I won't take it,' the girl said stubbornly.

Emma smiled. 'Does Gilles know what a strong-minded woman he plans to wed? Well, then, if you will not take the money, will you keep it for me? I could be robbed in the street, you know, and if I return here I may have need of it.'

'And if you don't?' Jeanne's face was miserable.

'Then you will know that I am safe among my friends and you will use the money wisely. Is that a bargain?'

Jeanne seized her hand and kissed it. 'I may never see you again,' she whispered. '*Mademoiselle*, you have been so good to me....'

'We shall meet again,' Emma promised. 'I don't lose my friends so easily. Now, hand me my bonnet and my gloves. Berthe must be growing impatient.'

She was not mistaken. Clad all in black, the house-keeper awaited her in the hall.

''Tis bitter weather to be walking,' she grumbled. 'Master said as how we might take the carriage...'

'I prefer to walk,' Emma told her coldly. 'I am much in need of the exercise.' This brought no response except for a look of sheer contempt, which Emma ignored. She set off at a brisk pace in the direction of the church spire, which was visible in the distance.

The narrow streets were crowded with people walking in the same direction. In spite of the efforts of the authorities to stamp out a religion that they regarded as subversive superstition, it was clear that they had not succeeded. The faith of the common people was still strong.

Keenly aware of the watchful eyes of the housekeeper and also of the man who strolled beside them, Emma felt relieved that no one had tried to speak to her in the street. Then, as she entered the church, her spirits lifted. Lit by the gentle glow of a thousand candles, the crib of the Christ Child lay before her as the voices of the congregation lifted in praise.

Emma moved forward to look more closely. Then she was surrounded by a group of children. In their midst she saw Marcel. He did not catch her eye, but a note was pushed into her hand. When she looked again he had disappeared.

She paused to light a candle and stole a quick glance at the note. It was brief and to the point, but the words leapt out at her. It advised her to use the first confessional box.

Chapter Seven

Emma's heart was thudding wildly. Surely Berthe must hear it? She stole a wary glance at the angular figure of the housekeeper, but the woman had seen a familiar face in the congregation and was beckoning to a friend.

It was Brigitte, the other maid. Emma groaned to herself. Now there would be another pair of eyes watching her every move. Both women were her enemies. Nothing would give them greater pleasure than to trap her.

She picked up her hymnal and joined in the singing, ignoring the pair of them. Never had a service seemed so long, although the sermon struck a chord in her breast. It was a plea for tolerance and understanding.

Emma looked at the speaker with interest. Even his magnificent gold-embroidered vestments could not disguise the fact that the priest was a short, squat man, not in his first youth. Yet she was beguiled by the beauty of his voice, and the sincerity with which he insisted upon the old truths.

Father Jacques was an unlikely hero, but somehow she sensed that Simon Avedon was not mistaken in him. This man would not hesitate to lay down his own life for others if the need arose. The knowledge strengthened her own determination.

She must escape, but how? Every exit from the church would be guarded. It was impossible to lose herself in the crowd. She would be seized at once. For the moment she could only follow the instructions in the note.

Some minutes before the end of the service she rose to her feet. A clawlike hand closed at once about her wrist.

'Where do you think you are going?' Berthe demanded.

'To confession. Have you some objection?'

'I'm not to let you out of my sight. Now sit down, miss! You ain't going nowhere.'

'Perhaps you'd prefer me to make a scene?' Emma looked about her. 'These people seem devout. I doubt if they would welcome a disturbance in their place of worship.'

They were already attracting attention, and clearly Berthe had been warned against it. As heads turned in her direction she took her hand from Emma's sleeve. 'No tricks!' she warned. 'I shall be waiting for you.'

Emma didn't reply. She slipped across the aisle and entered the first of the wooden cubicles standing by the wall. In the darkness she stumbled against a wooden stool that faced a small metal grille set into the panelling.

'Sit down, Miss Lynton!' a deep voice ordered.

Emma caught her breath as the shutter behind the grille slid back. Peering into the gloom, she could see only a hooded figure leaning towards her, a hand shielding his face.

'Simon,' she whispered. 'Oh, Simon, is it really you?'

'Who else?' came the teasing reply. 'Now, *mademoi-*

selle, your jailers won't believe that your sins will take long to confess...'

'Oh, pray don't joke!' she cried in anguish. 'You are in great danger—'

'Which will be even greater if we don't make haste,' he replied.

'But you don't understand! There is no escape from here. Every exit is guarded.'

'Not quite! Now if you will curb your unfortunate tendency to argue, I suggest that you reach out to your right and press your hand against the wood.'

'I don't know what you mean...' Frightened and confused, Emma felt desperate to touch him. She placed the palm of her hand flat against the metal grille and in a second his fingertips were against her own, sending an unspoken message of encouragement.

'Yes, like that!' he told her gently. 'Press firmly and the panel will move aside.'

She only half-believed him. The wall beside her looked so solid, but she did as he suggested, to her amazement, a section of the panelling swung outwards. She heard the click as the shutter behind the grille was replaced. Then Simon was standing in the aperture beside her, drawing her forward.

With a sob of relief she threw herself into his arms.

He held her to his breast for just a moment and she thought she felt his lips against her hair. He gave her no time to confirm this strange behaviour. Moving quickly, he pushed the panel back into place and secured it firmly.

Then he took her hand and began to lead her down a flight of steps that led into the darkness.

'Careful!' he warned. 'We dare not risk a light just yet.'

The staircase seemed endless, but it was not until they reached level ground that he paused to listen for sounds of pursuit. There was nothing.

'Good!' he said with satisfaction. Emma noticed that his eyes were twinkling. 'Your sins have taken long in confessing, *mademoiselle*.'

Emma could not raise a smile. A tear trickled down her cheek. 'I thought you were dead,' she told him in a broken voice.

'A cause for rejoicing, surely? After all, Miss Lynton, we have not been the best of friends.'

'No, but…well…you are my only hope of getting back to England.'

'Of course.' The teasing voice had disappeared. Now Simon was all efficiency. Taking a hooded robe from a hook upon the wall, he threw it to her. 'Wear this,' he said. 'It will serve as a disguise.'

Emma looked about her. Simon had taken a torch from an embrasure. Now, in its flickering light, she noticed the rows of tombs. 'Where are we?' she asked.

'We are in the crypt, *mademoiselle*. There is an exit into the graveyard.'

'I see. You seem to know the place well. Have you used this route before?'

'Many times, and I hope to do so again.'

'But your friend, Monsieur Jacques? Will he not be suspected?'

'For what reason? He is above suspicion. How could he be involved in your disappearance when, at this very moment, he is leading the faithful in prayer?'

'I should have known,' she cried bitterly. 'You think of everything, don't you?'

'I try.' His voice was imperturbable. 'After all, there is much at stake here, including your charming head.'

'Much you care!' Emma could not have said why she
was so incensed by his manner. Once again he had set
her at a distance. Even his teasing was preferable to that.
Had she imagined that kiss upon her head? She must
have done so. To Simon Avedon, the task of getting her
back to England was a duty and nothing more. She knew
it, so why did the thought annoy her?

It was just that she did not care to be regarded as a
package to be delivered to the appropriate authorities,
she decided, but Simon was in for a surprise.

Even as they had been speaking he was urging her
along.

'Make haste!' he insisted. 'We have not much time.
Once your escape is discovered all routes from the city
will be closed. We are not out of danger yet.'

Emma found herself running to keep up with his long
stride, but he didn't slow his pace until they reached the
lane that ran beside the graveyard. There he lifted a hand
and, as if by magic, Marcel appeared, driving a small
dog-cart.

'Get in!' Simon ordered. With effortless ease he slid
into the seat beside her and they set off at a brisk pace.

'Won't we be stopped?' she whispered. 'This cart is
a tempting prize.'

'It is also well known as the property of Father
Jacques. None of the locals will question two of his fellow friars on business for the parish. Keep your hood
close about your face.'

Emma did as she was bid. In spite of his assurances
she was fearful of discovery, but she could hear no hue
and cry behind them.

'You have done this before?' she asked at last.

'Many times, and I hope to do it again. This scheme
has proved its value in saving lives.'

'But the priest—Father Jacques—don't the authorities suspect him?'

'Why should they? Throughout your visit to the church he was in clear view of the congregation. Even at this moment he will be bestowing a final blessing upon his flock.'

'He must be a brave man.'

'None braver, *mademoiselle*!'

Emma shuddered. 'If Chavasse finds the secret exit from the confessional, his life will be forfeit.'

'He knows that, but it is a risk he is prepared to take. In any case, it is unlikely. I barred the door securely.'

'Don't be too sure. Chavasse will not hesitate to tear the place apart. He is capable of anything.' She heard a low laugh.

'I'm glad to hear that your stay with your friend has not been totally wasted. You seem to have changed your mind about him.'

'He is no friend of mine. He's changed. Now all he thinks about is himself.'

'And what brought about this sudden change of heart?'

'He tried to trap me into enticing my father back to France. I wrote the letter, but it carries a warning that my father will understand.'

'Chavasse read the letter, of course?'

'He did, but he overlooked the warning to beware of Greeks bearing gifts.'

Simon laughed aloud. 'What it is to have a classical education! My congratulations, Miss Lynton! I should have guessed that, with your devious mind, you would find some way to outwit him.'

'Sneer if you must!' she snapped. 'I could think of nothing else to do. I was a prisoner in that house, though he would not admit it. My safety was his main concern, or so he claimed.'

'We guessed as much. The street outside was watched, so we could not get a message to you, but my faith in you was unabated. All we had to do was wait.'

Emma did not take up his teasing challenge. She was silent for some time. Then, to her surprise, a large hand covered her own.

'Something is troubling you,' Simon said more kindly. 'Won't you tell me what it is?'

'If my father believes that I am being held against my will, he may still come to France, in spite of my warning.'

'Then we must assure him that you have escaped.'

'Oh, can you do that? Is it possible to get a message to him?'

'Chavasse is not the only person with access to a network of couriers,' he told her smoothly. 'Your father will be informed.'

'Oh, thank you!' she cried. 'Simon, there is one other matter. I must not be taken again. Failing all else, Robert Chavasse may offer a life for a life. My own for that of my father. I cannot let that happen.'

'It won't happen,' he assured her. 'Now, ma'am, since we appear to be dispensing with formality, may I be allowed to call you by your given name?'

Emma stared at him. Then she understood his meaning and colour flooded her face. 'I beg your pardon, Mr Avedon,' she said stiffly. 'I had no right…I mean, I had no intention of overstepping the bounds of propriety.' She heard a chuckle of pure enjoyment.

'May we not agree to ignore the rules of polite society, at least until we are back in England, Emma? We shall be much in each other's company for these next few weeks, travelling together, eating together and sleeping together.' He heard a little sound of protest. 'Always fully clothed, of course,' he continued.

Emma looked up and saw the amusement in his eyes. 'You are right!' she told him frankly. 'This is no time to be mealy-mouthed. I shall be happy for you to call me by my given name... Now, sir, where are you taking me?'

By this time they had left the outskirts of the city and were travelling fast away from the coast and into the foothills.

He did not answer her directly. 'We have a problem,' he announced. 'Piers has been injured, so we are likely to be delayed.'

'What happened?'

'They were almost through Marseilles when Mado was accosted by a drunken mob. Piers took a musket ball in the shoulder when he went to help her.'

'Is he badly injured?'

'He has lost a lot of blood.'

'But Pierre and Yves? Could they not help?'

'They'd been beaten to the ground when Joseph found them. He drove his horse into the crowd to scatter the ringleaders. It was enough to cause the rest of the mob to flee.'

'But they are all safe now?' Emma did not hide her anxiety. In their short acquaintance she had grown attached to the ill-assorted members of their little group.

'They are, but this is a set-back.' Simon frowned. 'Piers cannot travel for the moment. He feels that we should leave him.'

'Oh, pray don't do that! Alone and injured, he would not stand a chance if he were discovered.'

'I have no intention of leaving him,' Simon told her

calmly. 'But we must get you out of France. You said yourself that you would make the perfect bargaining counter for your friend Chavasse.'

'He is *not* my friend!' she cried hotly. 'Why must you continue to insist on it?'

'Possibly because you still have influence with him, *mademoiselle*. How did you persuade him to release Madame Diderot and her daughter?'

'You knew about that?'

'Naturally! The house in Marseilles had been under observation from the moment you arrived there. No one entered or left without my knowing of it, and Chabrol was followed to the prison with his message. We saw *madame* released on the following day... Monsieur Chavasse is not renowned for a tendency to mercy. What bargain did you strike with him?' His eyes were intent upon her face and Emma felt herself blushing, much to her own annoyance.

'If you imagine that Robert Chavasse made... er...advances to me, you are quite mistaken. If you must know, he thinks of me as little more than a stupid child, overindulged by her father and encouraged to think of herself as much cleverer than she is.' Her tone was icy.

'And *monsieur* was wrong, of course?' There was no mistaking the amusement in Simon's voice.

Emma rounded on him in fury. 'I *did* get myself out of the house,' she reminded him.

'That didn't surprise me in the least. I felt sure that your devious little mind would come up with some solution. All we had to do was wait.'

'You flatter me, sir! That same devious mind persuaded Robert to release his victims in return for my agreement to write to my father. Of course, he didn't know that I had included a warning with my letter.'

Beside her she heard a chuckle of amusement. 'Chavasse could not be more mistaken in you, could he? Tell me, why did you do it?'

'Do what?'

'Persuade him to release Madame Diderot and her daughter.'

Emma was silent for some minutes. 'I was disgusted,' she said at last. 'Robert encouraged Berthe to denounce the Diderot family because he wanted their house and their possessions, not because they were enemies of the State. I could not let him kill *madame* as he had done her husband.'

To her surprise a strong arm slipped about her shoulders. She looked up in alarm, but Simon was smiling at her. 'I'm glad you are on my side,' he teased.

Emma wriggled free of the encircling arm. His closeness was having the most disturbing effect upon her emotions. He'd kissed her once before and she had been unable to banish the memory of those warm caressing lips. What was she thinking of? This man had nothing more in mind than the need to do his duty. Those kisses had been given with the intention of deceiving Chabrol, and for no other reason.

'You are sure that you can get a message to my father?' she said at last.

'I am certain of it. Why do you ask?'

'I have been thinking. If my father knows that I am safe with you, he won't worry about me, and nor will he be tempted to return to France.'

'So…?'

'So there is no need for haste. I know what you do, and possibly I could help you.'

'In what way?' From the cool tone she could not guess what he was thinking, but it was not encouraging.

Emma persevered. 'I know this country. I speak the local dialect, and a woman is less likely to be suspected than a man.'

'But I thought that you were desperate to return to England. What has brought about this change of heart?'

'I can't bear the cruelty,' she told him frankly. 'What is happening in France at present is nothing to do with liberty, equality or brotherhood. It is simply an opportunity for unscrupulous men to further their ambitions at any cost. They shall not do so with my approval.'

Emma gave him a defiant look, fully expecting some acid comment upon her romantic notions. To her astonishment, he took her hand and raised it to his lips.

'Your offer is generous beyond belief,' he told her very gently. 'Sadly, my dear, I can't accept it.'

Emma pulled her hand away. 'Why not?' she demanded. 'I suppose you think me merely a stupid woman.'

'Have I said so? I think nothing of the kind, but I would ask you to consider. Let us suppose that you were seized again.' He stopped her protest with a lifted hand. 'No, Emma, let me have my say. It could happen to any of us, even the most experienced. Next time you would not be treated with consideration. I wonder if you have any idea of the horrors of French prisons?'

She did not answer him.

'Aside from that, you would have given Robert Chavasse the opportunity he seeks to persuade your father to return to France.'

'But I have warned him not to do so.'

Simon took her hand again and held it in his own. Then he began to stroke her fingers. 'Emma, I have no wish to frighten you, but you must understand the true nature of Robert Chavasse. He is not a Frenchman—' He fell silent, wondering if he should go on.

'Well, what does that signify?' she asked.

'He is of Sicilian origin, and the natives of that country have a somewhat direct approach to difficulties.'

'I don't know what you mean.' Emma was still smarting from his abrupt refusal of her help and she didn't trouble to hide her anger.

Out of all patience, he studied her hand again. 'Such pretty fingers,' he said quietly. 'I'm sure you would not care to lose them.'

Emma paled. 'What are you saying?' she whispered. 'Why are you trying to frighten me?'

'I'm trying to make you understand. Your father might receive a finger or an ear to persuade him to change his mind.'

'No, I won't believe it. That is too horrible. No human being could be capable of such brutality.'

'It has happened. Chavasse has far too much at stake to trouble his head with thoughts of pity or humanity.'

'Oh, Simon, are you sure?'

'Quite sure! I'd hoped to keep these horrors from you, but you must believe me, Emma. Perhaps you see now why it is so important to get you out of France.'

Emma hung her head. 'I have been very stupid,' she admitted miserably. 'But I did not know, you see.'

'That doesn't make you a stupid person, although you have an alarming tendency to believe the best of people, myself excluded, of course.'

'Oh, that isn't true!' she cried hotly. 'I was never so glad in all my life—I mean…I am pleased that you rescued me.' She could not tell him that for the past week she had longed to see him again with an intensity that

frightened her. She could not understand her own con-
flicting feelings.

The man beside her had none of the qualities that
might endear him to a woman's heart. His manners were
cool and distant and at times he did not hesitate to use
the most cutting sarcasm. And he wasn't even handsome,
she thought on a half-sob. As if that mattered. She would
entrust her life to him without a second's hesitation.

She could not look at him. The knowledge that she
had almost betrayed her feelings filled her with dismay.
Then she heard a short laugh.

'Ah, yes! Rescuers must always be welcome. Better
than Greeks bearing gifts, you will agree?'

Emma was forced to smile at this reference to her
warning, and suddenly she felt at ease with him. She had
strayed on to dangerous ground. She must not let it happen again.

Now she looked about her. This was wild country, far
inland from the coast. There was not a dwelling in sight.
'Have we far to go?' she asked.

'We are almost there. Do you see the valley ahead?
That is our destination.'

'And is it safe?'

'I believe so, Emma. These people have farmed the
land for generations. They are a law unto themselves. A
proud race with their own values, suspicious of strangers, and with scant regard for authority.'

'Then why should they help us?'

'Because of Pierre. He is one of their own. Without
him we might search for days without a hope of shelter.'

Emma fell silent as they made their way towards a
group of low stone buildings. The two men who came
to greet them were both young. They seemed to know
Simon well.

He handed Emma down with an instruction to remove the monk's robe. He took off his own, and handed both garments to the men. As they drove back to Marseilles, she realised that Simon had laid his plans well in advance. Who could guess that the men in the dog-cart were not the same two who had left the city earlier that day?

Simon wasted no time in hurrying her indoors. 'From now on you must not venture out,' he warned.

'Do you think that we were followed?'

'No, I don't, but we must take no chances. This farm is isolated, but Chavasse will be tireless in his search for you. There must be nothing untoward, even to the most casual observer.'

Emma shivered. Only in these last few hours had she fully understood the callous nature of her former friend. 'He won't take me alive,' she promised.

'Now, Emma, let us have no dramatics!' Simon teased. 'You must not joke about these matters. Marcel may even believe you, even if I do not.'

Emma had not been joking, but a glance at the boy convinced her that her words had terrified him. She smiled and took his hand.

'I can't resist the temptation to make game of Monsieur Avedon,' she insisted. 'Somehow we must make him smile, don't you agree?'

Marcel seemed convinced, but even so he took her hand and held it tight. '*Mademoiselle*, you would not do...what you suggested, would you?'

'Of course not! There will be no need. After all, we have Monsieur Avedon on our side. Who could possibly defeat us?' She had chosen her words with care, knowing that Simon would rise to the bait. She wasn't mistaken.

'How kind!' he murmured. 'You overwhelm me, *mademoiselle*!'

'I had hoped to do so, sir.' Emma gave him her sweetest smile. 'I can scarce believe my good fortune.'

At that he laughed aloud. 'Mercy!' he pleaded. 'Your tongue would flay a man alive! I thought we had agreed upon a truce.' His eyes were twinkling as he looked at her.

They were both smiling as they entered the long, low farmhouse kitchen.

Mado challenged them at once. 'So! I see that you have rescued your fine lady once again, *monsieur*. Now, perhaps, you will give some thought to the condition of your friend?'

'I had not forgotten him,' Simon told her quietly. 'How is Piers?'

Mado's eyes filled with tears. 'He has the fever,' she whispered. 'You may see for yourself.' She led them into a small room off the kitchen.

Piers was lying on a rough pallet. His eyes were too bright and he was flushed, but he stretched out a hand to Simon. 'You must go!' he whispered. 'Pray do not wait for me! I am putting you all in danger.'

'Nonsense, we are safe enough for the moment!' came the robust reply. Then Simon turned to Mado. 'Has the surgeon seen him?'

'We dared not risk it! Pierre extracted the ball, but there seems to be an infection.'

'It may respond to a poultice,' Emma suggested quietly. 'Herbs grow wild in the hills hereabouts. No doubt the mistress of this household has stored them for the winter.'

Mado sniffed at the suggestion, but Simon took Emma up at once. 'What do you need?' he asked.

Emma gave him her list. She was on familiar ground. Her father believed implicitly in the efficacy of natural remedies.

Mado eyed her with disdain as she infused the herbs with boiling water.

'That mess will do more harm than good!' she predicted scornfully. 'It looks disgusting! Are you trying to kill Monsieur Fanshawe?'

'No, Mado, I am trying to help him.' Emma refused to be drawn into an argument. 'The wound must be washed, or course. Can we remove his shirt without inflicting further pain?'

As the girl hesitated Emma lost her temper. She did not raise her voice, but her tone was cutting. 'Why don't we forget our differences?' she suggested sharply. 'We have an injured man here. As I understand it, he was injured whilst trying to help you. Will you not do the same for him?'

Mado flushed. Then she turned her head away, but she could not hide the tears that were pouring down her cheeks. 'It is all my fault!' she whispered. 'I was so sure that I knew the quietest route through the city. I wouldn't listen to him. We were surrounded before we knew it.'

Emma reached out to the girl. She could not bear to see a fellow human being in distress. 'We all make mistakes,' she comforted. 'Heaven knows, I've made enough myself. Now, Mado, let us try to make *monsieur* more comfortable. Do you slip his arm out of this sleeve and I will bathe the wound.'

Thankfully, Piers was drifting in and out of consciousness as she examined the torn mass of flesh. She worked quickly, with Mado's help, binding the poultice in place after drawing the edges of skin together.

Mado gulped. 'Will he...will he lose his arm, *mademoiselle*?'

'Of course not! Our patient is young and strong. Fortunately the musket ball did not shatter the bone, nor did it tear the muscles. This is a flesh wound, but the danger now is of infection. We must watch him carefully.' She looked at Mado's face and was disturbed by what she saw. 'When did you last sleep?' she asked.

'I can't remember!' The girl was swaying slightly. '*Monsieur* was delirious. I could not leave him. He might have hurt himself.'

'You won't help him by falling ill. Won't you try to rest?'

As Mado hesitated, Simon made the decision for her. He had entered the room unnoticed by either woman. Now his glance at Mado confirmed all Emma's suspicions. 'Do as Miss Lynton suggests!' he insisted. 'My dear, you are worn out! How shall we go on if you collapse? We should never cope with all our patients. If you sleep now, you shall return later to care for Piers.' Without waiting for a reply he took her arm and led her away.

When he returned he looked concerned. 'You women!' He shook his head in disbelief. 'You are prepared to kill yourselves rather than admit defeat.'

'Our sex has long training in dealing with adversity,' she told him coolly. 'How are Pierre and Yves? They too were injured, were they not?'

'They are battered and bruised, but the application of goose grease seems to be restoring them to health. How is Piers? Is his condition worse?'

'I think not.' Emma laid her hand upon the sick man's brow. 'He is resting more easily now.' She indicated the bowl beside her. 'When this infusion cools we shall use it to give him a strip wash.'

Simon sniffed at the aromatic liquid. 'Lavender?' he enquired.

Emma smiled. 'Of course! It grows wild hereabouts and I know of nothing more refreshing.'

'I do! Emma, had you forgot? You have not eaten all day.'

Emma stared at him, trying to recall. 'I'm not hungry,' she said at last.

'Nevertheless you will eat! Where is your common sense, my dear? Perhaps you have no objection to adding to my problems?'

Emma fell silent.

He held out a hand to her. 'Come!' he said. 'Let us dine together. Joseph will take your place here.'

Obediently, she laid her hand in his, conscious of the fact that, as always, his slightest touch seemed to heighten all her senses. Now, as the powerful fingers closed about her own, she had the strangest feeling that he was passing on to her some of his own strength. It was a comforting thought, but it had no basis in fact.

She was being fanciful. It had been a long day, and so much had happened since that morning. Her mind was playing tricks on her, and she was very tired. It didn't seem possible that she was now safe among her friends, and she owed it all to the man beside her. Unconsciously, she tightened her hold upon his hand.

Simon was at once aware of that convulsive movement. Now he looked down at her, a question in his eyes. 'What is it, Emma?' he asked gently.

'Oh, nothing! I am being foolish!' She attempted to withdraw her hand. 'I fear it will take me a little time to grow accustomed to being free again.'

'You are not safe yet,' he reminded her as they entered the kitchen, which was empty except for the farmer's wife. He seated Emma at the great wooden table and sniffed appreciatively as the woman ladled out her country soup. He waved aside her apologies for the simplicity of the fare.

'Nothing could be better!' he announced. 'This, with your fresh-baked bread and some of that delicious goat's cheese? Why, it is a feast fit for a king! Now, Emma, you must not insult *madame* by failing to eat your fill. We shall be lucky indeed to find another such cook in the course of our travels.'

As he smiled at the old woman she was clearly pleased by his compliments, although she blushed and disclaimed any special skills. Simon could be so charming, Emma thought drily. Sadly, he didn't trouble to waste that charm upon her.

'Where are the others?' she asked.

'Well, let us see.' He ticked them off on his fingers. 'Mado is asleep, Joseph is on duty in the sickroom, whilst Pierre and Marcel and Yves have retired to the barn.'

The farmer's wife looked troubled. '*Monsieur*, we have no accommodation here, other than for ourselves, and Mado is using the bedroom of our sons. There is only the hayloft. Must I ask my husband if he will give up his bed to the young lady?'

Emma was on her feet at once. 'You will do nothing of the kind!' she exclaimed. 'It is enough, *madame*, that you have risked your lives for us. I have slept in a barn before. I shall be happy to do so again.'

'Well then, *mademoiselle*, if you will excuse me? We keep country hours, asleep from dusk to dawn. *Monsieur* will show you to the loft.' She bobbed a curtsy and left them.

Emma looked at Simon and found that he was smiling. There seemed to be no particular reason for such amusement, so she challenged him. 'What do you find so entertaining, sir?'

'Just you, as always, my dear Emma. In your company there is never a dull moment.'

'I can't think why you should make such a statement, Mr Avedon.'

'Oho! We are back to formality again, are we? It won't do, Emma, especially as we are to sleep together.'

She coloured to the roots of her hair. 'You are insulting, sir. First you suggest that I am a figure of fun, and then you try to indicate that I…that I…'

'Would sleep in the arms of the nearest male? It is December, Emma. Worse things could happen to you. It will be mighty cold in the loft.'

Emma drew herself up to her full height. 'Pray do not let that trouble you, Mr Avedon. I have my cloak.'

'Of course you do! Why did I not think of it? There are the rats, of course.'

She eyed him nervously. 'What do you mean?'

'Why, ma'am, all farms are overrun with the creatures. Still, you won't mind a little company of that kind. Rats are said to be both friendly and intelligent. I'm told that in the past prisoners have made pets of them.'

Emma shuddered. She was terrified of the beasts, but if Simon thought that he could scare her into accepting him as a bedfellow he was much mistaken.

She stalked ahead of him into the barn, wondering at his motives. He had betrayed no softer feelings towards her, so she could not accuse him of designs upon her virtue. She doubted if he had ever considered her as a desirable woman.

She scowled at him. Doubtless his flippant remarks were intended to put her at a disadvantage once again. She could think of no reason for it unless he was beginning to see her as merely a confounded nuisance. Well, she would show him! In an icy silence she climbed the ladder into the loft, spread out her cloak upon the hay, lay down and closed her eyes.

He did not follow her, and from the sounds below she gathered that he was settling down himself.

'All right?' he asked.

'Perfectly all right, I thank you!' It was far from the truth. As Emma stared into the darkness she fancied that small bright eyes were watching her from every corner of the loft. Then, just as she was drifting into sleep, a warm, furry body ran across her foot.

Her screams brought Simon to her in an instant and, just as she had done in the church, she threw herself into his arms.

'What is it, my dear?' He was holding her close, stroking her hair and gentling her as he might have done a nervous foal.

'Oh, it was horrible!' she cried. 'A rat ran across my foot.'

'Did it bite you?'

'Well, no, but I can't bear the creatures…those long, hairless tails…ugh! My flesh creeps at the very thought of them.'

'I expect that it wasn't a very *large* rat,' he chuckled. 'And that scream must have frightened all of them back into their holes. It frightened me, I can tell you.' He made as if to leave her, but she clutched frantically at his sleeve.

'Don't go!' she begged. 'Perhaps you could shoot them if they come back.'

'Very well.' He took out his pistol and laid it on the ground beside him. 'I promise to fire at anything that moves, so you had best sleep very quietly.'

Emma settled down beside him, comforted, as always, by his sheer physical presence. Even so, she could not sleep.

'Something is still troubling you?' he asked.

'I feel so cold,' she told him in a small voice. 'My feet are like stones.'

'Come here!' There was laughter in his tone as he reached for her. 'Did I not warn you, Emma? When will you learn to trust me? I have no ulterior motive, my dear.'

If this remark was intended as reassurance, it had the opposite effect. There was something insulting in Simon's assurance that her charms had no effect on him. Naturally, she did not wish him to make improper advances, but he might at least have shown some interest.

Now he was all efficiency as he massaged her feet, restoring the circulation to them. 'Better?' he asked at last. 'Will you sleep now? I promise not to leave you.'

Emma did not argue further. Reassured, as always, by his presence, she closed her eyes. She did not even protest when he drew her into the circle of his arm, covering her with his cloak. 'Will…will you stay awake?' she begged in a low voice.

'I can't promise that, but I give you my word that no harm will come to you. Is that enough?'

'It is,' she whispered. 'I believe you, Simon.'

In the darkness she could not see his face. It was as well. His expression would have overturned all her previous notions of his feelings towards her.

Chapter Eight

When Emma awoke it was to find herself unable to move. A powerful arm lay across her waist, and her feet were trapped neatly between Simon's ankles. His head was resting upon her shoulder.

Emma looked down at him. In sleep he looked younger and much more vulnerable. An unaccountable impulse persuaded her to bend her head and kiss him gently upon his brow.

'Dangerous!' a deep voice chuckled.

Emma jumped as if she had been stung. 'Oh!' she cried. 'You are awake! Why did you not tell me?'

'I had no opportunity, *mademoiselle*. Besides, you were resting so comfortably. I had not the heart to disturb you.'

'What time is it?' she asked inconsequentially. What a fool he must think her. She wriggled out of his grasp.

'It is long past dawn,' he replied. 'High time we bestirred ourselves. We have much to do today.'

'Have you a plan?'

'Not as yet. We are safe enough for the moment. The goatherds will give the alarm if strangers enter the valley.'

'Why should they do that?'

'They are the farmer's sons and Pierre's nephews. They have been keeping watch, even as we sleep.'

When Emma did not answer him he challenged her.

'Well?' he said. 'You are very quiet, ma'am.'

'I was just thinking,' she said slowly. 'People are amazing, are they not? They will risk their lives for their beliefs.'

'That should come as no surprise to you. You are of the same mind, are you not?'

'I am, but would I have their courage? I am not brave, you see. In fact, I am a coward. If I were threatened, most probably I should give way.'

'Don't let it worry you. We do not know how we should behave in any particular situation. Put these matters from your mind.'

Emma tried to obey him, but it was impossible. Simon was beset with difficulties, not the least of which was how he was to transport Piers to a place of safety. Emma had given the matter some thought, but she listened in silence as he explained their predicament to his companions.

'Piers is resting more easily today,' he announced. 'Even so, we cannot move him. He can neither walk nor ride in his present condition. I suggest that we split up. Our enemies are searching for the English, not the French among us. Pierre could lead Yves and Mado and Marcel to a place of safety. At this present time we are a danger to them, and all their relatives.'

Marcel's face crumpled. '*Monsieur*, don't send us away!' he begged. 'We can still be of help to you. I drove the dog-cart, didn't I?'

Simon gave him a smile of rare sweetness. 'You did

indeed, Marcel. It is thanks to your bravery that Mademoiselle Lynton escaped from the church in Marseilles.'

'I could do it again,' the boy said eagerly. 'Besides, my sister won't go, will you, Mado?'

'No, I won't!' Mado lifted her chin. 'You can't make us leave, *monsieur*. We have every right to be here among our own people.'

'More right than we have? That is what you mean, I think, and I can't argue with that. But, Mado, do consider—'

'Perhaps you should consider, Monsieur Avedon!' Pierre spoke up at last. 'If I leave, who will guide you across the border?'

'I have made the journey before.'

'But not at this time of year, and with a lady and a sick man on your hands.'

'There may be another way,' Emma said quietly. She blushed a little as all eyes turned to her.

'Well, Emma?'

'I have been thinking. Madame Diderot and her daughter were taken safely to Perpignan, on the border, by a fisherman.'

'How do you know of this?' Simon demanded sharply.

'The man is the father of one of the maids employed by Robert Chavasse.'

She heard a snort of disbelief from Mado.

'Help from that nest of vipers?' the girl shook her head. 'You are easily gulled, *mademoiselle*.'

'I think not!' Emma refused to be drawn into an argument. 'The girl became a friend.'

'And you would trust her?' Mado looked her disbelief.

Simon stopped her with an upraised hand. 'You have proof of her good faith?' he asked.

'She knew of my plan to escape the house,' Emma told him steadily. 'She did not betray me.'

'And this fisherman? How did he travel to Perpignan?'

'That puzzled me for a time. *Madame* and her daughter could not have walked the distance—they were not strong enough. I doubt if Jeanne's father would have taken them on horseback. It would have been too dangerous. Their mounts would have been taken from them before they had travelled a mile.'

'So?' Simon's eyes were intent upon her face.

'Well, don't you understand? They must have gone by sea.'

'That's impossible!' Mado poured scorn upon the idea. 'By now there isn't a fisherman along the coast who won't have sold his boat for gold beyond his dreams.'

'There may be one. Jeanne's father does not only sail boats. He builds them too. Who is to say that he does not have some craft concealed in one of the inlets on this coast?'

'Why should he do that?'

'Seamen don't give up their chosen way of life so easily. Jeanne's father may be thinking beyond the present crisis.'

'That's true!' Pierre intervened again. 'These troubles cannot last. In time to come, those who sold their very livelihood for gold will have spent it. How are they to live without the tools of their trade?'

Simon was lost in thought. 'It may be the answer,' he said at last. 'To travel by sea would be the easiest way for Piers, but is the man prepared to help us? That is the question.' He turned to Emma. 'Will you speak to Jeanne?' he asked.

As she nodded Mado rounded on the pair of them.

'Must you risk our lives on *mademoiselle*'s word?' she cried bitterly. 'If she is caught in Marseilles again, she will be tortured until she betrays us.'

'Be quiet, Mado! *Mademoiselle* will not return to Marseilles. The girl will come here.'

Emma stared at him, 'How will you manage that?'

'Quite easily, I think. Does the girl attend Mass on Sundays?'

'Of course!'

'Then what more natural than she should attract the attention of a young man such as Yves here? She is not ill favoured, I imagine?'

'Not in the least! Jeanne is a pretty girl, but why send Yves?'

'He is the most suitable person for our purpose. Marcel is too young, Pierre is too old, and Joseph would be unlikely to approach a young lady of another race. I would go myself, but possibly I might be recognised. In any case, I am an unlikely candidate for any woman's affections.'

As he turned away he missed the look on Mado's face, but Emma did not. Simon might have a poor opinion of the softer emotions. The fact remained that he held a powerful attraction for the opposite sex, possibly because he made no effort to win them to him.

Not for the first time Emma was puzzled by his complex character. Did he need anyone at all? He had shown no sign of it. He appeared to be self-sufficient, but he travelled a lonely road, if that were the case.

Now he turned to Yves. 'Will you do it?' he asked.

'No, he won't!' Mado was furious. 'Yves has no part in this. As yet he is not a fugitive. You have no right to ask it of him.'

'Nor you to speak for him, Mado. Yves must make his own decision.'

'That's right.' Yves gave Mado an apologetic look, but his words were for Simon. 'I'll be happy to help if you will tell me what to do. More than anything I'd like to see Mado...I mean, I'd like to see you all safe.'

'Sentimental fool!' Mado turned away in disgust, but Simon caught her by the arm.

'Such charm!' he observed in ironic tones. 'Go on like this, my dear, and you will have the world at your feet.'

All the colour drained from Mado's face. It was a very public reproof and his words stung. Now her eyes glittered with unshed tears and Emma sprang at once to her defence. Mado was being impossible, but she was under a tremendous strain. She was overcome with pity for the girl.

'Mado is right to consider the dangers,' she insisted calmly. 'Shall we discuss this further before we make a decision?'

Mado stared at her unlikely champion. She had not expected support from Emma, but the knowledge that she had an ally persuaded her to suggest another plan.

'I could go to meet this Jeanne myself,' she said in a low voice. 'It would occasion no suspicion—just one woman speaking to another.'

'Unless you were recognised.' Simon dismissed the idea at once. 'Be sensible, Mado, our friend Yves here is the obvious choice.'

'I agree, *monsieur*!' The young man was eager to play his part. 'When shall I go?'

'The sooner the better, I believe. If necessary, we shall wait until next Sunday, but that is almost a week away. Emma, does the girl leave the house at other times, perhaps to visit her parents?'

'She is allowed just one half-day a month. I don't know when that will be, but sometimes she is sent to market when Berthe does not care to go.'

'Then that may be our best chance to contact her. Yves must watch the house for the next few days.'

'And how shall I know the young lady, *monsieur*? Perhaps there are many female servants.'

'Just three,' Emma told him. 'Berthe, the housekeeper, is an older woman. You could not mistake her for Jeanne, who is eighteen or so. The other maid is a bold-looking person with bright red hair. Jeanne is small and dark and rather shy.'

'And will she believe me if I claim to come from you, *mademoiselle*? She may suspect a trap.'

'Show her this!' Emma slipped a small amber cross from around her neck. It was a birthday present from her parents and she wore it night and day. 'She will recognise it.'

Yves took the jewel from her and slipped it in his pocket. Then he turned to Simon. 'What am I to say to her, *monsieur*?'

'You will tell her that Mademoiselle Lynton would like to see her. If she is agreeable, you will bring her here. Yves, this may be a fruitless errand, but it is possibly our only chance to get our wounded man away... You will do your best, I know.'

Yves flushed with pride. He drew himself up to his full height and executed a formal bow. 'I thank you for your trust in me, *monsieur*!'

Such exaggerated courtesy might have seemed comic in the surroundings of the farmhouse kitchen, but Simon did not smile.

'That trust is not misplaced, my friend.' He held out his hand with equal formality, and a look that assured the young man of his regard. 'Off you go, then. We shall wait to hear from you.'

Emma moved over to Mado's side. 'Yves is unlikely to come to harm,' she said quietly. 'At worst he can only be accused of making advances to a young girl.'

Mado bent her head. 'He is such a hothead, *mademoiselle*. I am not kind to him, but if I encouraged him who knows what he might do?'

'He will follow his orders, I believe. After all, he seems to value Simon's good opinion.'

'As all men do. It is ridiculous! He has but to raise his finger and they will jump through hoops for him.'

Emma chuckled. 'That wouldn't help us much in our present situation, but it is an entertaining thought, is it not?'

Mado gave her a reluctant smile. 'You must think me a crosspatch, *mademoiselle*.'

'No, I do not. I think you have good reason to be worried, as have we all, but we must do what we can to save ourselves. Now, do please call me by my given name. Yves has provided us with quite enough formality for one day, and, after all, I call you Mado.'

Another smile lit the girl's face briefly. 'Yves did rather overdo it, didn't he? Fortunately Monsieur Avedon did not laugh.'

'Of course not! We all appreciate what Yves is doing. The waiting will be the hardest of all. Perhaps we should try to occupy ourselves. There are so many of us to feed. *Madame* may allow us to help her, after we have attended to our patient.'

Mado followed her into the sickroom. They were both relieved to find that Piers was showing signs of improvement. Emma laid a hand upon his brow and noted with satisfaction that it was no longer burning to the touch.

'Shall I live?' His eyes were twinkling as he questioned her.

'Only the good die young, *monsieur*, and you, I feel, have many years ahead of you.'

'Unkind!' he mourned. 'Now, *mademoiselle*, since I have recovered my senses, perhaps you will tell me what is happening?'

'We have made a plan,' she said sedately. 'For the moment we need not trouble you with the details.'

'Miss Lynton, you are just as bad as Joseph. Even as he was bathing me with your excellent lavender preparation I could get no information from him.'

'That is because we have none to give, as yet.'

'I see!' He turned his face away. 'I am delaying you, I know. Why won't Simon listen to me? You should all be away from here. I am prepared to take my chances.'

'We don't intend to leave hostages to fortune,' Emma assured him. 'With luck we shall all be away from here before the week is out.'

'And am I not to know what you have in mind?' He was tossing uneasily, and Emma decided that honesty was the best policy. She told him.

'Thank you!' he said simply. 'It might work.'

'It will if you help us, Monsieur Piers. You must rest and try to recover your strength. Eat and sleep and pray and don't worry. By the end of the week you may be on your feet again.'

Piers closed his eyes with a sigh of contentment and, satisfied, the two girls slipped away.

Simon came to find them as they were working at the kitchen table slicing vegetables into an enormous cauldron. 'What did you say to Piers?' he asked. 'He seems easier in his mind.'

'We told him the truth, *monsieur*. Sometimes it is the best way.'

'I see. You did not think to ask for my permission?'

'We did not need it, sir.' Emma gave him an angry look. 'You have some objection, perhaps, to Monsieur Fanshawe knowing of our plans?'

'I had no wish to worry him.'

'He worries more about being left in ignorance. Now, *monsieur*, if you will excuse us we have much to do.'

'So I see,' he replied in a dry tone. 'Do you add cooking to your talents, Emma?'

'I am not helpless,' she replied.

'Good! Then I need not fear that either of you will poison me?'

'We might be strongly tempted,' she assured him. 'Sometimes you would try the patience of a saint.'

'And you are no saint, I think!' He was laughing as he walked away.

Emma examined the contents of the cauldron. 'This ancient bird must be tender by now,' she announced. 'The vegetables will not take long. Perhaps *madame* has another task for us.'

She was not left long in doubt. At that moment the farmer's wife entered the kitchen and lifted down a home-cured ham from one of the beams. She smiled at the two girls.

'I am not used to have such help.' She beamed. 'Will you slice this ham for me?' She handed Emma a fearsome-looking knife. At first glance Emma knew that it was razor-sharp.

The woman was all good nature, but Emma felt troubled.

'*Madame*, we are eating you out of house and home,'

she protested. 'Will you not allow me to make at least some small contribution to the cost?'

Madame shook her head. 'We country people are self-sufficient, *mademoiselle*. We spend little in the town. We rely upon our pigs and goats, hams, cheeses and our own vegetables to see us through the winter. We have more than enough for all.'

'You are very good,' Emma told her soberly. 'But seven extra people? It is too much!'

Madame smiled. 'One of your party has already left us, Miss Lynton, and your patient scarce eats enough to keep a bird alive. Now pray do not trouble your head about these matters. I have bread to make. With the stew it will fill up hungry men.'

Emma did not argue further. *Madame* was never less than courteous, but she left no one in any doubt that this was her home, and she was mistress of her domain.

Mado raised one last question. 'Your sons, *madame*? I am grateful for the use of their room, but please inform them that I shall sleep in the barn tonight.'

Madame threw up her hands, now covered in flour. 'Such nonsense! You will do no such thing, my dear. My boys will bed down in the barn. Perhaps you and your friend here will share the room?'

Mado looked uncomfortable. 'Miss Lynton…I mean, Emma…may not wish to share with me.'

'Why ever not?' Emma smiled at the girl. 'Let me assure you, Mado, that I am not brave enough to face the rats again.' It was not the true reason for her un-willingness to spend another night in the barn. She had worried all day about the unaccountable impulse that had led her to bestow a kiss on Simon Avedon.

He had not referred to it, either by word or look, and she had half-convinced herself that he truly was asleep when she had given way to that disastrous action. She had heard just the one word, 'Dangerous!,' but she put it from her mind. He could have been referring to their present situation.

She was speedily disabused. When he approached her late that night she told him of her intention to sleep within the farmhouse, and to share with Mado.

'Buried the hatchet, have you, Emma? Well, I don't know how you did it, but it is a worry off my mind.'

'That must always be a source of pleasure to us,' she replied in silky tones.

'On this occasion not to me,' he replied. 'What a joy it was to be awakened with a kiss.'

Emma glared at him. 'It was the impulse of a moment, sir, based only upon gratitude for your help. It meant nothing more.'

'Naturally, *mademoiselle*. No thought was further from my mind. After all, the redoubtable Miss Lynton is unlikely to be swayed by any protestations of devotion.'

'I have heard none from you, sir.'

'Nor will you do so, ma'am. I can think of nothing more likely to set you against the speaker.' He bowed and left her.

Emma reflected upon his words as she lay in bed that night. Was she really so unapproachable? It wasn't true, she decided, but, in any case, why should she care? Simon Avedon was the most impossible person she had ever met. He was cold, sarcastic, and ready with his taunts.

It was only surprising that he had listened to her suggestion to get in touch with Jeanne. Doubtless when, and if, Yves brought the girl to her he would raise all manner of objections to anything she suggested.

The colour rose to her cheeks. How ill mannered of him to remind her of that impulsive kiss! She had almost persuaded herself that he really had been asleep when she pressed her lips to his brow. No such luck, she thought bitterly. She would not be allowed to forget that moment of folly.

Why had she done it? Upon reflection it was an unpardonable act of stupidity. Another man might have imagined it an invitation, but not Simon. Oh, no, she thought ruefully. 'Dangerous!' Was that really all he had said?

He had laughed and treated the matter lightly, so why must he remind her of it later? It must be just another of his ploys to keep her off balance. What was he afraid of?

She dismissed the matter from her mind. It was of no consequence. Simon was useful for the moment. Without him she had no hope of making her escape from France. Or had she?

The next morning she was lost in thought for quite some time. When Jeanne arrived, she would discuss the matter with her friend. But Jeanne did not come that day, nor the next.

On the evening of the third day Emma was in despair. True, Piers was still improving slowly, but he was still unfit to travel. And meantime their continued presence at the farm brought greater danger to her hosts with each day that passed.

The enforced waiting was getting on her nerves. She had obeyed Simon's orders not to venture out, but late that night she could endure the confines of the farmhouse no longer. She opened the back door and gazed into the night. A frost was already glazing the buildings with a film of white, but overhead the stars were bright, scattered like diamonds across a velvet sky.

Then Simon was beside her. He hadn't spoken, but she sensed his presence in the darkness. 'You will catch cold,' he insisted. 'Come indoors, Emma. I can't have you falling sick.'

Emma did not reply. Another time she might have rounded on him sharply, reminding him that he did not own her. Now, entranced by the beauty of the moonlit countryside, she had no mind to quarrel with him.

'Did you hear me, Emma? This is no time for dreaming.'

'I wasn't dreaming,' she replied. 'But I *was* enjoying this peaceful scene. It's hard to believe that people are killing each other just a few miles away. What will become of France, I wonder?'

Instinctively he moved a little closer. 'Order will be restored in time, my dear.' His tone was gentler than she had expected.

Emma looked up at him. 'You love this country too, I think. What will you do after we return to England? Shall you return here on another similar errand?'

'I don't know yet. It will depend upon where my masters send me. We may be in for a lengthy war with France. Who knows what may happen?'

Emma shivered, but he did not remark upon the fact. Instead he slipped off his coat and placed it about her shoulders.

'Thank you,' she said simply. Then she gave him a shy smile. 'Sometimes you are a puzzle to me, sir.'

'I can't think why!' He turned his face away. 'Since

you will not come indoors, I have no choice but to prevent you from catching a chill upon the lungs.'

This time Emma was stung into a swift retort. The comforting moment of intimacy had been lost. Now he was setting her at a distance again. 'I quite understand,' she said with icy sweetness. 'If I were foolish enough to fall ill, I should be even more of an inconvenience to you. I have no intention of doing so, but you are right. The air has grown chill.' She slipped out of his coat, gave it back to him, and stalked indoors.

Simon caught her arm. 'Don't disappear just yet, Emma. We need to talk. The kitchen was deserted when I came to find you. Shall we sit by the fire in there?'

She nodded coldly. He was quite impossible. She wondered that he had any friends at all, since he was so ready to crush any overtures in that direction. 'I am very tired,' she announced. 'Please make haste to say what you have to say. I need to seek my bed.'

He gave her a long look. 'You are also worried, Emma. I have seen it in these past few days. I think you should consider that it may be difficult for Jeanne to get away. The housekeeper works her hard, I understand?'

'She does.' Emma forgot her irritation. 'But it isn't just that I find the waiting hard. I would not put the girl in danger for the world. Perhaps we should not have asked for her help.'

'The decision must be up to her. As I see it, nothing will be found amiss if she should succumb to certain blandishments from Yves. After all, these things happen every day.'

They do, thought Emma, but never to you, I fancy. 'How long will you wait?' she asked.

'Until the end of the week. After that, I believe that we must decide upon another plan. Piers is improving—'

'He is still not well enough to travel by road.'

'I know that, Emma, but let us not cross our bridges before we come to them. All we can do now is to wait.' His smile lit up the room. 'Try not to worry so. War, you know, is said to be ninety-per-cent boredom and ten-per-cent action.'

'I prefer the action,' she said with feeling. 'It's better to be doing something to change the situation.'

'There speaks the amateur,' he teased. Then, as her face fell, he took her hand. 'Don't lose heart, my dear! Until now you have kept up well. So well that I am often inclined to forget that...well, it is no matter.'

Emma was curious. 'Oh, no!' she challenged. 'You cannot leave it there. What is it that you have been inclined to forget?'

'Just that, as a young lady of fashion, you are unaccustomed to adversity.' The mask of indifference was in place once more.

Emma could have struck him. She jumped to her feet and swept out of the room without another word.

That night she prayed that Jeanne would arrive before the end of the week. Then the clever Mr Avedon would be forced to admit that even a young lady of fashion had some brains in her head. Her suggestion that they might escape by sea might prove to be ill founded, but to date it was the only plan they had. And, if it worked, Simon would be forced to admit that women were not the feeble-minded creatures that he so clearly thought them.

It was not until noon on the following day that her prayers were answered. A bustle in the stable-yard announced the arrival of a horseman. Then, before she had time to rush to the door, Jeanne was hurrying towards her.

Emma threw out her arms to fold the girl in a warm embrace. 'We had almost given up hope...' she admitted.

Jeanne's eyes filled, as she clung to Emma. 'I can't believe that you are safe, *mademoiselle*. Monsieur Chavasse has been behaving like a madman since you escaped. He is turning the countryside upside down. I was persuaded that he must find you.'

'For the moment we are thought to be safe enough,' Emma assured her gently. 'But we cannot stay here long. We are putting our friends in danger. Father Jacques has not suffered, I hope?'

'No, *mademoiselle*. He was saying Mass when you disappeared, so no one could accuse him of helping you.'

'I see. The route of our escape was not discovered, then?'

Jeanne's eyes grew round with wonder. 'It is still a mystery. Berthe said that it was witchcraft.'

'But *monsieur* did not believe her, I imagine?'

'No!' The girl's lips quivered. 'I do not like her, as you know, but there was no need to beat her so severely. She...she has a broken jaw, and cannot leave her bed. *Monsieur* accused her of gossiping with her friends instead of watching you. Brigitte was beaten too, and Chabrol has been threatened if he does not find you.'

'Thank heavens that I did not allow you to accompany me!' Emma said with feeling. 'Won't you be missed, my dear? How were you able to come to me today?'

A faint smile touched the girl's lips. 'I asked for permission to visit my father,' she explained. 'Since he is a fisherman, he would know if enquiries had been made about a boat. Monsieur gave me permission to leave at once.'

'That was clever of you, Jeanne! I wondered if Berthe had warned Monsieur Chavasse that you had been my personal maid.'

'She did, but I pretended that I believed *monsieur* when he claimed to be worried about your safety. I said that I would do anything to see you safely under his protection again.'

'And he believed you?'

'He did, *mademoiselle*.' The girl dimpled. 'Monsieur does not have a very high opinion of the lower classes. In his view, they are unable to think for themselves.'

'Shrewd girl! You understand him well, I think. Now tell me, Jeanne, did Yves explain our position to you?'

'He said that Monsieur Avedon would explain.'

It was at this moment that Simon entered the room. 'Is someone taking my name in vain?' he asked cheerfully.

Jeanne blushed, but Emma took her hand and led her forward. 'This is my friend, Jeanne,' she announced. 'At great risk to herself she has come to help us.'

Simon bowed with grave courtesy. 'You have courage of the highest order, Mademoiselle Jeanne. Nothing I can say would express our appreciation...' He motioned to her to a seat beside the fire and poured her a glass of wine. 'I trust that no suspicion has fallen upon you?'

'Not as yet, *monsieur*.' Jeanne gave him a shy smile. 'After all, I have given no cause, but if you will tell me how I can help *mademoiselle* I will gladly do so.'

Simon wasted no time. He saw at once that the girl was well able to understand their predicament. She listened in silence as he outlined their difficulties, but it was not until invited to do so that she spoke.

'As I understand it, *monsieur*, you are suggesting an escape by sea?'

'With a sick man it is our only chance.'

'And you wish my father to help you?'

'We have no right to ask it of him,' Emma said warmly. 'He would be risking his life to save our own.'

'He would not consider that, I think. My father has a firm belief in right and wrong.'

'That is commendable,' Simon intervened. 'But the dangers must be pointed out to him. You have already told us that Monsieur Chavasse is obsessed with recapturing *mademoiselle*. He will stop at nothing to achieve that end.'

'You do not know my father!' Jeanne's smile was warm. 'He has been offered a fortune to sell his boat, but he will have none of it. He is watched, of course, but Father takes great pleasure in outwitting the authorities, and this coast is wild. There are many little inlets where a man may hide small craft.'

'So you think there may be hope?'

'Let me ask him, *mademoiselle*. He claims to owe you a great debt for your rescue of Madame Diderot and her daughter. I think he will be glad to help.' She rose to her feet and held out the little amber cross. 'It was only when I saw this that I knew that a message came from you.'

Emma slipped the cross around her neck, smiling as she did so. 'Then Yves did not offend you, Jeanne? I thought you might have sent him away unheard.'

'Not when I saw the cross, *mademoiselle*.' Jeanne held out the small leather purse. 'Will you take the gold? I kept it safe for you.'

'You must continue to do so. I may need you to use it on our behalf...' She saw the expression on the girl's face. 'My dear, I know that your father will not take payment if he agrees to help us. I was thinking more of supplies of clothing.'

Satisfied, Jeanne nodded. 'Now I must go. I shall tell Monsieur Chavasse of a rumour that you went back to Toulon.'

As she turned away, Simon took her arm. 'You must take great care,' he insisted. 'We are dealing with a ruthless man. Pray do not put yourself in danger.'

A smile was his reward. 'I shall have some news for you within a day or two, *monsieur*.' Then she was gone.

Emma watched until Yves was out of sight, his pillion passenger riding behind him. A lump formed in her throat and she was very close to tears.

'What is it, Emma?' As always, Simon was aware of her feelings. 'Jeanne will be careful, I am sure of it.'

'I know.' Emma's lips were trembling. 'I pray that there will be no mischance. After all, there is no reason in the world why Jeanne should risk her life for me.'

'Do you not know that you attract devotion, Emma?' Simon's tone was light, but there was an odd note in his voice and, as she looked up at him, he turned away.

Chapter Nine

'Now you are making game of me!' she cried indignantly.

'Am I? Why do you find it strange that people should care for you?'

'I don't!' Emma was at a loss to answer him. 'I mean…well…my family cares for me, but I don't expect total strangers to be willing to put themselves in danger.'

'People are amazing, are they not?' he teased.

'I don't find Jeanne's bravery amusing,' she told him coldly. 'I shall never be able to repay her.'

'Perhaps you have already done so.'

'Now you are speaking in riddles again. What do you mean by that remark?'

'You have seen her as a person and not a servant, Emma. Did you not embrace her as a friend when she arrived? She knows she is valued, not merely because she may be able to help us. You respect her, and that means much to a girl who seldom receives a civil word from her employers.'

'I like her,' Emma said simply.

'As you like Marcel, and Pierre and Piers and Joseph?

Each of them would offer you the same support. Even Mado is softening towards you.'

Emma coloured. 'You do not mention yourself, *monsieur*.' The words were out before she realised their importance. Then she could have bitten her tongue.

'Me?' Simon's voice held nothing but amusement. 'I am your slave, my dear. I thought you knew it.'

Emma glared at him. She was furious, not only with him, but with herself. It must have sounded as if she were begging for a compliment from this obnoxious creature who took such delight in giving her a sarcastic set-down. Worst of all, she had given him the opening herself. In future she would think carefully before she spoke.

'Nothing to say, *mademoiselle*?'

Emma was too incensed to notice the look that accompanied his words. Had she done so, she might have been aware that much rested upon her reply.

'No, I have not!' she snapped. 'It is impossible to hold a conversation with you, sir. You take nothing seriously.'

'You are mistaken, Emma.' He was no longer laughing. 'One day I hope to prove it to you. Now, if you will excuse me, I have certain matters to attend.' With that he walked away.

Emma watched him go with a strange sense of dismay. She had said something to upset him, but she could not think what it was. She shrugged. If Simon insisted on behaving like a fool, he must not expect her to be deceived. Claiming to be her slave, indeed! Should she have simpered and fallen into his arms? She could well imagine his reaction. It would have given him yet another opportunity to sneer at her gullibility.

He deserved the harsh words she had thrown at him,

but for some strange reason the thought gave her no satisfaction. After all, this was no time for the little party of refugees to be quarrelling among themselves. Perhaps she had been too hasty, but it was not too late to make matters right with him. She went to the door just in time to see him riding away.

Disconsolate for some unaccountable reason, she wandered back into the kitchen where she found the farmer's wife alone.

Madame was examining the contents of a basket with evident delight. 'See, *mademoiselle*! Your young friend has been so generous! Fish, of all things! We see it seldom in the country. Today we shall have bouillabaisse. Such a treat for all of us!'

Emma looked doubtful. 'Bouillabaisse? Is that not a fish stew?'

'You are not familiar with the dish?' *Madame* was astonished. 'In Marseilles it is traditional.'

'We lived in Lyon,' Emma explained. 'Such fish as reached us there was never fresh. I'm afraid it gave me a dislike of such food.'

Madame laughed. 'I shall hope to convert you, my dear. Let me show you how the dish is made. Later you shall taste it. Then you may decide. First we must prepare the vegetables.'

She set Emma to peeling and chopping carrots, onions, leeks and potatoes whilst she cleaned the fish. The trimmings she simmered in a small amount of water to create a richly flavoured stock, before taking down an enormous cauldron and splashing olive oil into the base.

'Now we sauté our vegetables, *mademoiselle*, to bring out the flavour of each one. Tomatoes next, I think, together with plenty of herbs. Then we may add the fish and the stock.'

Emma watched as she cut the assortment of fish into bite-sized pieces. Some varieties she recognised, but others she did not know at all. Their ugliness disturbed her.

'Don't judge by appearances, *mademoiselle*!' the farmer's wife said gaily. 'Today I shall promise you a new experience.' She turned to her bread dough, which was proving by the fire and began to shape it into loaves. 'How is your patient today?' she enquired.

'He had a better night, I thank you, *madame*. The fever has abated, but it has taken its toll, I fear. Monsieur Fanshawe is still very weak.'

'Then we shall build him up with plenty of good food,' *madame* said firmly. 'There is nothing like home cooking to restore a man to health. If I may say so, you look much in need of a restorative yourself, as does Mado. You girls have worn yourselves to the bone, caring for *monsieur*.'

'It was worth it,' Emma told her warmly. 'It is such a pleasure to find him looking so much better.'

'Well, take care that you do not fall sick, *mademoiselle*. I should not care to be in Monsieur Avedon's company should that happen.'

'Certainly he would find it a serious inconvenience,' Emma said drily.

'Rather more than that, I fancy.' *Madame* gave her a sharp look, but Emma would not be drawn into a discussion of Simon's motives. She made haste to change the subject.

'Where is everyone this morning?' she asked casually.

Madame betrayed no surprise at the sudden change of conversation. 'They are busy about the place. There is always much to do. The fences must be repaired, and the shed needs a new roof.'

Emma smiled. 'I had not thought that Monsieur Avedon would turn his hand to carpentry.' It was a round-about way of asking where Simon had gone that morning.

Madame was undeceived. 'He is not here, *mademoiselle*, as I thought you must know. He left with my eldest son to find the quickest and easiest route to the coast.'

'Will it be very difficult? Monsieur Fanshawe may have to travel on a litter.'

'This is rough country, *mademoiselle*, and the cliffs at the coast are sheer, but Bernard has lived here all his life. Monsieur Avedon could have no better guide.'

Emma stared at her in wonderment. 'Why are you helping us?' she asked at last. 'You and your family, I mean? You are putting your lives at risk for total strangers.'

Madame gave her a steady look. 'I hope we all know right from wrong, Miss Lynton. We cannot agree with what is happening in France at present. Certainly, there were abuses under the old regime, but that is no excuse for wholesale murder.'

She reached over to throw a pinch of saffron into the pot and followed it with mussels and two small lobsters.

'Great heavens!' Emma cried. 'The king himself could not have dined upon a more luxurious dish.'

Madame sighed. 'No, he could not, poor soul! What an end for a simple man who asked for nothing more than to be allowed to repair his collection of clocks and locks. He could have been exiled. There was no need to send him to the guillotine.'

'And his wife?'

'The Austrian? Marie Antoinette was hated in this country, *mademoiselle*. Folk claimed that she was a spy. Perhaps it was true, though for myself, I doubt it. As a mother I could only sympathise with her. She lost her eldest boy, you know.'

'I heard that the Dauphin had died, but there is a second son, is there not?'

'Aye, but what will become of him? His whereabouts are secret. These murderers may already have done away with the boy.'

Emma shuddered. 'Surely not? He is just a child! How can he pose a threat?'

'Folk may rally round his cause, ma'am. I doubt if we shall see him alive again.' *Madame* looked at her companion. Perhaps she had said too much—Emma had grown pale at the thought of such an atrocity. She took down a bowl from the shelf. 'Will you see if your patient is awake, Miss Lynton? He must eat if he is to regain his strength and this nourishing broth will do him good. Later he may take a little of the fish if he should fancy it.'

Emma walked into the sickroom to find Mado in a chair beside the bed. Piers was awake, but his eyes were troubled as he looked at the girl.

'Emma, can't you persuade her to rest?' he whispered. 'She is killing herself with worry and lack of sleep.'

Emma laid a gentle hand on Mado's shoulder. As the girl's eyes flickered open, they flew at once to Piers.

'Is he worse?' she cried.

'Indeed not! *Monsieur* is so much better today that I am about to bring his meal. Our hostess has worked all morning upon her famous bouillabaisse. Now she insists that we must try it.'

Mado shook her head. 'I could not eat, Emma. I am not hungry in the least.'

'Just wait until you smell the dish! I believe you will

change your mind… Besides, we cannot insult *madame* by refusing her hospitality.'

'It would choke me.'

Emma lost all patience. 'Then Monsieur Avedon will choke you if the food does not. He has made his feelings very clear to me. He will not have sick females upon his hands.'

Mado looked stricken. Her eyes filled with tears. 'I'm sorry,' she faltered. 'I had not thought of that.' She buried her face in her hands.

'You are tired, my dear. Why not seek your bed for an hour or two? It will restore you, and *madame* will set some food aside for you. Later you will enjoy it.' Emma urged the girl gently from the room.

When she returned she was carrying a bowl of the fragrant broth, redolent with herbs, but Piers shook his head as she approached him.

'Great heavens!' she cried. 'Am I also to coax you into eating, *monsieur*? I had thought better of your good sense!'

'I will make a bargain with you, Emma.' Piers eyed her steadily. 'I will eat if it you will do something for me…'

'And what is that?'

'Persuade Simon that he should leave me here. God knows, I am hoarse with trying to convince him. I know well enough that I am delaying you, the Lord knows for how long.'

'He won't do it!'

'He might…that is, if you were to ask him.'

'Me?' Emma stared at him in astonishment. 'Why should he listen to me? Simon thinks me an obstinate fool.'

'You are mistaken, Emma. He has the highest regard for both your courage and your character.'

'*Monsieur*, you are the one who is mistaken. Your friend loses no opportunity to give me a sharp set-down and to sneer at me.'

'And that tells you nothing?'

'It tells me that he dislikes me and thinks me a mighty inconvenience to him.'

Piers chuckled. 'You are right in one respect at least. You *are* a mighty inconvenience to his peace of mind.' He eyed her curiously. 'You see nothing strange in his behaviour, *mademoiselle*?'

'Indeed I do! It is all a mystery to me. I know he is your friend, but a more arrogant, infuriating, sarcastic creature I have yet to meet.'

'And yet?'

'He is brave,' she admitted. 'I would not have you think that I don't appreciate the fact that he has rescued me on two occasions.'

'Anything else?'

Emma smiled. 'You are determined to have me acknowledge his virtues, *monsieur*. Well, then, he is charming with Marcel, and the soul of courtesy to those who might be considered beneath him.'

'Does this not show you that he has a softer side?'

'He does not reveal it to me. He speaks in riddles, and I am tired of his cryptic remarks.'

Piers laughed aloud. 'He is afraid of you, my dear!'

Emma stared at him. 'I can only imagine that your fever has returned, *monsieur*! What a thing to imagine…!'

'It isn't imagination. It is true! For the first time in his life, Simon is faced with a situation over which he has no control.'

'He has made his plans, *monsieur*. He will have confirmed to you his hopes for an escape by sea.'

'Yes, he has done so, but from some situations there is no escape. Simon is facing one such at this moment.'

Emma surprised a twinkle in his eye. She could not mistake his meaning. 'Oh!' she cried indignantly. 'Pray don't tell me that he has been entertaining you with his nonsensical stories of some secret passion?'

'He did not need to tell me,' Piers said solemnly. 'I have seen it coming for some days.'

'My dear sir, what can you mean from that remark?'

'Listen to me, Emma. Simon is very dear to me. We grew up as boys together. He is no stranger to rejection. Perhaps if I tell you something of his history?'

Emma was silent, and Piers took her silence for assent. 'His parents were a devoted couple,' he continued. 'Sadly, his mother died in giving birth to him. The Duke was distraught. He blamed himself, but he could not love the boy. The very sight of Simon brought back all his pain. Can you imagine what it was like for a young child to be banished from his father's sight and never to know the reason?'

'It was monstrous!' Emma exclaimed. 'Was he further ill treated?'

'He was well housed and fed, and he received an excellent education. All he lacked was love.'

'The most important thing of all…' Emma sat lost in thought. Then she looked at Piers. 'Why are you telling me all this?'

'It is important that you know. You must not misjudge my friend. Simon has learned to wear a mask of coolness and indifference. The qualities in him that you dislike are those which have helped him to survive.'

'I see. But surely things are different now? His father

must have changed. Time is said to be a great healer, is it not?'

'A popular fallacy, Emma! In some cases it is true, of course, but for the Duke the agony is still as raw as it was some thirty years ago.'

'Poor man! It is a tragic tale.'

'Not less for Simon,' Piers reminded her. 'It has left a scar. Now he protects himself in ways that are all too familiar to you.'

'Protects himself from what?'

'From giving his heart, my dear.'

'He does not appear to need anyone,' Emma said slowly.

'That is what he would have the world think. It is not true. We all need someone, Emma. Don't you agree?'

'I do.' Emma smoothed the fabric of her skirt. 'Does Simon see his father now?'

'Occasionally. There was some slight chance of a reconciliation years ago, when he reached his majority. They are a military family and the Duke intended Simon to join the army. His refusal to join the colours widened the rift still further. Harsh words were spoken and Simon was accused of cowardice. The charge drove him away.'

'I should think so!' Emma was indignant. 'Whatever else, he is no coward.'

'His father will not have it so. Now he believes that Simon drifts about the world, intent upon his own pleasures.'

'Could you not have spoken to him, Piers? You might have told him the truth.'

'I dared not speak on his behalf.' A grim smile touched the sick man's lips. 'Simon forbade it utterly, on pain of ending our friendship.'

'Stubborn as always?' Emma gave him an answering smile.

'As always!' Piers agreed.

Emma eyed him with concern as he lay back against his pillows and closed his eyes. 'I am tiring you, *monsieur*. Rest now. I shall come back later.'

She rose and made as if to leave him, but he caught her hand. 'Shall you be better friends with Simon from now on?' he pleaded.

'I believe so. I have not been kind, in spite of all that he has done for me. Now I shall regard him in a different light.'

'Not with pity?' he asked anxiously. 'That he could not bear.'

'Not with pity, sir, but perhaps with more understanding.'

'That's good! Now, ma'am, I have kept my bargain as you see. You will give my compliments to *madame*? Her broth is truly excellent. Later I shall beg to taste her delicious fish.'

He was pale, but Emma felt that he was resting more easily after their conversation. Simon was lucky to be able to call him friend, she decided as she returned to the others.

The men had returned from their various tasks about the farm and there was a general air of anticipation as they seated themselves about the great pine table.

'Something smells good!' Marcel announced. '*Madame*, I am so hungry…'

'I'm glad to hear it, child! Have you washed your hands and face?'

Marcel nodded as he reached for a hunk of the fresh-baked bread.

Madame rapped sharply at his fingers with her wooden spoon. 'We have not yet said grace,' she reminded him.

Undaunted, Marcel bent his head until the prayer was ended. Then he looked about him. 'Where is Monsieur Avedon?' he enquired.

Emma too was wondering. Simon had left early in the morning. Surely it was time that he returned. She'd been ashamed of her behaviour even before she had spoken to Piers. Now it was important that she made things right between herself and the difficult creature who was occupying her mind to the exclusion of all else.

She sensed his presence before he entered the room, but she kept her eyes fixed firmly upon her plate. It was not until he seated himself beside her that she turned her head.

'A successful morning, sir?' she enquired politely.

He gave her a long look, nodded briefly and then turned to the others. 'We have found a good route to the coast,' he announced. 'The track is wide enough for Piers to travel by cart if he is still unable to walk by the time we leave. There is a suitable inlet beneath the cliffs where a boat may land—'

'Always supposing we find a boat, *monsieur*,' Joseph reminded him.

'Indeed, but we have great hopes of Mademoiselle Lynton's friends. We should hear from them within a day or two.'

Pierre frowned. 'The cliffs are steep, Monsieur Avedon. It won't be an easy descent, even for the strong and fit.'

'Agreed, but the place we have chosen has one great advantage. There is a ruined castle on the headland. With that to guide him, our fisherman will find us easily enough.'

'There is still the problem of getting Monsieur Piers down to the beach.'

'I believe there may be a solution. If we construct a litter and fasten our friend securely, it should be possible to lower him by rope.'

'A dangerous move...'

'Less dangerous than staying here, Pierre. To date we have been lucky not to be discovered, but our good fortune may not hold. Chavasse will have intensified the search for us. He won't give up his prize so easily.'

'And you believe that *mademoiselle*'s friend will find a boat for us?'

'We can't be sure, but I believe that she will do her best.'

'And if she is unsuccessful?'

'Why, then we must change our plans...' Simon had seen the look of terror on Marcel's face. He turned to the boy. 'Now, what do you say, young man? This litter for Monsieur Piers? Will it be possible for you to help me build it?'

Marcel gulped. 'I shall try, *monsieur*. When must we start?'

'At once, I think. Do you go with Joseph and Pierre, find some stout wood and cut it into lengths. I shall join you shortly. First I must speak to *mademoiselle*.'

When the others had left the room he turned to Emma. 'How is Piers today?' he asked.

'He is much better, but the fever has left him weak. The musket-ball drove cloth from his shirt into the wound. That is what caused the infection.'

'I see. Then it is as well that we do not move him today.'

Emma was silent.

'Well?' he prompted.

'He hopes that you will agree not to move him at all. In his present condition he believes that he is a danger to us all. He fears to delay us and to make a quick escape impossible if we are discovered. He says that you must leave him here.'

'Do you agree?'

'No, I don't!' she replied. 'But I don't know how you are to convince him.'

'That won't be difficult, Emma. I shall remind him of the consequences if he is found beneath this roof. *Madame*, her husband and her sons will all be executed.'

Emma caught her breath. 'Of course, how stupid of me! I should have thought of that myself. Once he understands he will agree to leave.'

'Of course. Now, where is Mado? I hope she has not disobeyed my order not to venture out of doors.'

'Mado is too tired to disobey you,' Emma told him drily. 'She blames herself for the injury to Piers. In trying to make amends she has worn herself to the bone. I insisted that she get some rest.'

'Sensible of you! What of yourself?'

'I am not tired in the least.'

'Made of stern stuff, eh?' He was smiling down at her, and Emma's heart turned over. The smile transformed his face, lighting up the room. Now she saw something of the delightful person he might have been, under happier circumstances. His friend's words came back to her.

'I'm glad you won't leave Piers,' she replied simply. 'It is not merely because of the danger to the family here, I think…'

'And what else do you think?'

'I think you wear a mask, *monsieur*. You would have us believe that you have a heart of stone. It is not true, I suspect. Piers is your friend and you would defend him with your life.'

'Great heavens, Emma! Must you be so dramatic? I thought I had explained why Piers cannot stay here.'

'So you did!' Emma's lips curved in a little secret smile. 'And now, sir, you will turn your hand to carpentry? Marcel is flattered beyond belief by your request for help.'

'The child was terrified. I needed to distract his attention.'

For the first time in their acquaintance Emma sensed that her companion felt uncomfortable. He turned away.

'No, you shall not escape so easily,' Emma insisted. 'This morning I was rude to you. I wish to make amends.'

'Indeed? And what do you propose, *mademoiselle*?'

When he looked down at her Emma saw the light in his eyes. It was her turn to feel uncomfortable.

'Well…' She faltered. 'I said that it was impossible to hold a conversation with you. That is not so, and I admit it.'

'Good! I'm glad to hear it. We shall have many conversations in the future, I believe, but for the moment you must excuse me.'

As he made to leave her she stretched out a hand to clutch his sleeve. 'Simon…you do believe? I mean…do you think that we shall escape to England?'

'Nothing is more certain, my dear.' He raised her fingers to his lips and kissed them. Then he was gone.

Emma felt perilously close to tears. Simon was the most unpredictable creature she had ever met in her life. At one moment he was driving her away from him with his coldness and his sarcasm. At the next he was drawing her to him with an unexpected display of charm and tenderness.

She scrubbed angrily at her fingers as if to banish the memory of those firm lips against her skin. Simon was teasing her. It was probably all part of his plan to throw her off balance, but why should he wish to do so?

Piers's words came back to her. Was Simon really afraid of betraying a softer side to his nature? She thought back over their recent conversation, and realised that it could be true. Something had changed in their relationship. Simon had not looked so ill at ease before, and it had happened when she had challenged him about his feelings for his friends.

Had she found a chink in his armour? She hoped so. She recalled the words of one of her father's favourite poets. John Donne had said that no man was an island. How true that was! Simon could only damage himself if he retreated into his shell and kept the world at bay.

Emma pondered the question. Why should it matter to her? Piers was kinder, and a more delightful companion, but in her eyes the two men were not to be compared. There was a quality in Simon which was all important to her, though she could not find the words to describe it.

Vainly she tried to brush the matter from her mind. This difficult man meant nothing to her, nor could he ever do so. It was just that in his company, for reasons she could not explain, she felt more alive and the world seemed a different place. She had learned to listen for his step, to welcome the very sound of his voice, even when he was teasing, or, more often, issuing orders with which she often disagreed.

She trusted him, of course. If anyone could succeed

in returning her to England it would be Simon Avedon, but what would happen then? Would he deposit her with her family as one might deliver a troublesome package and then disappear? Suddenly she felt desolate. Life without him seemed bleak indeed. She shook her head, as if that simple action could drive the unwelcome thought from her mind, but it was in vain.

What was happening to her? In the past no man had ever occupied her mind to this extent. Sternly she told herself that it was time to gather her shattered wits. She was tired. That would account for her confused state of mind, as would the frustrations of waiting for news from Jeanne. Once the delay was over and they resumed their journey she would feel more herself again.

Then her name was spoken softly and she turned to find Simon standing in the doorway. She had no time to compose herself and the look upon her face brought him to her with outstretched hands.

Then she was in his arms and his cheek was against her hair. Through the fabric of his shirt she felt the pounding of his heart close to her breast.

'What is it?' he asked in a low tone. 'This waiting is hard, I know, but you must not allow it to wear you down.' As he spoke he stroked her back, gentling her as a man might soothe a nervous filly.

The comfort of his embrace was a revelation to Emma, and as she realised the true nature of her feelings for him she tried to pull away. He did not release her.

'Look at me!' he insisted. 'You haven't answered my question.'

Emma was given no time to do so. A cry of outrage filled the room. Then Mado ran towards them with up-raised fists. She struck at Simon first, but he caught her wrists and forced her to a halt.

'What is this?' he demanded sternly. 'Have you run mad?'

The girl was breathing heavily and her pallor was alarming. 'You should know!' she cried. 'How could you lead me on when you had no intention—'

Simon stopped her with an upraised hand. His face was almost as pale as her own, but his voice was steady as he answered her. 'That's right, Mado. I had no intention of deceiving you. When have I ''led you on'', as you are pleased to state? Great heavens, girl, have we not enough to trouble us? You are allowing your imagination to run away with you.'

His voice was icy and Emma knew that he was furious, but Mado was too distressed to heed the warning signs.

'I might have known that you'd deny it,' she cried in anguish. 'You are like all the rest. I'll do until something better comes along. Why choose a gypsy girl when your fancy piece here is more than ready to throw herself into your arms?'

Simon looked as if she had struck him and Emma decided to intervene.

'You are mistaken, Mado,' she said quietly. 'I am not feeling quite myself today. Monsieur Avedon noticed it, but there is nothing between us, in spite of your suspicions.'

'I don't believe you!' the girl cried hotly. 'He was holding you in his arms.'

Simon gave an exclamation of disgust. 'Let us be done with this.' His cold gaze transfixed the girl. 'This nonsense is the outside of enough, Mado. We must part company without delay. I have felt it for some time—'

He was unprepared for her reaction. She sank to the ground, buried her head in her hands and burst into uncontrollable sobbing. Simon looked at her in consternation and for the first time in their acquaintance Emma saw him at a loss for words.

'Leave us!' she whispered. 'I will make things right with Mado, but we must not embarrass her further.'

Simon seemed about to speak. Then he thought better of it. With a long look at Emma he left the room.

'There now, he has gone.' Emma raised Mado to her feet. 'Don't distress yourself, my dear. Won't you sit down and let me explain?'

'There is no need,' the girl said dully. 'It is you he loves.'

'That isn't true!' Emma insisted. 'You must have seen how bitterly we disagree on everything under the sun. Besides, I do not know Monsieur Avedon as well as you do. I met him for the first time just about two weeks ago.'

'Then he has not offered for you!'

'Great heavens, no! It is just that today I was not feeling very brave. He could see that I was frightened and he tried to comfort me. This waiting is getting on my nerves. Don't you feel the same?'

'I suppose so...but I've tried so hard to please him.' Mado's face crumpled again. 'I thought he cared for me.'

'Of course he does, but not perhaps in the way you imagine. Simon's only concern at present is our safety. He has had little time to think of other matters. I'm sure he admires your bravery, as do we all.'

'Perhaps I've been too brave...' The girl looked wistful. 'I could change... If he thought that I was terrified...?'

'Don't add to his burdens, Mado dear. I'm sorry if you were distressed by finding us together in that way.

The fault was mine and I'm ashamed of my own weakness. It is just that sometimes I feel dreadfully alone. You have Marcel and Pierre, but I can't help wondering if I shall ever see my own family again…' Her voice broke and she turned her head away.

Mado stared at her. Then, on an impulse, she threw an arm about Emma's shoulders. 'I'm sorry!' she whispered. 'I hadn't realised… I've been so selfish, Emma, in thinking of my own concerns. Can you forgive me?'

Emma smiled and patted her cheek. 'There is nothing to forgive.'

'Monsieur Avedon may not feel the same. How shall I face him after making such an exhibition of myself?'

'I'll speak to him if you wish. He will understand.'

To her astonishment Mado bent and kissed her cheek. Then, as if ashamed of this show of affection, she hurried away, leaving Emma to her own thoughts.

Chapter Ten

Those thoughts did not bring her any peace of mind. The events of the past hour had shaken her to the core. How could she forget the bliss of those few moments when Simon had held her close, safe in the shelter of his arms? If they had not been interrupted by a furious Mado, she might have allowed herself to believe that Simon truly cared for her. He had comforted her with uncharacteristic gentleness.

But that was all. She would not allow herself to imagine that his purpose was anything other than to calm her down. He could not allow any member of his ill-assorted group of refugees to give way to despair. They needed all the courage he could give them if they were to escape.

A sense of doubt assailed her. Had he taken Mado in his arms on a previous occasion with the same end in mind? If so, she could understand the girl's outrage. Simon seldom showed his softer side, but when he did it was enough to turn any woman's head, including her own.

She stood by the window for some time, gazing out at the winter landscape. Then, although he had made no sound, she knew that Simon had returned. She spun round to face him, undeterred by his grim expression.

'Well?' he demanded. 'What was that all about?'

To her own surprise, Emma was tempted to smile. Simon had some sterling qualities, but an understanding of the female sex was not amongst them. 'I don't quite understand you, sir.'

'Of course you do! I'm speaking of that nonsense with Mado. I saw the girl just now, but she ran past me without a word. Now she is with Piers. I hope she isn't upsetting him with her ridiculous flights of fancy. I can't think what has got into her, can you?'

Emma had no difficulty in understanding very well. Mado's outburst had been caused by plain, old-fashioned jealousy. She herself might have felt the same if the tables had been turned and she had found Simon and Mado locked in an embrace.

She brushed the thought aside. Simon's relations with the opposite sex were none of her concern. Even so, she had no intention of enlightening him as to the true reason for Mado's anger. She had promised the girl that she would make things right with Simon and now she must try to do so.

'Mado is tired and overwrought,' she said quietly. 'She is suffering from a lack of sleep. Have you any idea of the number of nights she has spent in the sickroom, caring for Piers?'

'Of course I have, but, as I told her, it is sheer folly to tire herself to the point of collapse.'

'Simon, have you thanked her for her kindness, or did you order her from the room?'

'I suppose I did both...' Simon looked baffled. 'Damn it! Why must women be so difficult? Say a kind word and the next thing they get some notion into their heads…I mean, they read meanings into words that were never intended. You heard her. She accused me of ''leading her on'', as she terms it. Great heavens, one might imagine that I had made advances to the child.'

Emma hid a smile. 'Mado is not a child. She is a woman grown, and she longs to be appreciated. Just think of what she has suffered in these past few months! With her parents gone she has Marcel to care for. She must wonder what is to become of them if ever they reach England. Is it so strange that she should wish to cling to you as the one person who has offered her hope?'

Simon frowned. 'She must know that I would not abandon them, but that is no excuse for these hysterical accusations.'

'I believe she is afraid of losing your support.'

'If she goes on in this way, she will succeed in doing so.' His tone was grim.

'Nonsense, sir! Don't try to gammon me.' Emma faced him squarely. 'You would defend both Mado and her brother with your life, in spite of your threats to send them packing. Is that not so?'

He had the grace to admit it, but his expression did not lighten as he began to pace the room. 'What am I to do now?' he asked. 'Mado will not speak to me. Dear Lord, have we not problems enough without the worry of a foolish girl to set the cat among the pigeons?'

'It must be hard for you,' Emma agreed drily. 'After all, it is a severe trial for any man to find himself so admired.'

He gave her a sharp look. 'Spare me the sharp edge of your tongue, *mademoiselle*! Perhaps I might have handled things better, but—'

'But you have had a dreadful shock? Bear up, *mon-*

sieur, clearly it is your fate to be the object of adoration among the female sex. When we reach London I expect to hear you described as the town's most eligible bachelor.'

'But not by you, I fancy.' Simon glared at her.

'Oh, most certainly not by me, Mr Avedon. Pray don't forget that I have spent much time in your company. I am under no illusions as to your opinions on the subject of women.'

Emma gave him her sweetest smile, but it hid a wounded heart. She had come so close to making the same mistake as Mado. If the girl had not burst in upon them when she did, Emma herself might have melted into Simon's arms and confessed her love for him. The thought of his probable reaction made her shudder. His anger would have stripped her of all self-respect and the scars upon her soul would never have healed.

She had had a lucky escape. She knew that now and she would not make the same mistake again. Simon had made it all too clear that the occasional act of kindness on his part must not be misconstrued. In future she would keep him at a distance.

From the expression on his face at that particular moment, she guessed that from now on it would not be difficult. Clearly her disparaging words had struck home.

He bowed. 'Too kind! If that is your assessment of my character, I will trouble you no longer with my company.'

He did not trouble to hide the fact that he was furious, but Emma did not attempt to soothe his injured feelings. She let him go without another word. It was a small triumph in a way. At least she had managed to puncture his hateful self-esteem by telling him exactly what she thought of him.

Her scathing words were fully warranted, were they not? She told herself that she wouldn't have taken them back, even had she been able to do so, but a small voice within her warned that it wasn't true. Sarcasm was an unpleasant weapon to use against this man who had done so much to help her. Why had she lashed out in such a way? After all, she had seen his look of shock when Mado had flown at him like an avenging fury, accusing him of deceiving her.

And it wasn't true, Emma admitted miserably. Whatever his faults, Simon was an honourable man. He would never have stooped to trifling with the affections of this girl who was so dependent upon him. Mado had allowed her imagination to run away with her with disastrous consequences.

And she herself had promised to try to heal the breach between them. Unfortunately she had succeeded only in annoying him still further. It was little wonder that his opinion of women was so low when one of his companions had claimed to be the object of his love whilst the other had chosen to flay him with her tongue.

Emma sighed. She had been at odds with this difficult man from the moment that they met. Of course it shouldn't matter, but honesty compelled her to admit that, in recent days it had begun to matter very much indeed. How could she blame him for his anger when Mado had accused him of everything but rape? No man of spirit would have borne it.

As to her own behaviour? Her nose wrinkled in disgust. Simon was not the only person who might have handled matters better. She could have advised him to ignore the episode. After all, their ill-assorted company had been forced to live together without respite for much too long. It was little wonder that nerves were stretched to breaking point. Now the most trivial annoyances loomed large as their lives were overshadowed always by the threat of danger.

It was unlike her to lose her self-control in such a way. Why had she allowed herself to be tormented into fighting yet another battle with Simon? They had had their differences before on many an occasion, but lately Emma had sensed that they were growing more in charity with each other.

She had welcomed that better understanding long before she understood the reason for her satisfaction. She knew it now. She was hopelessly in love with him and all to no avail. Less than an hour ago Simon had made it clear that he was a stranger to the softer emotions. He regarded them as mawkish sentiment. They had no place in his life and would never do so.

For Emma the shock had been severe. After all, he had taken her in his arms and held her close. What a fool she had been to imagine that she meant anything to him! He had given way to the impulse of a moment, much as he might have thrown an arm about Marcel's shoulders.

In her anger she had thrown caution to the winds and quarrelled with him yet again. It was dispiriting to realise that she had been driven to such folly. And folly it was! They must continue in each other's company until they reached England, and, with the dangers that lay ahead, each member of their party must trust the others. She could not change Simon, so she must make a greater effort to get along with him. For a start, she thought wryly, she must learn to hold her tongue, and, as her mother was fond of insisting, she must try for a little conduct.

It was a worthy resolution, but it did not solve the

present problem of how to make things right with Simon. Oh, if only Jeanne would return with news for them! Petty quarrels would be forgotten if she could offer them some hope of escape from this place. Kind as *madame* and her husband were, the enforced confinement within the four walls of the farmhouse had begun to make it feel like a prison.

Emma took herself to task at once. It was high time she pulled herself together. Self-pity was the last thing she needed. Others were risking their lives for her. She should be grateful to them, rather than bemoaning her lot.

She made her way to the sickroom, to find Piers alone for once. 'No Mado?' she asked lightly.

He gave her a quizzical look. 'Simon came to find her. Some question of discussing Marcel's future after we reach England, so I understand.'

'Really? I thought he did not wish…I mean…'

'He must have changed his mind. Emma, what have you been saying to him? I do not often see him in such a state. Have you had another difference?'

'We have. Mr Avedon was kind enough to favour me with his true opinion of my sex. It did not agree with my own.'

She heard a laugh of pure delight. 'Serves him right! I would have given much to be there. I take it that you sent him to the rightabout?'

Emma looked crestfallen. 'I was cruel,' she admitted. 'I can't think how it happens. We seem to be getting on so well and then we quarrel dreadfully.'

'A battle of the Titans!' he assured her solemnly. 'I expected nothing else.'

She gave him a reproachful look. 'I don't find it amusing, sir. We need to be united in our aims.'

'I'm sure you are, my dear, although I suspect that you are approaching them from different directions. There is no word from Jeanne, I take it?'

'Not yet. Perhaps that is the reason why we are all at odds with each other. The waiting is a strain for everyone.'

'It will end,' he comforted. 'Cheer up, Emma! To date we have been lucky. We are all safe and well.' He grimaced. 'That is, except for me. I had hopes that you would bring your influence to bear on Simon. Surely he sees that you must leave me here? In my present state I shall delay you. That must put you all in danger...'

'It would be far worse if you were to be taken here. We have no guarantee that the searchers will not find this place eventually. Should you be found here, I'm sure you can imagine the fate of the farmer and his wife and his sons.'

Piers was silent for some time. 'You are right,' he said at last. 'The fever must have addled my wits. Give me your arm—I must make shift to get about on my own.'

'Don't give yourself a set-back!' she pleaded. 'You are not yet strong enough.'

He shook his head in disbelief, but Emma was right. When he set his feet to the ground and tried to stand, he almost fell into her arms.

'What's this?' Simon rushed forward to catch his weight. 'Fool! Are you trying to kill yourself? Emma, I thought you had more sense than to encourage Piers to leave his bed.'

'I didn't!' she cried hotly.

'It was the height of folly!' Simon was furious. Then he looked at Emma's stricken face. 'My apologies, *ma-*

demoiselle,' he said stiffly. 'It would appear that I have misjudged you.'

'Yet again!' she retorted sharply. The unwarranted criticism had stung and she was close to tears. Not trusting herself to say another word she hurried from the room.

It was some time later when he came to find her. She could not look at him, but when he spoke it was in a chastened tone.

'Piers has been telling me of your conversation,' he began. 'He understands now why he cannot stay here. I wish to thank you for that...'

Emma nodded briefly, but she did not answer him.

'And I must tell you that for the second time today I have been taken to task. My character has been explained to me in no uncertain terms. Apparently I have much to learn... Emma, may I hope that you will take me in hand?'

Astonished, she turned to look at him and saw the pleading in his eyes. Even so, she was disposed to tease him. 'The task would be beyond me, sir!' she said demurely. 'I fear it is the work of a lifetime.'

'Quite! Oh, my dear, I have a lifetime to offer you. Won't you agree to share it?'

Emma was too startled to reply. She sat down suddenly, aware that her legs were refusing to support her. 'I...I thought that you disliked me,' she stammered in confusion. 'I know I have offended you today, but I had not thought you capable of mockery. This is unworthy of you, sir.'

He stared at her in disbelief. 'Mockery?' he repeated slowly. 'Can you possibly believe that I would insult you in such a way?' His face was dark with anger.

Emma quailed before that look. 'If I am wrong, I beg your pardon,' she said stiffly. 'I must have mistaken your meaning, sir.'

A firm hand gripped her chin and tilted her face to his. 'I think not, Emma. My meaning was clear enough. Is it so difficult to believe that I should want you for my wife?'

'It is incredible!' Emma's hands were shaking and she tried to conceal them in the folds of her skirt. 'Why, only an hour ago, you told me—'

He hushed her with a finger against her lips. 'I know what I told you,' he groaned. 'Sometimes my folly knows no bounds. Oh, Emma, could you ever consider an arrogant, ill-tempered brute who loves you to distraction? I'll try to change, I promise you.'

'You mean you would fight this urge to love me to distraction?' she said demurely.

Simon looked deep into her eyes. What he saw there caused him to sink to his knees beside her. He raised her fingers to his lips and covered them with kisses.

'I think I've loved you from the moment I first saw you,' he whispered. 'I hadn't meant to speak so soon. I'm sorry if I startled you, but I had to know if there was any hope for me…'

Emma hesitated. She had promised herself that she would not reveal her true feelings to this man who had accused her sex of reading meanings into words that were never intended. She had sworn not to make the same mistake as Mado, but surely this was different. His friend's words came back to her. Simon had suffered rejection all his life from those he loved. She would not add to it from a misplaced lack of trust or a want of courage.

'You have surprised me,' she admitted. 'I thought that

we were enemies.' Her smile took the sting out of her words.

'Beloved enemies, perhaps?' He took her hands and raised her to her feet. Then his arms were round her and he held her to his breast. 'You have not answered me,' he said tenderly. 'Tell me, Emma, given some time, do you think that you could learn to love me? My sole concern will be your happiness.'

Emma reached up and stroked his cheek. 'I don't need time,' she told him. Then her lips curved in a delicious little smile. 'Can it be possible that you did not guess?' she teased. 'I thought I'd given myself away...'

He held her away from him, searching her face for the confirmation of his dearest hopes. Then he kissed her and the world was lost to them. Emma found herself swept away on a dizzying tide of passion. It was unlike anything she had experienced before. She clung to her lover as wondrous sensations consumed her. Suddenly, all the glory of the world seemed to be revealed. Now at last she understood the force that had led poets to put their innermost thoughts into words. When he released her she was breathless, but she still clung to him.

'Sweet witch!' he chided. 'You would tempt a saint! Have mercy, Emma, I'm not made of stone!'

'I thought you were,' she teased. 'On occasion, sir, I suspected that you had met the Gorgon.'

'Ah, yes, was not that the creature which turned men into statues?' He gave her a wicked grin. 'I am no statue, Emma, as I hope to prove to you as soon as we are wed.'

Emma touched her bruised lips. 'I believe you have proved it already, Simon. Oh, my dear, have we any right to be so happy when there is such chaos about us?'

Simon took her in his arms again. 'Love is an affir- mation of life,' he insisted. 'We should see it as a small bright candle in our darkened world—something that lasts when all else falls apart.'

Emma was deeply moved by his words. She reached up and took his face between her hands. 'You make me feel ashamed,' she confessed. 'I thought you so unfeeling…'

'Not unfeeling, Emma…never that!'

'Then I must give you credit, sir. You are an accomplished actor!' Emma pretended to frown. 'From your behaviour I should never have guessed that you had the least affection for me.'

'Piers knew,' he assured her with a smile. 'You would have pity on me if you knew how often I have been taken to task for my ill behaviour towards you. It is not pleasant, you know, to be accused of cowardice in the face of…'

'Love?' she suggested. 'Perhaps we have both been blind.'

Simon settled her comfortably within the shelter of his arms. 'Thank heavens we are blind no longer, Emma. Oh, my dear, is this really true? Can you be sure of your own feelings? You are very young and without experience of the world. I would not have you accept me from some misplaced sense of gratitude.'

Emma could not resist the temptation to tease him. 'You may be right. It may be that I am mistaken. Perhaps if you were to kiss me again I could come to some decision.' She looked up at him with an invitation in her eyes.

'Minx!' Simon's smile transformed his face. 'Come then! Let me persuade you!' As he sought her lips Emma threw her arms about his neck and raised her face to his.

This time Simon could be in no doubt that Emma's passion matched his own. As he held her she murmured

inarticulate words of love, offering herself without reserve to his demands.

It was he who ended that wild embrace at last.

'My dearest love, we can't go on like this,' he whispered.

'Why not?' Emma ached with a longing that she did
not understand. 'I thought you wished me to convince
you of my love.'

'I am convinced, my darling. I think myself the luck-
iest man alive, but you must not tempt me into folly.'
He held her away from him, striving to control the passion that overwhelmed him. 'Emma, it is very late. I
must let you seek your bed.'

'So soon?' She looked at him in dismay, unwilling to
lose the magic of the past hour. 'I am not tired in the
least.'

'I am,' he lied. If he did not leave her now, he knew
that his iron self-control might snap. Emma was too
young and inexperienced to understand the full power of
his emotions. 'My journey to the coast was arduous, but
we'll talk again tomorrow.' He dropped a gentle kiss
upon her brow. 'We have so much to discuss. What of
your father, Emma? Will he agree to give me your
hand?'

Emma clung to him. 'My father is a clever judge of
character. How could he fail to love you as I do?'

'Perhaps you are a little biased,' he teased. 'I can't
hope for such generosity from him.'

'You do not know him,' she said firmly. 'I trust his
judgement in all things. He will not fail us, Simon.'
Emma looked down at the lean, brown fingers entwined
so closely with her own. 'I need a promise from you,
though...'

'You shall have anything within my power to give you,' he said tenderly. 'What is it, my love?'

Emma hesitated. She had no wish to return to the thorny subject of Mado's infatuation, but it could not be avoided. Confirmation of the girl's suspicions might spur her into making fresh accusations, especially as Emma herself had assured her earlier that day that Simon had not offered for her and had no intention of doing so.

Simon slid a finger beneath her chin and tilted her face to his. 'Won't you tell me what is worrying you?' he begged.

Emma would not meet his eyes. 'You will think me foolish,' she whispered. 'But would you mind if we keep our secret to ourselves for the time being?'

For answer he hugged her close, but he was laughing. 'Ashamed of me already, Emma? Can it be that you are having second thoughts?'

'Of course not!' she cried indignantly. 'It is just that…well…our friends may find it strange to find that—'

'That we have discovered that we love each other? Oh, my little goose, it will come as no surprise to Piers, at least!'

'I was not thinking of Piers,' she told him quietly.

Simon stared at her for a long moment. Then his expression changed to one of disbelief. 'Mado? Don't you trust me, Emma? You can't believe that there was any truth in her accusations?'

'No, no, of course not!' Emma reached up to kiss his cheek. 'But you are a hero to both Marcel and herself. They may not wish to share you.'

'Emma, this is nonsense! Piers has done as much for them as I have myself, and young Yves is risking his neck for them even at this moment.'

'It makes no difference, my dear. Perhaps we have no choice as to where we give our affection. Mado does not think herself in love with either Piers or Yves.'

'Nor is she in love with me! This is but a foolish fancy on her part. Did you not try to explain it to her?'

'I did. I thought she understood that the terrors of these past few weeks have left us all so vulnerable. She did agree, but we can't be sure of her true feelings at this moment. I would not see her distressed again.'

Simon dropped a kiss upon her brow. 'Nor would I, Emma. You are right, and it shall be as you wish.' His eyes began to twinkle. 'From now on I must guard my expression when I look at you…'

'Indeed you must!' she told him with mock severity.

'But of course you must do the same,' he teased. 'At this present moment you would deceive no one.'

Emma looked up at him with misty eyes. 'At this present moment I have no desire to do so,' she confessed. Then she blushed a little. 'Perhaps we might contrive to quarrel again? It is just that I can't think of a subject on which we might disagree.'

He gave a shout of laughter. 'Give it time, my love! You'll think of something, I make no doubt.'

'Do you think me argumentative then?' Emma had been kissing his fingers, each in turn. Now she shot him a mischievous little look.

'An impossible minx!' he told her firmly. 'The problem of what to do with you has exercised my mind for days. You disobey my orders, never miss an opportunity to take up the cudgels against me, and favour me at frequent intervals with scathing attacks upon my character.'

'I wonder that you care for me at all,' she said in a low voice.

'Do you, my darling?' Simon took her in his arms again. 'Then let me tell you why I love you more than life itself. I can't believe my own good fortune in finding a strong, courageous girl who isn't afraid to speak her mind.'

'Is that so unusual?' she whispered.

'Certainly, when it is allied to a perfect form, and a face that a man would die for.'

Hot colour rushed to Emma's cheeks. 'You are making game of me, my love!'

He caught her to him then, showering kisses upon her eyelids and her cheeks. 'Not so!' he said thickly. 'I have not told you one-half of the reasons why I adore you, Emma, and with each day I love you more. Your loyalty, your kindness—'

Emma stopped him with a finger against his lips. 'You will turn my head,' she teased. 'Could it be that you are a little biased, sir?'

'I am talking nonsense,' he admitted. 'A recital of your virtues does nothing to describe my darling Emma, who is a woman unique in all this world. Oh, my dear, when we return to England, I promise to do everything in my power to protect you, to cherish you...'

'And to love me?'

'Do you doubt it, dearest?'

For answer she offered him her lips, and as his mouth sought her own the world was lost to them.

Simon was the first to regain his self-control. It was only by making a supreme effort that he tore himself away from her embrace. Then, taking her firmly by the hand, he led her to the doorway. 'Until tomorrow, Emma. Sleep well, my love!'

'Until tomorrow,' she agreed. His last, long, lingering kiss then banished all hope of falling into a dreamless sleep. As Emma climbed the stairs to her room she had a curious floating sensation. The world about her seemed unreal.

Could it be true that Simon returned her love? She had not even dared to hope that he cared for her so deeply. Had she not sworn to keep her distance and never to face the agonies of a broken heart? Yet in this last hour all her stern resolution had vanished like snow in summer. She had promised herself to him without reserve, matching his caresses and his words of love with her own.

Did she regret that open-heartedness? In all truth she did not. She could no longer doubt him. He had come to her to offer her his heart and to claim her own. It would have been less than honest to prevaricate and to take refuge in a display of maidenly modesty. She had always despised such missish affectations. It was not her way. Even at the risk of humiliation she had not been afraid to tell him of her love, and her generosity had been rewarded.

How could she ever forget the expression in his eyes when he knew at last that she was his? That look of heartfelt devotion had lifted her spirits to the skies. Now it did not seem to matter that they were still in danger, in a country far from their own, and facing an implacable enemy. To Emma the world was still a wonderful place and she was tempted to sing her happiness aloud.

The sound of regular breathing in her room brought her back to earth. Mado had left a single candle burning; by its feeble light Emma could see that the girl was sound asleep. She sighed with relief. In her present state of mind it would have been difficult to hide her joy. By morning she would have recovered much of her composure, or so she hoped. This was not the time to upset her troubled companion further.

She undressed quickly and slipped into bed, but sleep eluded her for some time. Her mind was in a whirl. There were plans to make for her future life with Simon. Would he continue with his dangerous work after they were wed? She already knew the answer to that question. Much as she longed to keep him safe and by her side, he was not the man to shirk his duty to his country.

For a dark moment her heart misgave her. Then common sense returned. Simon, above any man she knew, had an uncanny ability to survive. His plans were always laid with care, and he took no unnecessary risks. On that comforting thought she fell asleep at last.

When she awakened it was still dark. Something had disturbed her, but although she listened for some time she could hear no sound. Closing her eyes, she drifted off again. Whatever it was had not disturbed the girl in the other cot. Possibly there were mice behind the wainscoting.

When next she opened them it was to find that the darkness had lightened imperceptibly. Emma threw her coverlet aside. It must be late. In these dark winter mornings, dawn came slowly and with reluctance.

Glancing across at her companion, she noticed that Mado had not stirred. Emma decided not to wake her. The girl must be exhausted after those long days and nights spent in the sickroom.

Shivering as her bare feet touched the wooden floor, she padded across to the ewer on the washstand and poured the icy water into the bowl. It was so cold that she caught her breath as she splashed it on her face, but it banished the last traces of sleep. Then she eyed her crumpled garments with distaste. They were dusty, wrinkled and badly in need of washing. It seemed impossible that she must wear them once again.

Then her lips curved in amusement. Simon must certainly love her for herself and not for her appearance. At this moment her own mother would have collapsed with shock to see her first-born looking like a gypsy.

Still smiling, she made her way down to the farmhouse kitchen to find the menfolk breakfasting on sausages and ham and eggs, washed down with flagons of local wine.

'You are alone?' The farmer's wife turned from her blazing fire, a wooden spoon in her hand. 'Mado has eaten nothing for days, Miss Lynton. Will you not persuade her to break her fast?'

'She is asleep, *madame*. I thought it best to let her rest.'

'But for so long? Is she quite well?'

'Perhaps I had best make sure…' Emma hurried back to her room.

At first glance it seemed that all was well, but the recumbent figure in the makeshift cot did not stir when Emma spoke to her. 'Mado? Mado, wake up!' Emma bent down, intending to grasp the girl's shoulder, but her hand grasped only a pillow.

Startled beyond belief, she threw back the coverlet to discover that the bed was empty. Linen, pillows and coverlet had been carefully arranged to give the impression of a sleeping figure.

Where was Mado, and why had she played this trick upon her friends? None of them could give her an answer and surprise gave way to consternation when a search of the house proved fruitless.

'The poor maid has been confined long indoors. Mayhap she went out for some air,' Joseph suggested.

'In this weather?' Simon's face was grim. 'Besides, I gave strict orders that—'

'Oh, to perdition with your strict orders!' Emma was too distressed to mind her tongue. 'This is no time to insist upon your authority.'

Worried though he was, Simon could not repress the glimmer of a smile. 'Did I not predict that we should be at odds with each other again before too long?'

'You did, and we are!' Emma refused to be mollified. 'Will you not think about Marcel?' She gestured towards the huddled figure in the corner of the room, aware that the child was sobbing bitterly.

Simon went to him at once. 'Now then, what is all this?' he asked gently.

'She has left me, *monsieur*!' Marcel turned a tear-stained face to him. 'I shall never see her again.'

'This is nonsense, lad, and you must know it! Your sister would not leave you. Now then, I shall need your help to search the outbuildings. For all we know, Mado may have heard some noise outside. Perhaps she decided to investigate.'

'She would have roused us, Monsieur Avedon. We were sleeping in the barn.'

'She may have tripped and fallen. Come, we must lose no time in finding her!' Simon turned to Emma. 'You heard nothing untoward, I suppose?'

Emma stared at him as memory returned. 'I can't be sure. Something wakened me in the early hours but I don't know what it was. When I heard nothing more I went to sleep again.'

Simon did not comment upon this information, although he suspected that Emma had been disturbed only by Mado's attempt to leave their room without detection. In spite of his comforting words to her brother, he had little hope of finding her close at hand. Mado's mysterious disappearance indicated that the girl had some destination in mind.

What could she be thinking of? Any ill-judged action at this time might ruin all his plans for their escape. He shrugged his shoulders. What was done was done. He could not change it. All he could do now was to await developments. Meantime, he would lead the search for Mado.

As he had half-expected she was nowhere to be found upon the farm. Nor had she been seen by the farmer's sons as they kept watch for strangers upon the only road.

'I'll saddle the horse,' Joseph suggested. 'There is but one way out of here. She can't have gone far.'

'I can't think why she has gone at all.' Simon groaned in exasperation. 'Some maggot in her head, I make no doubt!'

'She may have thought of some way to help us,' Emma said stiffly. 'You have an unfortunate habit, sir, of believing the worst of everyone.'

'Not of everyone, I assure you, *mademoiselle*, but give me credit for some concern, at least.' He looked about him. Then, satisfied that Marcel was not within hearing, he voiced his private worries. 'This is a serious matter, Emma, and I fear for Mado's safety.'

Emma refused to believe him. 'You are jumping to conclusions,' she cried. 'Surely you don't imagine that Mado has been abducted?'

'No, I don't!' he told her grimly. 'At this moment I suspect that she is trying to reach Marseilles with some mistaken notion of finding help for us. It would be like her.'

'Is that so very dreadful?' Emma asked. 'She is devoted to her family and friends.'

'Devoted enough to help them up the steps to the guillotine, my dear. Don't you realise that if she is taken, as she must be, not only her own life will be forfeit?'

Chapter Eleven

'No!' Emma's voice was high with panic. 'Why must you try to frighten me so? You are guessing, Simon. You have no proof that Mado has gone to Marseilles.'

'Where else would she go, my dear? There isn't another town for miles. You won't expect me to believe that she is strolling about the countryside for pleasure on this January morning?'

'Of course not. Oh, Simon, I can't believe that she would leave of her own free will. I know that you have dismissed the idea, but is there no possibility that she may have been abducted?'

Simon looked at her in disbelief. 'From your room at dead of night without disturbing you? That isn't possible, Emma. You would have heard more than the slight noise that awakened you. Besides, who knows the farmhouse well enough to find your room in darkness without arousing the household?'

'I've given some thought to that,' she admitted.

'And your conclusion?'

Emma turned away from his stern gaze. 'You may think me foolish, but is it not possible that Yves may have decided to take her away from here? Mado has been keeping dangerous company and the boy knew it. After all, it is we who are sought by the authorities.'

'And do you believe that she would go with him?'

'No, I don't. She would not leave Marcel, but she may have been taken against her will.'

'That is unlikely, Emma. However, you may have a point.'

'Well, do pray tell me what it is,' she cried impatiently. 'You will not have it that Mado has been abducted. Why else would she return to Marseilles?'

'Possibly to find Yves?'

'What nonsense! Why should she search for him? She thinks him just a stupid boy.'

'Does she? Emma, your powers of observation must have deserted you. Those two young people are much closer than you think. Their bond was formed in childhood. Mado likes to tease the young man, but that is a woman's prerogative, is it not? It does not alter the fact that she has perfect trust in him.'

'So?'

'So she may have sought his help for all of us—' He held up his hand to still her protests. 'We know that there is nothing he can do, but Mado may not share that feeling. She may have gone to him in desperation.'

'I know that feeling....' Emma eyed him steadily. 'Do you know what I find worst of all about our situation? It is the sense of helplessness. If only we could take some action!'

Simon took her in his arms and tilted her face to his. 'It is hard, I know,' he told her tenderly. 'This waiting has told on all of us, but it will end, my darling. Meantime, there is something we may have overlooked.'

'About Mado's disappearance?' Emma's face lit up. 'Have you guessed where she might be?'

'I think we should speak to Piers.'

Emma looked doubtful. 'Is it wise to worry him? I would not give him a set-back for the world.'

'He will have guessed that something is amiss, with all the bustle in the household. Not to know the reason for it will have him chafing with impatience. Would you not feel the same?'

'Of course. It is just that he is still so weak. How can he help us, Simon? He will have seen nothing since he is still unable to leave his bed.'

He smiled at her then. 'You do not know him as I do. That quiet and charming manner persuades people to confide in him. Behind it lies a mind as sharp as a blade...'

Emma grew thoughtful. 'I see. Well, it's true that Mado has spent many hours in his company, but if she had told him of a plan to leave he would not have kept it from us.'

'I don't doubt it, nor would Mado. I don't imagine she would risk his opposition by speaking of it openly.'

'Well, then?'

'She may have given away some small clues without realising that she was doing so. Come, let us talk to him! I promise not to tire him out.'

As he had half-expected, Piers was sitting up in bed, his eyes fixed on the door.

'I have been waiting for you,' he announced. 'Simon, what is going on?'

'There is no easy way of saying this.' He shot a worried look at the gaunt face. 'The truth is that Mado has disappeared.'

'I see! I won't ask if you are certain. You will have

searched the place, I know. When and where was she last seen?'

Emma sat down in the only chair. 'It was in our room last night. I thought that she was sleeping, but this morning she was gone.'

'And you heard nothing?'

'I did. Some slight sound awakened me in the early hours. Then I heard nothing more, so I ignored it. Oh, if only I had paid more attention!'

Piers threw his eyes to heaven. 'How you ladies love to blame yourselves where no blame can be attached! Hindsight is a wonderful thing, but it does not help us in the least. Mado has been suffering from the same affliction. She blames herself not only for my injury, but for the fact that it has delayed our escape. Nothing I could say has changed her mind, and it has preyed upon her sadly.'

'Then it must be as I am beginning to suspect.' Simon perched on the end of the bed. 'Mado is determined to make amends. She must have gone to seek what help she can.'

'You have some ideas?' Piers looked closely at his friend.

'I have, but I'd like to hear yours first. Where will she have gone?'

'Marseilles, without a doubt. There is nowhere else within her reach.'

'And to whom?'

'I'm not sure. Let me think! She spoke often of the young man, Yves, but he is in no position to aid in our escape. He could, however, accompany her to someone else.'

'There is no one else,' Emma told him miserably. 'Who in Marseilles would risk their lives for us?'

'You have a short memory, Emma. What of your friend, Jeanne?'

'Oh, pray heaven that she would not be so foolish as to seek her out! At least she does not know Jeanne's whereabouts. In any case, were we not supposed to wait for Jeanne and her father to perfect their plans?'

'Mado will wait no longer, my dear. Piers has confirmed my own suspicions.' Simon began to pace the room. 'How will she find the girl?'

'She will find Yves first, I believe. Is he not supposed to be wooing Jeanne?'

Emma's blood ran cold. 'But if his home is being watched, she will be seen.'

A large hand covered her own and gave it a comforting squeeze. 'Yves is not known to the authorities, my love. He is under no suspicion.'

'You don't know Robert Chavasse,' she cried in anguish. 'Jeanne was my personal maid in his household. She was the only friend I had. The housekeeper may have warned him that I would have no one else about me. If all else fails in his search, he may decide to question Jeanne again, especially as she has suddenly acquired a strange admirer.'

Piers was silent for some time. 'You could be right,' he said at last. 'The young man may be watched. Certainly we should not underestimate Chavasse...'

Emma put her head in her hands. 'Is there nothing we can do?' she whispered.

'We can hope, my love.' Simon slipped an arm about her shoulders. 'Let us not cross our bridges before we come to them. Mado is impulsive, but she may not be entirely foolhardy. She may have concealed herself in the hope of seeing Yves or Jeanne.'

'There is another possibility.' Piers frowned in an effort to recall. 'She questioned me about the harbour at Marseilles on at least one occasion. She claimed to be intrigued by Jeanne and her family and wondered where they lived. I thought little of it at the time, believing that she was simply attempting to divert me. Now I no longer think so…'

Simon stared at him. 'The harbour? I wonder? Any of the fishermen would direct her to Jeanne's father. Besides, the busy wharves are an ideal place to hide.'

'But what could she hope to gain by going there?' Emma was mystified.

'How can we tell, my dear? She may have hoped to hasten our escape by pointing out the urgency of the situation.'

'But Jeanne knows that already.' Emma looked at the worried faces of her companions. 'Is it not possible that we are both wrong? Mado may simply have grown tired of this waiting and the situation here. She may have had no other thought in her head than to get away.'

'Are you suggesting that she left in a fit of pique?' Simon's frown deepened. 'Is that likely, Emma?'

'No, it isn't,' she admittedly miserably. 'She was unhappy, but she would not have left Marcel. She must be intending to return.'

'Then let us hope that she succeeds in doing so. Personally, I could wring her neck!'

Piers smiled at last. 'You must be looking forward to that delightful prospect. In the meantime, we can do little else but wait.'

Simon nodded in agreement. 'I'll get Marcel to help me finish the litter. That will keep his mind occupied for the moment.'

Emma decided to follow his example. 'Can I help?' she asked.

'Not unless you have some knowledge of carpentry, my love!'

'I can't lay claim to that, but *madame* will find some tasks for me, I am sure.'

The farmer's wife had already anticipated the need to keep Emma busy. One glance at the girl's desolate expression persuaded her of the need for occupation. For the rest of the day she set about teaching her own method of marinating meat in a special concoction of herbs and spices.

In spite of her worries, Emma was intrigued. 'You leave it overnight, you say? That seems a lengthy business. Does it make a difference to the flavour, *madame*?'

'Not only to the flavour, but also to the tenderness, Miss Lynton. It will improve the toughest meats and I use it also for our ancient, stringy hens, although I vary the ingredients.'

Emma eyed her companion with affection. 'I believe that cooking is a pleasure for you, ma'am. Is that not so?'

'It is, my dear. As a young bride I decided that since I must do it every day I had best learn to enjoy it. And then, you know, there is little to compare with the satisfaction of feeding those with hearty appetites.'

Emma smiled. 'I need no convincing, *madame*. Even Monsieur Piers is beginning to enjoy your dishes.'

'Ah, the poor gentleman! He has been sorely tried. You think him improved?'

'He is a little better with every day that passes, thanks in large part to your nourishing broths.'

Madame looked pleased, but she would not claim all the credit. 'And to your nursing, *mademoiselle*,' she insisted. 'You and Mado have spared no efforts on his behalf.'

'Mado has done too much,' Emma told her quietly. 'She would not rest.' Her eyes filled. 'I dread to think what has become of her.'

'Well, worrying won't help her, my dear. Now, let us get on. There is so much to do. We waste nothing on the farm, you understand, and this is a busy time for me. We have not the fodder to overwinter our stock, so much of it has been culled. We smoke our hams and make spiced sausages at this time of year. The seasonings help to preserve them.'

Emma looked doubtful and *madame* smiled. 'I shall not ask you to make sausages,' she teased. 'Perhaps instead you will help me to press this boiled tongue?'

She reached into a nearby cupboard and brought out a deep, straight-sided earthenware dish. 'I have prepared the meat and taken out the small bones,' she explained. 'Now we arrange it in a circle within the dish and weight it down. Will you do that for me, *mademoiselle*?'

Emma did as she was bidden, realising as she did so that this kindly woman intended to keep her fully occupied until they had some news of Mado.

She was not mistaken. As she laid a small clean plate over the meat and placed the weights on top of it, *madame* was already preparing to make her daily batch of bread.

'Have you worked with dough before?' she asked.

Emma managed a smile. 'I've tried, *madame*. The wonderful smell of baking has drawn me into our kitchen on many an occasion, but Cook despaired of me. My efforts were uneatable. Father teased that I was planning to break his jaw.'

'Then you must try again. It goes better with practice.

Kneading must be done with a steady rhythm, closing the palm of the hand. Let me show you. I made up the mixture earlier so it is ready for use.'

Fascinated, Emma watched the deceptively easy process as *madame* worked the dough. 'Would you like to try?' the older woman asked at last.

Emma gave her a doubtful look as she took her place at the table, but with a little more instruction she became more proficient.

'Now then, we are ready for the proving.' *Madame* turned the mixture into a large bowl, covered it with a cloth and a thick blanket and set it close to the fire. 'It will rise again,' she announced. 'Now, let me test the heat in my bread oven.' She reached a hand into the brick-built aperture and nodded. 'It will be hot enough by the time we are ready... Now, *mademoiselle*, you must be thirsty. What do you say to some home-made lemonade?'

'That would be wonderful, *madame*. You are very kind, especially as I have so little experience in the kitchen. I fear I am more of a hindrance than a help to you.'

'Nonsense, my dear. Many a young lady would have thought it quite beneath her dignity to spend her time with me.'

'I hope I am not so foolish. Thanks to you, I have not been left to brood on Mado's disappearance, but I cannot help but wonder what has become of her.'

'Worrying about it will change nothing,' the older woman told her firmly. 'We shall know soon enough. Our menfolk won't give up the search until dark. If she has met with some accident and been injured, they will find her. Now, my dear, let us put our bread in the oven.

We are low on supplies and possibly we may have to pack some food for them to carry in their search.'

She wasn't mistaken. Towards noon the men returned in ones and twos, pausing only to slake their thirst with the rough, red wine of the region. They refused to sit at the table, choosing instead to take the provisions with them before resuming their task.

'You have found no trace of her?' Emma stopped Pierre.

'Nothing, *mademoiselle*, and nor has Joseph, though he rode to the outskirts of the city. She could not have outpaced the horse on foot.'

'You forget. She had a start of several hours.'

'Even so, some wagoner may have taken her up if she was making for Marseilles. Either that, or she is lying injured somewhere in the countryside—' Emma heard a choking sob. Unnoticed, Marcel had entered the room and was gazing at them in despair. She stretched out an arm to him. 'Don't give up hope!' she pleaded. 'I have been speaking to Monsieur Avedon. He believes that Mado has gone to Marseilles.'

'But why would she do that, *mademoiselle*?'

'Why, to find Yves, of course. He is an old friend, is he not?'

The boy eyed her doubtfully. 'She didn't say anything to me.'

'Perhaps she hoped to be back again before we missed her.'

'Then you believe that she will come back?'

'Nothing is more certain!' Emma told him cheerfully. 'She will bring Yves with her, I feel sure. Then we shall have some better news at last.'

'*Monsieur* believes this?'

'That Mado is in Marseilles? He does, I can assure you, and so does Monsieur Fanshawe.'

'Well, she might have told me…' The boy's face clouded. 'I could have gone with her.'

Emma sighed. 'I thought you were my friend,' she told him sadly. 'Mado told me often enough that you would look after me.'

Marcel looked shamefaced. 'I want to look after both of you, *mademoiselle*.'

'And so you shall. When Mado returns, she will be glad to hear that you have helped us all so much today. The men are full of praise for the tireless way you have searched for her.'

'But we haven't found her, have we?'

'That's true, but at least we know that she is not lying somewhere about the farm. Now, did I not understand from Monsieur Avedon that you were to help him finish the litter for our injured man? We shall have need of it when we set off, you know, and that may be sooner than we think.'

'You mean if Mado returns today with news for us?'

Emma smiled at him. 'We must not be too impatient. It may take her some little time to find Yves. We must not expect her back today.'

Marcel was not completely satisfied with her explanations, but he left her at last and went in search of Simon.

Emma sighed with relief. There was little she could have said to comfort the boy, but she had done her best to allay his fears for his sister's safety. Unfortunately, she had not succeeded in stifling her own and, as that endless day wore on, they increased, especially when, at dusk, Simon called off the search for Mado.

He met with some opposition from his companions.

The farmer and his sons insisted that they must continue, as did Pierre. Eventually, Simon was forced to tell them of his belief that the girl had eluded them and returned to the city.

'Surely not, *monsieur*?' The farmer dismissed the notion out of hand. 'That would be the height of folly! In any case, no woman could walk so far in the darkness and along a rough track.'

'You don't know Mado!' Pierre announced. 'Once away from the farm here, she might wait for daylight before she made for the main road into Marseilles.'

'And someone may have taken her up,' one of the young men pointed out. ''Tis market day. There would be no shortage of carts and wagons.'

Simon nodded. 'That is likely.' He looked round at the circle of solemn faces. 'We have done all we can here,' he said quietly. 'Now we must wait.'

Emma felt a sense of despair. Certainly there was no alternative but to wait. Simon would not hear of an expedition into the city to find the girl.

'A waste of time,' he announced in a tone that brooked no argument. 'That would be as sensible as searching for a needle in a haystack. Now, if you will excuse me, I have work to do.' Taking up a lantern, he motioned to Marcel to follow him as he left the room.

Emma was left to wonder at his astonishing ability to dismiss all fruitless worries from his mind. For Simon, what was done was done. He could not change the past, but he could influence the future. It was an enviable trait of character, and she wished that she could cultivate it herself. After all, there was nothing to be gained by indulging in vain regrets, but it was hard not to wonder if there was not more that she might have done to convince Mado of the need to wait.

Slowly she made her way to her room. After her day's work in the kitchen she felt tired and grubby. She longed to change her clothing, but guessing correctly that the farmer's wife would not do so, she could not be seen to be setting herself apart from the others.

The water in the ewer on the washstand was icy, but she poured it into the ornate basin, reflecting as she did so that *madame*, with her usual kindness, had allowed her unexpected female guests the use of what was clearly a family heirloom.

Emma scrubbed at her face and hands, grateful for the use of the home-made soap, until she had washed away all traces of the day's exertions. There was no mirror in the room, but common sense informed her that this was no time to worry about her appearance. She smoothed her hair and sat down upon the bed, wondering, as she did so, at the unexpected events of the last few hours.

It had been a day of violent contrasts, beginning with an overwhelming sensation of happiness. The knowledge that Simon returned her love had changed the world for Emma. Even the commonplace objects in the sparsely furnished room had taken on some special significance. She felt that the scales had fallen from her eyes and that life could not have seemed more wonderful. To love and be loved in such a way was beyond her childhood dreams, but sadly that happiness had been banished in an instant. Apprehension had succeeded it.

With Mado's disappearance all the terrors of the past few weeks returned to haunt her. Had the girl been taken by Chavasses's men? Was she being tortured, even at this moment, to make her reveal the whereabouts of Emma and her friends? It did not bear thinking about, but she couldn't dismiss it from her mind.

She walked over to the one small window and stared

into the darkness. How could she make even a pretence at patience, when there was so much at stake?

When the door opened she didn't turn her head. Supper must be ready. 'I'm sorry, *madame*,' she whispered. 'Give me another moment and I won't keep you waiting.'

Strong arms encircled her. Then Simon's cheek was pressed against her own. 'My dearest love, this will not do. I cannot bear to see you so distressed. Will you not trust me? All will yet be well, I promise you.'

Emma melted into his arms. She was perilously close to tears. 'I don't know how you can be so sure,' she said in a piteous tone. 'We don't yet know what has happened to Mado. Pray don't tell me that no news is good news.'

'Why not, Emma? We know, at least, that Mado is not lying injured somewhere in this neighbourhood. The men would have found her.'

'But…if she is in Marseilles? I can't bear to think of her in so much danger. Suppose she is even now in the hands of Chabrol…that fearsome creature with the eye-patch?'

'Suppose she isn't? You mustn't allow your imagination to run away with you, my darling. That way you are likely to suffer through torments that don't exist. Just consider, Emma, if Mado had been captured we should even now be barricading ourselves against an onslaught from Chavasse's men.'

Emma's eyes grew huge. 'You think she would have betrayed us? No! I won't believe it.'

Simon held her close. 'She would not do so willingly, my love, but you can have no idea of the depths to which such men will sink in order to gain their ends… Suppose, for example, that Mado was threatened with rape?'

'That could not be!' Emma shook her head. 'Robert would never allow it!'

'No? He has done so in the past, I can assure you.'

Emma was silent. She could no longer defend Chavasse against his accusers. Too much had happened in this past few weeks to convince her that he was not above reproach.

Simon kissed her cheek. 'Don't let us dwell upon possible horrors, my darling, until we have evidence to the contrary. I prefer to believe that at this moment Mado is seeking out her friends. We need only wait a little longer.'

'I wish I had your patience.' Emma sighed.

He laughed at that. 'You have not been in battle, Emma. It is said, you know, that the life of a soldier is but ten-per-cent action. The rest is boredom.'

'Then I would never make a warrior.'

'Nonsense! You are a splendid warrior in your way, though at this moment my thoughts are not upon battle.' He bent his head and pressed his lips gently into the hollow of her neck. 'We have had so little time alone, my love. It has not been enough for all I wished to say to you.'

Emma caressed the bent head. 'Sometimes there is no need for words,' she whispered as she twined her fingers in the dark locks. 'When I look into your eyes, that tells me all I need to know.'

'Then kiss me, Emma! Let us shut out the rest of the world for a little time at least.' His mouth sought her own in a caress that told her of his passionate love and his need of her.

Emma clung to him, rejoicing in that love. She returned it in full measure, clasping her arms about his neck and drawing him ever closer.

'I feel so safe when I'm with you,' she whispered at last. 'I want this moment to last forever.'

'There will be many, many others,' he told her tenderly. 'A lifetime won't be long enough for us…' His hands rested lightly upon her shoulders as he held her away from him and gazed at her beloved face. 'You are everything to me, my darling, and this day will live for ever in my memory. I had never hoped to win you…'

'I'm yours and always will be, Simon.' She reached up and drew his face down to her own once more. 'I too will remember this day for all of my life. This morning I was rejoicing in our happiness in spite of our present danger.' Her expression changed. 'Oh, how I wish that Mado could be found. I've tried to thrust that worry from my mind, but it is always there.'

Simon took her hand. 'Let us join the others,' he suggested. 'We have Marcel to consider. I managed to divert him for a time whilst we built the litter for Piers, but he must not be left to brood about his sister's possible fate. He must eat, and sleep. Then, perhaps, by morning, we shall have some news…'

His hopes were not realised until late the following day. Darkness was fast approaching when the sound of a horseman reached the sombre group assembled in the kitchen.

As the men raced for the door Simon stopped them with an upraised hand. 'Careful!' he warned. 'Don't show yourselves just yet!'

'But it's Mado! Mado and Yves!' Evading all attempts to stop him, Marcel raced into the stable-yard. He clutched at the rider's stirrups and then burst into tears.

'Stop that caterwauling, you silly boy!' Mado swung

down from the pillion without waiting for assistance. 'Be quiet, or I'll box your ears!'

'Your own are in much greater danger, Mado!' Simon's voice was cold. 'If anyone is in need of a thrashing it is you!'

His words fell upon stony ground. 'You won't say that when you hear my news,' the girl replied in haughty tones. 'Well, are we to stand out here for the rest of the day, or am I allowed to come indoors?'

Emma stepped forward and took her hand. It was clear that Mado was unsure of her welcome. As she looked round at the angry faces she could have been in no doubt of the enormity of her offence, but she tossed her head, determined to brazen it out.

'We are so glad to see you safe and well,' Emma told her quietly. 'We have been worried about you.'

'And you may regard that as the understatement of the year!' Simon seized Mado's arm and thrust her into the kitchen. 'This place has been in turmoil since you disappeared. Dear God in heaven, whatever possessed you?'

Mado glared at him. 'You were doing nothing!' she accused. 'We might have spent the rest of our days here for all you cared. I wasn't prepared to wait!'

'So it was Mado to the rescue? How touching! I take it that we may now make our escape unhindered by our pursuers?' The cutting sarcasm brought a painful flush to the girl's cheeks and Yves stepped forward.

'You are not being fair, *monsieur*!' he said in a low tone. 'Will you not hear what Mado has to tell you?'

Simon rounded on the young man. Clearly, he was in no mood for excuses. He was about to make an angry retort when Emma laid a gentle hand upon his arm.

'Mado has news for us,' she pointed out. 'You must listen to her. It may be important.'

Simon controlled his fury with an obvious effort. Then he threw himself into a chair and began to tap his fingers on the table. 'Well, get on with it!' he said roughly. 'You might begin by telling us where you have been for this past two days.'

Mado seemed disposed to sulk but, prompted by Yves, she gave them a halting account of her movements since she left the farm.

'I went for help,' she said defiantly. 'I knew we could find it only in Marseilles and I thought Yves might know of something.'

'But how did you get there, girl?' Pierre stared at her in wonder. 'We asked, but we heard nothing of you on the road.'

'A farmer took me up. He was on his way to market.' Mado blushed a little. She did not care to recall the type of payment the man had demanded.

'I see!' Simon was quick to read her expression. 'You are unharmed, I trust?'

'Oh, yes!' she replied in airy tones. 'I hit him with the largest of his marrows!'

This was too much for Simon. The stern mouth quivered and he lifted his hand to shield his face. He could not disguise the fact that his shoulders were shaking.

Emma heaved a sigh of relief. It seemed that the worst was over, but it took her beloved a little time to regain his composure.

'How did you find Yves?' he asked at last.

Mado gave him a defiant look. 'I know you think me a fool, *monsieur*, but I was careful. I did not go to the Chavasse house in case the street was still being watched.'

'So?'

'So I decided to wait for Jeanne near her father's cottage. I...I thought that she could tell me where to find Yves—' Mado stopped, aware of the accusing looks of her companions. For the first time it occurred to her that she had caused a good deal of worry and heartache. 'Someone had to do something!' she snapped.

'Indeed! And you have done so much!' Simon's tone was withering. 'Won't you enlighten us, my dear? Exactly how was Yves to help us?'

Mado glared at him. 'I thought he might have spoken to Jeanne's father about the fishing boat.'

'Jeanne herself must have done that. She was to arrange our escape and send us news. Had you quite forgotten?'

'No, Monsieur Avedon, I had not. It did not occur to you, I suppose, that she might have been unable to send that news?'

Emma paled. 'What has happened? Is she ill?'

Mado shook her head. 'No, *mademoiselle*, she is not ill, but she is being closely watched. Since Chavasse could find no trace of you in spite of his endless enquiries, he has turned his attention to his servants.'

'It was the housekeeper's idea,' Yves said quietly. 'She has always hated Jeanne, and more especially since *mademoiselle* here asked for Jeanne to be her maid.'

Emma gasped. 'I thought I had protected her,' she cried. 'She was not with me at the church when I escaped. Oh, please tell me that she has not been harmed!'

'Not for the moment, *mademoiselle*, but Chavasse watches her as a cat might watch a mouse.' Yves blushed a little. 'She sent me away, you know. Too many questions were being asked about her new admirer. She feared for my safety.'

'Then how did Mado find you?'

'I spoke to Jeanne myself at the fish market,' Mado announced with some trepidation.

'You did what?' Simon looked at her in disbelief. Then his face grew dark with anger. 'You realise, do you not, that you might have betrayed her to our enemies?'

'I took care not to do so. I wore my shawl around my head, and stood behind her in the crowd. No one noticed anything amiss.'

'I hope you may be right, though I doubt it.'

'You need not do so, *monsieur*!' Mado had flushed in the face of his fury. 'I thought you'd be pleased, but it seems that I can do nothing right. After all, Jeanne told me where to find Yves, and now we have brought you the news you wished to hear.'

'Have you any reason to believe that Yves would not have brought me that news himself without your interference?'

'Possibly, but there is no harm done. We were not followed.'

'You seem very sure of that. I wish I could believe you.'

'Does it not stand to reason, Monsieur Avedon?' Yves reached out and drew Mado to his side. 'Had we been followed, the farm would have been surrounded. You are too hard on Mado, sir. She could not know that the plans for your escape were well in hand. Had it been otherwise, she hoped to find some help for you elsewhere.'

'From you, sir?' Simon's cutting tone brought hot colour to the young man's cheeks.

'I should have done my best, *monsieur*,' Yves said

with dignity. 'In the event, it will not be necessary. Do you want to hear the plan?'

'Go ahead, if you will be so good.' Suddenly, Simon felt ashamed of his attitude.

In his anger he had been provoked almost beyond endurance, but it could not excuse the use of sarcasm towards this boy whose courage could not be doubted. 'You must forgive me, Yves, I fear I am behaving like a parent who beats the child who has just escaped from death, even as he is rejoicing in that escape.'

Yves gave him a brilliant smile. 'I understand, sir. It is a common reaction, but from now on all will go smoothly for you. In two days' time Jeanne's father will bring his fishing boat into the cove below the cliffs. He has chosen a night when there will be no moon, but you must wait until full dark. He will take your party off from there and sail across to the Gulf of Perpignan.'

There was no denying the buzz of excitement in the room. Were they really on their way at last after the long days of waiting? The men shook hands all round, and even Mado began to smile.

'There, you see! I did the right thing after all,' she told them proudly.

'No, you did not!' Simon frowned at her. 'In future you will obey my orders to the letter, or it will be the worse for you. We are not out of danger yet.'

Marcel tugged at his sleeve. 'Don't be cross with Mado,' he pleaded. 'Are you not glad to have her back again, *monsieur*?'

Simon looked down at the anxious little face and forced a smile. 'We are all delighted to have her back, my lad, but she must not go off on her own, you know. Just think how worried we have been! Thankfully all is well. Now, are you not pleased that we have finished the litter for Monsieur Fanshawe?'

'Oh, yes!' Marcel turned to Emma. 'Do you know, *mademoiselle*, it is in the shape of a triangle and can be drawn behind a horse. The North American Indians use such things when they are moving camp. Monsieur Avedon saw them when he was in their country.'

Simon smiled at his enthusiasm. Nor did he attempt to curb the excitement of the others. Spirits had been fading due to the enforced delay, but now the hope of rescue lifted them. He did not voice his underlying fears, though he could not dismiss them. At that moment he would have given much to have known the plans of Robert Chavasse. The man would not give up, when so much was at stake. The capture of his enemies had become an obsession. Success would bring him honour, recognition and everything he most desired.

None of Simon's concern was apparent as he joined in the discussion of their plans to reach the coast, but Emma was undeceived. By this time she knew him almost as well as she knew herself and she sensed his underlying tension.

That evening she waited until the others had sought their beds before she questioned him.

'You are still worried, are you not, my love?'

He found that he could not lie to her. 'I won't be easy in my mind until we are aboard the vessel and on our way to Perpignan,' he admitted. 'Much may still go amiss.' Then he looked at her stricken face. 'Forgive me, dearest! I have no wish to worry you.'

Emma shook her head. 'I'd rather know the truth. What is it you fear? Mado is convinced that she was neither recognised nor followed in Marseilles. She must be right, else we should have had Chavasse's bullies about our ears by now.'

'Possibly!' Simon was unconvinced, but he did not pursue the subject. Instead he looked long into Emma's eyes. 'I wonder if you have any idea how much I love you,' he said quietly. 'Whatever happens in the next few days, you must always remember that.'

Chapter Twelve

His words chilled Emma's soul. Was he preparing her for the possibility that they would not escape? Every instinct rejected the idea. She and Simon had so much to live for and she would fight for their future until her dying breath.

'Don't say that!' she whispered. 'Now that we have found each other I never want to leave you. You are my life!' She threw her arms about him and rested her head against his breast. 'Nothing must be allowed to separate us, Simon. I'd prefer to die rather than that we should be taken by Chavasse.'

She felt the arms about her tighten. For just a moment Simon's cheek rested against her hair. Then he held her away from him.

'Look at me!' he ordered.

Emma was too distressed to obey him. She hid her face against his coat, aware that all her courage had deserted her and unwilling to betray her anguish.

He would have none of it. A firm hand cupped her chin and raised her face to his. 'You must have faith,' he told her softly. 'You read too much into my words. I was not bidding you farewell, my love. That will not happen as long as we both have life. I am asking that you trust me implicitly. We do not know what may happen in these next few days. It may be that in certain situations your trust could be stretched to breaking point. Will you promise me now that the bond between us will not be broken?'

'Need you ask?' Emma gave a shaky laugh. She felt light-headed with relief as she offered him her lips.

In that embrace she sensed his urgent need of her, but his kiss was tenderness itself. Now she wondered how she could ever have thought him hard and arrogant. The cold unfeeling mask that he showed to the world no longer deceived her. She knew in her heart that this was a man whose love for her was all that she could ever have desired. That he was a passionate creature she could not doubt, but his gentleness amazed her. Simon would never frighten her with his rough demands. When she came to him it would be of her own volition, willing and eager for the consummation of their desire for each other.

Now she abandoned all shyness and wound her arms about his neck, showering his face with kisses, and whispering words of love. The strength of her longing for him no longer had the power to surprise her. She wanted him so much.

For a long moment he held her close as passion threatened to overwhelm them. Then, with a supreme effort of will he released her, holding her away from him with his hands upon her shoulders. 'Wicked Emma!' he teased with a smile. 'Are you trying to destroy all my good resolutions?'

Emma blushed a little at his words. She knew how close they had come to throwing caution to the winds.

'I'm sorry!' she whispered. 'You must think me a wanton!'

He laughed at that. 'Possibly!' he teased once more. 'But do you hear me complaining, my love? Mutual passion such as ours is rare indeed. The bond it creates will never be broken, but for us it cannot be satisfied in snatched moments such as this. When I make you my wife, it will be in very different circumstances and well worth the wait. Do you understand?'

'I think so,' Emma whispered.

'Believe it, Emma! When I make you mine you will come to me in all honour and from your father's hand. I reverence you, my darling, and I would not have it otherwise, would you? This will be no hole-in-corner affair with stolen moments of passion. You are worthy of more than that.'

Emma looked up at him with misty eyes. 'I know that you are right,' she faltered. 'But we can't foresee the future. Suppose that…?'

He took both her hands. 'There you go again!' he scolded gently. 'You are allowing your imagination to run away with you once more. Shall I tell you something? In the past I have found that at least one half of my worries never happened. I've learned not to waste the time in fruitless speculation. One day at a time is enough for me.'

'Wise counsel!' Emma sighed. 'But it is not so easily followed. I wish I could do the same.'

'You are tired, my love. Things will look better in the morning.' He bent his head and pressed a lingering kiss into each of her palms. Then he closed her fingers. 'There!' he whispered. 'Keep these kisses with you for tonight. Tomorrow I shall redeem them with interest.'

Emma did not doubt it. He was hers alone, and with

that knowledge much of her courage returned. With a last embrace she left him, determined that she would not fail him on the morrow.

In their chamber she found that Mado was still awake. Something was troubling her and clearly she was disposed to talk.

'Emma, will Monsieur Avedon ever forgive me?' she asked in a low voice. 'I think he hates me now after all the trouble I've caused.'

'Nonsense! He lost his temper with you, but it was because he had been so worried, as he explained to Yves. You are still our dear Mado, and we could not bear to think of you lost or injured or in danger. Simon understands that you believed that you were acting for the best.'

Mado raised a tearstained face. 'I wanted to help,' she whispered. 'You have been so good to us, and I feared that we had stayed at the farm too long... Was that so foolish?'

'No, the same thought had occurred to me! I wasn't happy about exposing our friends to danger by lingering here, but now our worries are at an end. We have only to survive tomorrow, and then we shall take ship to safety.'

'I hope so, Emma. Yves thinks that I should not take Marcel to England. There, we have no friends and we do not speak the language... He believes that it might be best for us to seek safety close to Perpignan and the Spanish border. Then we should not have to leave our beloved France.'

'And have you decided what to do?'

'Not yet! I thought I would ask Monsieur Avedon, that is, if he will still speak to me.'

Emma smiled. 'By tomorrow he will have recovered his composure. A good night's rest will benefit all of us. Do try to sleep, my dear! All will happen for the best, I am sure of it.'

Strangely enough, it was true. In some mysterious way Simon had passed on his own philosophy to his beloved, and stiffened her resolve. She would follow his example and try to take one day at a time without weakening her courage by indulging in imaginary terrors.

There would be much to do on the following day as the little party made their preparations for departure. Still planning happily, she fell into a dreamless sleep and awakened feeling much refreshed.

It was as well. The next few hours seemed endless. She'd planned to busy herself by helping *madame* to pack provisions for their journey, but Simon had already made his wishes known.

'Just some bread and some of your goat's cheese, *madame*!' he insisted. 'We must not burden ourselves with too much food, though it is good of you to offer it.'

Madame was moved to protest. 'Consider, *monsieur*! You cannot be sure when you will eat again, and there are enough of you to share the weight.'

He shook his head. 'We don't know what awaits us. It may be that we shall need to travel at speed.'

'But you will at least take a little wine with you? It is a great restorative if any of your party should fall sick.'

He smiled his agreement, thought he felt obliged to contradict her. 'Our journey will be short,' he insisted. 'It is but a few miles to the sea.'

* * *

She was forced to be satisfied with that, though later she drew Emma aside to confess her worries.

'Suppose you are delayed, *mademoiselle*? You will not find provisions at the coast.'

Emma laid an affectionate hand upon her arm. 'It will do us no harm to lack a meal or two, *madame*. You have fed us right royally in these past few days. That is sure to suffice us.'

'And Monsieur Fanshawe? He is but a shadow of his former self. How will he survive?'

'I have spoken to him this morning,' Emma assured her. 'Whilst we have been chafing under the delay, it has given him time to recover much of his strength. He tells me that he is almost completely well again.'

Madame sniffed in disbelief. 'I too have seen him,' she announced. 'He is deceiving you, Miss Lynton. His colour is not good. Here, take this, and hide it in your skirts! You may have need of it!' She thrust a flask of brandy into Emma's hand. 'I shall prepare an extra parcel for you. You need not mention it to Monsieur Avedon. Even the cleverest of men can behave like fools at times.'

Emma hid a smile. 'I know it well!' she agreed. 'However, *monsieur* has excellent reasons for wishing us to travel light.'

'Possibly, but you will take the parcel?'

'I will, and I thank you for it.' Emma hesitated. '*Madame*, may I give you a present? You and your family have done so much for us without the least thought of gain. We are deeply in your debt, and I should like to redress the balance.'

Madame tightened her lips and shook her head. 'Are you like the rest of your countrymen?' she asked shortly.

'I know that you English think us an avaricious race who would sell our souls for a handful of coins.'

'There may be some who think like that,' Emma agreed. 'After all, there are fools in every country. I am not one of them. You are proud, I think, and find it difficult to accept a gift, even if it is meant in friendship. It is so much easier to give than to receive, but if you won't take anything for yourself, won't you allow me the pleasure of giving to your sons?'

Madame looked indecisive. Proud though she was, she had all the shrewdness of the French peasant, and farming was a hard life. Should she deny her boys such an opportunity in these troubled times? If ever they were forced to flee, they would have need of money and she and her husband had little to give them. Still she hesitated. 'You will have need of your gold, *mademoiselle*. Who knows what awaits you on your journey to England?'

Emma took a small leather bag from her pocket and laid it on the table. 'This is little enough,' she announced earnestly. 'Pray don't regard it as payment. It is not meant as such.' On an impulse she kissed the older woman's cheek. 'Nothing I could offer you could repay your kindness.'

'You are very good, my dear!' *Madame*'s composure snapped. She sat down suddenly and buried her face in her hands. 'What a world this is!' she whispered. 'I shall not rest until I know that you are safe.'

When Simon entered the room it was to find the two women in each other's arms. 'What is this?' he asked lightly. 'Let us not say our farewells just yet. The rendezvous is not until tomorrow.'

Madame was quick to pull herself together. 'At what time do you plan to leave, *monsieur*?'

'I believe we should make a start at noon. We must reach the coast before dusk. We dare not risk those cliffs in darkness....'

'Will you not have a long wait on the shore, sir? There will be little shelter from the icy winds.'

'The walls of the ruined castle will offer us some protection and along the shore there is a cave of sorts.' Simon looked at Emma. 'Will you come and speak to Piers?' he asked. 'He insists that he is well enough to make the journey on foot.'

'But that is nonsense!' Emma cried warmly. 'You cannot persuade him otherwise?'

'I've tried without success. Now I must rely on you.' He turned and led the way to the sickroom.

They found Piers fully dressed and sitting in a chair. He greeted Emma cheerfully, although his eyes were wary as he turned to Simon.

'I see that you have summoned reinforcements,' he accused. 'Why won't you believe that I am fully recovered?'

'Because you aren't,' Emma told him bluntly. 'You have not tried to walk above a yard or two, and, as yet, you have not left this room. If you collapse, you may put us all in danger.'

'I know that, Emma, but the danger may be greater if we stick to Simon's plan. Suppose for a moment that we are challenged on the road? How will you explain away a wounded man being carried on a litter?'

'We do not travel on the public roads,' Simon told him stiffly. 'Our route to the coast is by the cart track.'

Emma had an inspiration. 'Suppose we took the farmer's horse and cart?' she suggested. 'You could not object to that, especially as Mado and Marcel and I could use it too.'

'Out of the question!' Simon snapped. 'We must take the litter. Piers, there is no other way of lowering you down the cliffs.' His face was set, and clearly he was controlling his rising anger only with an effort.

'I've told you...I'll get there on my own two feet!'

'Or break your neck! Dammit, man, must you be so stubborn?'

Emma decided to intervene. 'Must we decide today?' she asked innocently. 'Why don't we wait until the morning? Then we shall have a better idea of how we should go on.'

'As you wish!' Simon turned on his heel and stormed out of the room.

Piers gave her a rueful grin. 'Emma, am I being unreasonable? I am thinking only of your safety. Simon will not have it that we may be under observation, but it could well happen. Without me, you might pass as refugees, but a wounded man cannot possibly go unnoticed.'

Emma was silent. There was much truth in what he said.

'There is another point,' he continued. 'Simon has issued his instructions. If we are challenged we are to flee in opposite directions.' He gave her a wry smile. 'That will be difficult if I am lashed to some form of litter.'

'I understand,' she said quietly. 'But it would not apply if you were in the cart.'

'Then you are convinced that I am still too weak to make the journey without help.'

'I'm not sure!' she lied. 'Why not get all the rest you can? We do not leave until noon tomorrow. There is still time to decide.'

He seemed satisfied by her words, but Emma was still troubled. She could understand his reasoning, but in her heart she knew that if they did arouse suspicion, whether with a wounded man or not, there was little hope for any of them.

Was she being foolish? They had seen no strangers in the vicinity of the farm and *madame*'s sons had reported nothing untoward. Surely if Mado had been followed they would have been under siege by now.

Simon was unprepared to listen to her excuses for his friend. His face was dark with anger, but Emma persevered. 'Don't you see that he is thinking more of our safety than his own?' she pleaded.

'He's a fool!' her lover growled. 'Dear God in heaven, can't he see that he has no choice?'

Emma stroked his cheek. 'He will know it soon enough. Piers will find that although his mind is willing, his body will not obey him.'

Simon held her close. 'How wise you are!' he said. 'Thanks to you, my love, we have avoided an outright confrontation, and I am glad to have it so. Piers is my closest friend. I should not care to lose his good opinion in an argument.'

'You won't do that,' Emma soothed. 'Piers is devoted to you, but you must consider his position. Since he was injured he has felt himself to be a burden. He is determined not to continue to be so. My love, would you not feel the same?'

'I suppose so!' he admitted grudgingly. 'Very well, I'll say no more at present. I must hope that you are right!'

Emma hoped so too. She slipped her arms about her lover's neck. and pressed her lips into the hollow of his throat. For a time at least she hoped that he would cast aside the heavy burdens on his shoulders in the sure knowledge of her love for him.

He was silent for several moments, and when she looked into his eyes she could see that he was deeply moved. Starved of affection from childhood, he regarded that love as a treasured gift beyond his wildest dreams.

'Don't look at me like that!' she whispered.

'How then should I look at you, my darling?'

Emma smiled. 'Possibly not at all if you cannot hide your affection. What will the others say?'

Now it was his turn to smile. 'Do you think that they are in any doubt?'

Emma blushed. 'I don't know. *Madame* has hinted once or twice…'

'She has done more than hint to me,' he told her drily. 'If you must know it, Emma, I have undergone an inquisition at that lady's hands…'

'Oh, I am so sorry! Perhaps I should have been more careful in my conversations with her. What has she said to you?'

'What has she not said? I have been questioned as to my intentions towards you, warned that you are very young and without the protection of your family, and told that you would be an easy prey for some unscrupulous adventurer.'

Emma tried to hide a smile. 'An adventurer? Well, I suppose that you do give that impression.'

He pretended to be injured. 'If that is what you think of me, I have no hope of winning you. Must I withdraw my offer for your hand?'

'Don't you dare to do so!' Emma clung to him. 'I should complain to *madame* that, in addition to your other faults, you are naught but a deceiver. A poor maiden has no chance against such a villain.'

Simon threw up his hands in mock despair. 'A better chance than a mere man in the company of females, I fancy. Emma, I surrender! I promise to love and cherish you for the rest of our lives. Will you seal that bargain with a kiss?'

She came to him willingly, seeking his lips with a passion that matched his own. 'Dear love!' she whispered. 'Never leave me! You are my life!'

He kissed her again until she was breathless. After that there was no need for words, and Emma marvelled at her own good fortune. Who could have guessed that she and Simon would find love in such unpromising circumstances? Here in this ravaged land, torn with terror and destruction, they had pledged their troth in an age-old affirmation of human values. Life would go on, and man would survive in spite of his own folly.

On the following morning Simon called the little group together. Piers had left his bed to join them, but he was swaying on his feet.

Simon affected not to notice his friend's pallor. 'We shall leave for the coast at noon,' he said without preamble. 'The safest plan is to take the farm cart—'

'Not the litter?' Pierre asked. 'How shall we lower *monsieur* down to the beach?'

Emma had expected a protest from Piers, but none was forthcoming. It was clear that he felt wretched. She eyed him anxiously, afraid that he might collapse at any moment.

'The cart is long enough to hold the litter,' Simon explained. 'We shall lay it flat and cover it with straw. *Monsieur* and the ladies may then travel in some comfort to our destination.' Emma looked at Piers, but his eyes were closed. It seemed that he was in no condition to argue. She heaved an almost audible sigh of relief.

It was a good plan. The farm track was little used except by the farmer and his family, but in the case of a chance encounter she and Mado would be out of sight and so would their wounded friend. A few men accompanying a horse and cart would be unlikely to arouse suspicion, especially if they had some reason for their expedition.

Simon had thought of that. 'If we are challenged, we are collecting seaweed.' He looked at the farmer. 'You use it to fertilise your land, do you not?'

'Indeed, *monsieur*! The winter storms cast it up in quantities along the shore. We wash away the salt and use it freely.'

'Good! I was tempted to suggest that we might be gathering gulls' eggs from the cliffs, but it is too early in the season. The collection of seaweed will do well enough.' He looked from one face to another. 'Any questions?' he asked. 'If so, speak now! We must all be clear in our minds as to our future plans. There must be no confusion.'

Yves cleared his throat. 'You speak of being challenged, *monsieur*. If that should happen and our enemies are undeceived what are we to do? Must we fight?'

'That will depend upon the numbers ranged against us, but you have a good point. Lives must not be thrown away to no avail. If the odds are too great, I will give the word and we must scatter.' He smiled at the young man. 'Hopefully it will not come to that. With any luck we shall be well away from here before the night is out. If not, we shall rendezvous at the ruined castle in the morning.'

He looked about him at the circle of solemn faces. 'It

may well be that naught will go amiss today, but understand me clearly. If we are attacked I want no false heroics, or individual acts of gallantry. We act as a team or not at all. If it should come to the worst and I order you to run, you must obey me. Is that understood?'

They nodded their agreement. Only Mado looked mutinous.

'That is the coward's way!' she muttered.

Emma lost all patience with her. 'Don't be stupid!' she cried sharply. 'Have you not heard it said that one may live to fight another day? How will it serve to die at the hands of our enemies? For my own part, I intend to survive by whatever means I can.'

Mado flushed, but she took no further part in the discussion.

'Very well then. Let us make a start!' Simon turned to the farmer's wife. '*Madame*, I have no words to thank you enough for your courage and your hospitality. It has been far more than we had any right to expect. Will you accept our heartfelt thanks?'

Madame was unable to reply. She had grown fond of all her unexpected guests, and now she was even more afraid for them. She turned away, unable to bear the sight of that little party preparing to leave the safety of her farm for a journey that must be fraught with danger.

Emma laid a comforting arm about her shoulders. '*Madame*, you must not worry so,' she said gently. 'Our plans have been laid with care and this is an isolated spot. Who is to see us upon an old cart track? We shall be at the coast and aboard our ship before the day is out.'

'I pray that you may be right, my dear, but who can tell? Are you not afraid?'

Emma could not lie to her, but she forced a smile. 'I

have lived with fear so much for these past few weeks that I am almost accustomed to the feeling. Even so, I must confess to a certain strange sensation in the pit of my stomach. It will pass, *madame*, once we are on our way.'

'I hope so, my dear child. My prayers go with you.' The farmer's wife straightened her shoulders. 'There now, you must pay no attention to the ramblings of an old woman. Courage is inclined to desert us as our joints grow stiff. It is different for the young and you could not wish for a better leader. Monsieur Avedon will take care of you. Forgive me, *mademoiselle*! I have no wish to be a prophet of doom.'

Emma hugged her again. 'Never that, *madame*! And you shall not claim that your courage has deserted you. How many, I wonder, would have offered sanctuary to us in these troubled times? Aside from that, you have fed us, scolded us, and kept our spirits high.'

Madame gave her a reluctant smile. ''Tis true. I have never learned to guard my tongue, as my man is fond of telling me. You did not take it amiss, I hope.'

'Not in the least!' Emma gave her a demure look. 'You cannot imagine what a pleasure it was to see *monsieur* confounded upon occasion. I note that he did not argue with you.'

'Few men do!' *madame* told her grimly.

Simon had heard her words, but he did not reply directly. Instead, he demanded the attention of his friends once more. 'Before we leave I must ask you all to check the farm with care. Nothing must be left here to give away our hiding place. I need not tell you what discovery would mean for our kind host and hostess.' He turned to the farmer and his wife. 'Should aught go amiss, my friends—I mean, should you be questioned by the authorities—you must claim that you sheltered us only under extreme duress. Your own lives and those of your sons were threatened at gunpoint. You had no alternative but to agree to our demands. Is that clear?'

They nodded and he was satisfied.

Then *madame* gave him a worried look. 'It is not yet noon, *monsieur*. Surely there is time for you to eat before you go? Some of my good soup, perhaps?'

Simon was loath to agree, but it was a sensible suggestion. They had a trying journey ahead of them and possibly a long wait upon the beach. He smiled at her. 'Have you not done enough for us?' he asked. 'You have given us supplies of bread and cheese. We shall not starve in these next few hours.'

'That is not the same, *monsieur*. There is no substitute for good hot food.' She bustled over to the fire and began to ladle out the soup.

Simon made no demur. Long experience of harsh conditions on the battlefield had convinced him of the value of full bellies. Cold and hunger could sap the courage of the bravest. He sat down with the others and began to eat.

Piers alone seemed preoccupied. He took up his spoon and then he laid it down again.

'Is something troubling you?' Simon asked. 'Can you think of aught I have forgotten?'

Piers gave him a long look. 'There is one matter,' he said slowly. 'I would have it clear before we leave.'

'And what is that?'

Piers hesitated. He knew that his next words would not be welcomed and he would have spared the ladies, but it was important that the whole party was in agreement. 'I have been considering the question of what we do if we are attacked,' he replied. 'You said that we must scatter, did you not?'

'I did. You disagree with that?'

Piers smiled faintly. 'Not in the least. It is an excellent plan for the rest of you, but I could not make shift to hide. I want your word that you will leave me.'

Emma gasped. 'Leave you to our enemies?' she cried. 'We could not do that!'

'You must!' he told her firmly. 'Better that one of us is taken, rather than all.'

'But, Piers, you don't know Chavasse! He would not care that you are wounded. He would treat you ill, I know it!'

'That will not happen, Emma.' Piers held Simon's gaze. 'I shall have my pistol with me.'

'What nonsense!' Emma was too disturbed to mind her tongue. 'What can one man do against Chavasse? Do you suppose that he will come alone?'

'No, I don't think that.' He turned his head away, but not before Emma had seen the glance that passed between himself and Simon.

A dreadful suspicion crept into her mind. If the pistol was useless as a weapon of defence, there could be only one other use for it. She began to tremble. Now she understood. Rather than let himself be taken alive and tortured into giving away his friends, Piers would shoot himself.

'No!' she cried fiercely. 'You shall not sacrifice yourself for us. Anything rather than that! I am the one they want. They will not harm me. If I surrender to them you may all escape—'

'Such dramatics!' Simon exclaimed lightly. 'Emma, that imagination of yours is in full flow again. Now come, it is time we left. Forget all these imaginary terrors! We must concentrate on the task in hand.'

Piers did not stir at once. Instead he looked about him. 'Are we in agreement then?' he asked. 'None shall stay behind for me?'

Simon threw his eyes to heaven. 'Have it your way!' he cried in exasperation. 'Dear God, was ever a man so persecuted by his friends? Let us go, I beg of you. Emma, have you checked the house for evidence of our stay?' She nodded in silence as he looked at the others. 'The barns and the stable?'

A last he was satisfied with their assurances. With a last bow to *madame*, he opened the outer door and peered across the yard. All was silent as he led them to the waiting cart and it was the work of moments to lay Piers upon the thick bed of straw. Mado slipped in quickly and Emma took her place on his other side. She began to sneeze as further bales were loaded to conceal their hiding-place, but the straw was light and she pushed it aside a little to allow her to breathe more easily.

'Comfortable in there?' Simon asked in a low voice.

Suddenly Emma was seized with a strong desire to laugh. The incongruity of her situation had come home to her. What was she doing on this cold January morning, bundled into a farm cart beside a wounded man and a gypsy girl, with every chance of being seized by her enemies before she could escape from France? No, she decided, she would not have described her position as comfortable, but that was not what Simon had in mind. She murmured her assent, as did the others.

Satisfied, he gave the word to move off and the cart trundled out of the stable-yard towards the ancient track to the coast. It was not an easy journey as Emma soon discovered. Winter rains had gouged deep ruts in the lane into which the heavily laden cart sank all too frequently. It took the combined strength of all the men to haul them free, with the farmer urging his horse ahead and the others pushing from the rear.

Piers made no sound, but Emma suffered with him as they jolted through seemingly endless potholes. He must be in agony from his wound. She reached out and took his hand, pressing it in sympathy. 'We can't be far from our destination,' she comforted. 'Can you hold on, my dear?'

She felt the answering pressure. 'Don't worry about me, Emma. Look to Mado! She is very quiet.'

To their relief this provoked an angry outburst from their companion.

'Would you have me chatter then, *monsieur*? If you must know it, I am cold and bruised black and blue from travelling in this hellish conveyance. Monsieur Avedon should have let me walk with the others as I wished to do.'

'We aren't there yet,' Emma reminded her. 'I had not thought that the journey would take so long.'

Simon was walking beside the cart and he had heard their conversation. At his word of command the cart came to a halt. 'It is kind of you to consider the horse, Mado,' he said with heavy irony. 'You are right, of course. Come along! Out you get! The less weight for the animal to pull the better. We shall make better time if you walk with the rest of us.'

There was silence from the girl. Then she climbed out of the cart and Emma prepared to do the same.

'Stay where you are!' Simon ordered. 'One foolish female is more than enough for me. Mado, you will keep up with us, or back you go.'

'You allowed Marcel to walk,' she cried indignantly. 'Do you believe that I am weaker than my brother?'

Simon gave her a cold look. 'You are beginning to bore me,' he announced. 'Keep your ill temper to yourself! I'll have no tantrums from you, my girl! Have we not enough to concern us? For once you might consider others rather than yourself.'

Mado turned away. The stinging words had brought tears to her eyes, but she would not let him see them. She longed to apologise, but Simon was already striding far ahead. She could not know it, but anxiety had caused him to speak more sharply than he had intended.

He knew that they were already in trouble. Their journey to the coast had taken twice as long as he had planned, due to the poor condition of the track. It had deteriorated badly since he had last inspected it a week ago, and he was under no illusions. It was vital that they reached their destination before dusk. It would be difficult enough to lower a wounded man down the steep cliffs in daylight. In darkness it would be impossible.

Tirelessly he urged the little party onwards, grateful for the last brief glimpses of the setting sun. It could have been worse, he thought grimly. Cloud and rain would have brought the winter night upon them more quickly. Thank heavens he had allowed time in his plans for such accidents as a broken wheel or the horse going lame.

Even so, he was relieved beyond measure when he caught his first glimpse of the sea. A difficult operation lay before them, but he had rehearsed it in his mind. He would take it step by step. The priority was to get Marcel and the women down the steep path to the beach. He led the way himself, warning of the steep incline and advising them to take it slowly. He wanted no mishaps and none occurred.

He clapped Marcel upon the shoulder. 'Well done!' he said. 'Will you take the ladies to yon cave? It will afford them a little shelter, and perhaps you will find some driftwood. Take my tinderbox. A fire will not be seen from above.'

'Will it not be visible from the sea?' the boy enquired.

'I think not, if you are careful to build it where the cave curves deep into the cliff.'

Marcel nodded. He was happy to be trusted with the care of the ladies, and what boy could resist the lure of building a fire.

Simon left them gathering driftwood. There was little time to lose as brightness was fading from the day. He regained the cliff top to find that Joseph and Pierre had worked fast. Piers was already lashed firmly to the litter; as Simon looked at him, he managed a faint smile.

'So far, so good!' he joked feebly. 'Was that not what the man said as he fell from a window and passed the second floor?'

Simon laughed, though there was little to amuse him in their present situation. 'We don't plan to have the same thing happen to you,' he said lightly. 'You must trust to our strong arms to lower you to the shore. The ends of the ropes will be secured to the horse for added safety. He will not be so easily overturned. Are you ready?'

Piers nodded. 'Go ahead! The sooner this is over, the better it will be for all of us.'

Simon was in full agreement. Piers had suffered grievously on the journey from the farm. Now his pallor was alarming. His friend could only guess at what it had cost him to joke about the ordeal that lay ahead. He realised that there was no time to lose.

Now his orders were brief and to the point. Yves and Pierre he sent down to the beach to await the litter. His own strength, together with that of Joseph and the farmer's sons, would be equal to taking the weight of their burden. Once in place, he did not hesitate, straining to hold the litter steady as it disappeared over the edge of the cliff.

Minutes later he heard a shout of triumph from below, and the pressure on his shoulders was released as the ropes slackened. His feeling of relief was overwhelming, but now it was time that he and Joseph joined the others. He turned to the farmer, holding out his hand.

'What can I say, my friend? No words of mine can express our gratitude to you for your help. You have risked your lives for us and we shall not forget it.'

'No need for words, *monsieur*. We did as we thought right. No man shall tell me who I may or may not welcome to my home. That must be my decision. Now go with God! Send word to us when you are safe. My good woman will not rest until she hears that news.' He paused. 'We shall return to this place tomorrow, just to make sure that all has gone well with you.' With that he motioned to his sons. They put the horse between the shafts and turned to retrace their journey to the farm.

Simon wasted no time in returning to the beach. Glancing about him, he was pleased to see that it appeared to be deserted. The others had obeyed his instructions and concealed themselves in the cave.

He hurried to rejoin them, pleased to see that they were enjoying the warmth of a roaring fire.

'May we eat our picnic now?' Marcel asked eagerly.

'A splendid idea!' Simon smiled his approval, but his

eyes were upon Piers. Emma was kneeling by the wounded man and it was clear that she too was worried.

'How is he?' Simon asked quietly.

'Exhausted, as we might expect. Simon, he is much in need of careful nursing. Pray heaven that we shall not have long to wait before the ship arrives.'

'It will be full dark within the hour and Joseph is keeping watch. Be of good heart, my love. Our plan is working well. Soon we shall be safe.' He sat on the ground beside her and slipped an arm about her shoulders. 'I'm sorry that this is so hard on you, my darling.'

'Others have suffered more than I,' she pointed out. 'Besides, I am with you. I would not have it otherwise. In years to come we shall laugh when we remember our adventures.'

He raised her fingers to his lips and kissed them. 'I don't deserve you,' he said earnestly.

Emma dimpled. 'No, you don't!' she teased. 'Mayhap I should seek another...'

'Don't you dare!' he warned. 'I should make short work of a rival.'

'You have none!' Emma reached up to caress the dark curls. 'My love, you are all I could desire. My only wish now is that we return to England. Then we shall be able to lead a normal life together.'

He did not disillusion her. How could he explain that in these troubled times his life could not be normal? Conscious that he was deceiving her, he strolled to the entrance of the cave and called to Joseph. 'No sign yet?' he asked.

There was a long pause before Joseph answered him. 'A vessel is rounding the point, *monsieur*. It is ill lit. Must we wait for the signal?'

'Indeed! You know the code. Check it before you show a light.'

Eyes straining into the darkness, they waited as the fishing boat approached. Then, satisfied by the signals, Simon indicated that they should reply. Quickly he called to the others. 'Come, there is no time to lose! Joseph and I will take Piers between us.'

'Nay, *monsieur*, I'll carry him myself!' The giant negro picked up the wounded man as if he weighed no more than a bag of feathers and set off down the beach to the boat, which was fast approaching the shore.

Chapter Thirteen

Emma did not recognise any of the seamen. She had half-expected to see Jeanne's father among them, but in the darkness she could not distinguish faces and none spoke to her. Their silence did not trouble her. Simon had spoken to the bo'sun and was told that the captain of the vessel had urged the utmost haste.

It was what he had expected. As they had travelled through the quiet countryside they had not seen a living soul, but they would not be safe until they were aboard the ship and well out at sea.

Even then they might be stopped, but he thought it unlikely. As yet their enemies were fully occupied with holding down the cities that had fallen to them and searching out the hated aristocrats. Madame Guillotine needed fresh fodder every day, and victims were captured more easily on land than at sea.

He lifted Emma in his arms and waded through the shallow water to the boat. The others already aboard and at a word of command the crew began to row.

Simon glanced back at the shore and saw to his relief that the beach was still deserted. There were no signs of pursuit. Within minutes he would have his little party safely aboard the fishing vessel.

Jeanne's father had done well for them, he thought with satisfaction. The ship was larger than he had expected and to climb aboard would not be easy, even with the aid of the stout nets already hanging from the side.

Beside him Emma could not suppress a feeling of unease. She caught at his sleeve 'Can this be Jeanne's father's boat?' she whispered. 'I had not thought it would be so big.'

'Who else would keep this appointment with us, my love? This ship may seem large to you, but remember, it must carry all our party and the crew. The captain would be aware that a small fishing smack would be inadequate. Doubtless if his own vessel was unsuitable he would have made other arrangements.'

Emma did not argue, but her feeling of unease persisted. She looked up as they came alongside, but all seemed to be well.

'Piers must go first,' Simon insisted. He waited as Joseph slung the wounded man over his shoulder and began to climb. Then he signalled to the others to follow.

Marcel raced up the netting like a monkey, calling to Mado and Yves to match his agility. They were not far behind him, but when Pierre attempted the climb he found it difficult. Simon sprang to his assistance, pushing the old man ahead of him. Then, as hands reached out to offer help, he came back for Emma.

'Hold on and don't look down, my love. I am behind you. I won't let you fall.'

Emma reached for the netting. It took all of her courage to entrust herself to the swaying ropes, but she tried to hide her terror.

'Take it slowly,' Simon urged from below. 'You are almost there. Just one step at a time.'

The climb seemed endless, but at last she reached the deck. Looking down at last, she shuddered. The sea seemed so very far below and she had always been afraid of heights.

As hands reached out to her she pushed them away. 'Thank you, but I am perfectly all right,' she said with dignity. In the darkness it was difficult to distinguish faces. Only a single lantern swayed above them, doing little to dispel the shadows. She strained to see the others. Had Piers survived the rough-and-ready method of getting him aboard? She had expected her friends to cluster about her, filled with excitement at the successful completion of their plans, but all was silence.

To her surprise, one of the seamen still held her by the arm. As she tried to pull away from him, she stumbled over what she took to be a heavy sack. Then she heard a moan and, as the lantern cast its feeble beam across the deck, she gasped in horror. Joseph was lying at her feet and beneath his head she could see an ominous stain. Piers lay beside him motionless.

Then she heard a scream of terror and Marcel ran towards her. 'It's a trap!' he shrieked. 'Go back!'

The warning came too late. Emma knew it as the grip on her arm tightened. Her first thought was for Simon. She spun round just as he prepared to climb aboard and threw herself against the men who were offering him their hands.

'No!' she cried. 'We are betrayed!' With the last of her strength she struck out, knocking him off balance. He fell back without a cry and she heard the splash as he plunged into the sea below.

'Bitch!' A vicious blow across the face sent her to her knees. 'You'll pay dear for that, my lady.'

Emma's head was spinning. She offered no resistance as two of her captors grabbed her arms and hustled her below. They thrust her ahead of them into a large cabin, but she could sense their unease.

'Where is Avedon?' Robert Chavasse ignored her for the moment. When they did not reply, his face darkened. 'Are you deaf?' he enquired. 'I asked you a question.'

Both men began to speak at once and he raised a hand for silence.

'You!' He pointed to the man on Emma's left. 'I'll ask you again… Where is Avedon?'

'Drowned, I should think,' the man said sullenly. 'It weren't our fault we didn't get him aboard. The wench here pushed him back into the sea.'

'Indeed!' Robert's voice was silky with menace. 'Now why would she do that, I wonder? Something or someone must have warned her.'

The men were silent.

Then their master raised his stick and smashed it down upon the desk before him with such force that the noise was deafening. His face was contorted with rage. 'You'll suffer for this!' he promised. 'I'll have the skin off the back of every man on deck. Did I not make it clear that all the prisoners were to be taken?'

'We took all but one,' the first man ventured rashly.

'Why, so you tell me…' His master's eyes were glittering strangely. 'A pity that the one who escaped was the most important. What went wrong?'

'We almost had him, master. Then the child shouted a warning and the wench here twisted out of Henri's grip and reached the rail before we could stop her.'

'Outwitted by a woman? Well, it does not surprise

me, especially in this case. The young lady has deceived better men than you. Such a quick thinker, aren't you, Emma? Now I believe I must think up some special punishment for those who can neither control a child nor hold a woman safely captive.'

Emma shuddered as she met his gaze. She encountered a look of such malignancy that she could be in no doubt as to the depths of evil to which this man could descend. It was clear that he enjoyed inflicting physical pain and his own men were terrified of him. She could sense the animal panic in those beside her.

Now she stored away that knowledge. In future she might possibly put it to some use. For the moment it was important to divert his attention from Marcel. The boy's youth would not save him from a beating or worse if Robert decided that his warning was the reason for the ruin of his plans.

She found her voice at last. 'I needed no warning from the child,' she said coldly. 'Is it usual to leave your victims lying on the deck? It does give rise to speculation, even to those of limited intelligence.'

Robert looked at her. 'And your own intelligence is far from limited, Emma. I know that well enough.' He sighed. 'You see my difficulties, don't you, my dear? I am forced to work with idiots who cannot follow the simplest of instructions.' With the speed of a striking snake he lifted his stick once more and brought it down with sickening force across the shoulders of the nearest man.

'Get out of my sight!' he snarled. 'Send Chabrol to me with his prisoners.' He turned back to Emma. 'Do sit down, my dear! We must not tire you further. The journey ahead of us is likely to take some hours, depending upon the weather, but we should make Marseilles by morning.'

Emma did not answer him.

'Nothing to say?' he asked pleasantly. 'Perhaps you are considering the probable fate of your beloved. What a chance you took! Let us hope that he can swim.'

'At least he is out of your clutches!' she cried in triumph. 'Any fate is better than that!'

'Perhaps so, although I understand that death by drowning is most unpleasant.' His eyes did not leave her face.

Emma betrayed no emotion. She would not give him the satisfaction of knowing that his words had struck home. She had thrust Simon out of danger, as she thought, but now she shuddered inwardly at the memory of that fearful drop into the winter sea. Simon might be lying dead or injured and at the mercy of the waves.

She was given no time for further thought as the door flew open and Chabrol entered the cabin. Ahead of him he thrust two figures who had been so badly beaten that they were almost unrecognisable.

Emma stared at them in horror. The man had a huge contusion on his cheekbone and above it his left eye was closed. Beside him a young girl swayed, half-fainting, as she struggled to stand upright. Her gown had been ripped asunder from neck to hem and her feeble efforts to hold it closed were unavailing.

'Well, Emma, I hope that you are proud of yourself,' Robert said in mock-sadness. 'You alone have brought your friends to this…'

'My friends?' Emma looked more closely. Then she walked over to the girl and smoothed away the dishevelled hair.

'Jeanne?' she whispered uncertainly. There was no reply. The girl's eyes were blank with shock, but Emma could no longer be in any doubt as to her identity. White with fury, she swung round upon Chavasse. 'I might have guessed!' she cried. 'Defenceless women and old men are ideal victims, are they not?'

'You left me no choice, my dear.' Chavasse gave her an injured look. 'I had to find you and you did not make it easy. Chabrol will tell you how we searched. By the way, I must advise you not to anger him. His interest in you is not slight since his back still bears the marks of the whipping he received when you disappeared…'

Emma ignored him. She threw her arms about the shrinking girl and coaxed her into a chair. 'Don't worry,' she said softly. 'This man will get his just deserts if it takes me a lifetime to repay him.'

Chavasse laughed. 'Such optimism! It is altogether admirable, is it not, Chabrol? Apparently it has not occurred to you that your lifetime is likely to be short. Believe me, I shall not make the mistake of underestimating you again. It was fortunate indeed that Berthe remembered your surprising affection for this young lady.'

It was then that Jeanne's father spoke to her. 'I'm sorry, miss, but they threatened to rape her.' He forced out the words through battered lips. 'I could not let that happen.'

'Of course not!' Emma laid a comforting hand upon his arm. 'I should have done exactly the same if someone I loved was threatened.'

'Touching!' Chavasse sneered. 'Get back to the wheelhouse, man! It's time we were under way.'

Chabrol hesitated in the doorway before dragging his captive away. 'Must we give up the search for Avedon, *monsieur*? The men in the boat can find no trace of him.'

'Leave it! Get them back aboard! He may be dead already, but if not, it is no matter. We have the bait that will bring him to us.' He smiled at Emma. 'What pleasure it will give me to watch my tethered goat awaiting the approach of the tiger. Will you try to warn him, Emma? That would be difficult if you were to lose your tongue.'

Emma faced him without a tremor. Suddenly her courage had returned, even in the face of his threats. Simon was not dead. He would come for her. She was sure of it. Their destiny was bound together, no matter what the danger. She even managed a smile. 'I think you have forgot,' she said. 'I should not be the tiger's intended victim.'

'But he will be mine!' Robert's smile did not reach his eyes. 'This time he will not escape me.' He looked at her in triumph. Then his mood changed. 'Enough of this!' he said abruptly. 'I must not keep you from your friends.'

He strode to the door and threw it open. Then he motioned to the man who stood on guard. 'Take them below!' he ordered. 'I shall join you shortly.'

Emma slipped an arm about Jeanne's waist. 'Lean on me,' she said gently. 'You shall not be further harmed, I promise.' Both men laughed, but Emma ignored their jeering.

Then, infuriated by her calm expression, Robert grasped her arm. 'Always the optimist, Emma? Have you not heard? It is cruel to raise false hopes.'

She faced him then. 'You seem very sure that they are false. It is possible that you are mistaken...'

He laughed again. 'You have been reading too many Gothic novels, my dear. Will your hero come to your rescue single-handed? I confess, I should like to see him

capture this vessel on his own. If he can do so, he will
deserve his victory.'

Emma did not answer him. There was nothing to say.
She did not need Chavasse to tell her that she was
clutching at straws. With all his skill and courage Simon
could not hope to overcome so many of his enemies
alone, even if he had survived that perilous fall into the
sea.

Her mind was racing. If, by some chance, she could
disable or even kill Chavasse, it would avail her little.
It might discourage some of his men, but not the fearsome Chabrol. Was there no solution? Bargaining with
Chavasse was out of the question. He no longer trusted
her. Even so, she refused to consider their situation
hopeless, though she could rely on little assistance from
her friends.

Joseph would have been her main hope, but she could
not banish from her mind the sight of his body lying on
the deck. Had they killed him outright? Piers too might
be dead. Sick though he was, he would have been handled as roughly as the others. She must not think like
that, she told herself. Why imagine the worst? Simon
himself had warned her not to meet disaster halfway.

There was still Pierre, elderly though he was, and
Jeanne's father, too. Marcel she knew to be unharmed,
and she prayed that the same was true of Yves. She had
seen nothing of Mado.

The reason was not far to seek. As her captor held his
lantern high, he thrust her ahead of him in to the ship's
hold. She stumbled and almost fell over the bound figure
of Mado. The girl had been gagged, but above the filthy
cloth her eyes still blazed defiance. She thrust out her
legs and tried to trip the guard, but he was too quick for

her. His savage kick brought an immediate protest from Emma.

'Yon wench needs to be taught some manners,' he scowled. 'Wait till we get her to Marseilles. There's worse than a kick in store for her, I can tell you. Damme if she didn't sink her teeth into my hand and me just trying to help her.'

'I can imagine,' Emma replied coldly. She had seen the lascivious look upon the man's face. Peering into the shadowy corners of the hold, she tried to catch a glimpse of Yves, knowing that he would not let such threats to Mado go unchallenged. He was lying with his head in Marcel's lap, clearly unconscious. His clothing and that of the boy were heavily stained with blood.

Emma sank to her knees beside them. 'What happened?' she asked in a low voice. 'Is Yves badly hurt?'

Marcel was too shocked to speak. It was Pierre who answered her. 'They clubbed him, *mademoiselle*, just as they did Joseph. They are both dazed. You'll get no sense from them at present.'

'And Monsieur Piers... Is he...is he dead?'

The old man reached out and took her hand. 'He lives, my dear. They thought it not worthwhile to harm him further.'

'Not for the present, at least.' Chavasse had joined them. Now he signalled to his companions to hold their lanterns high, illuminating the sorry-looking figures of his captives. 'I wonder...?' he mused as he looked down at Piers. 'We can afford to take no chances.' With great deliberation he raised his cane and, using all his weight, pressed down hard against the injured shoulder. Piers gave a groan of agony and then fainted.

'Why, you savage!' Emma flew at Chavasse, clawing for his eyes, but he brushed her aside with a single thrust

of his arm. The man beside him lifted a hand to strike
at her, but she stood firm in front of her friend. Chavasse
would not be allowed to torture him again if she could
help it.

'No, leave her!' Chavasse held the man back. '*Mademoiselle* has much to learn and her lessons won't be
easy. Pray. don't injure that lovely face! Our friend Chabrol would take it much amiss. He has such plans for
her…' He was smiling as he went aloft, leaving his prisoners in darkness.

'Miss, what are we to do?' Marcel's voice was high
with panic. 'Do they mean to kill us?'

'Of course not,' Emma lied. She might have added,
'Not just yet…' but there was no point in distressing the
child still further. 'If they had meant to kill us they
would have done so already.'

'Then are we to be prisoners? I hope not. They are
such cruel men.'

'That's true, but we must not let them win. I'll loosen
your bonds. Then you shall untie Mado's gag. I want to
talk to her.'

Marcel jumped at the chance to be of help. Within
seconds he had removed the filthy cloth from his sister's
mouth.

'Ugh!' Mado spat in disgust. 'I shall die of poisoning.'

'But not just yet, I beg of you!' Emma tried to lighten
the situation with a joke. 'I need you well and strong if
we are to put our heads together to see what can be
done.'

Mado snorted in disbelief. 'Are you a magician then?
Yves and Joseph are unconscious and Monsieur Piers is
barely alive.'

'We must do what we can to help ourselves,' Emma

insisted. 'I have not been bound. Marcel shall release you and then we can untie the others.'

'And how will that help us, *mademoiselle*? Are you suggesting that Chavasse won't discover that we have been freed?'

'He has satisfied himself that we are not a danger to him. I doubt if he'll visit us again. If he does we must dissemble... Just keep the bonds loosely about your hands and feet—'

'But I still don't see—'

'Hush! Listen to the wind! Soon we shall be under way.'

'You seem mighty anxious to return to Marseilles, Miss Lynton.' Pierre's voice was sad. 'We can expect no help from there. Now, had Monsieur Avedon been alive—'

'Of course he is alive!' Emma's angry tone concealed her own anxiety. 'We boarded this vessel close to the shore. Why should not *monsieur* have gained the beach?'

'Mayhap he did.' The old man sounded defeated. 'Even so, he can do naught to help us.'

Emma lost her temper. 'Oh!' she cried. 'Must you be beaten before you start? We must fight whilst there is life within us.'

Mado sniffed. 'Typical of the English!' she sneered. 'Fools to the last. Won't you accept defeat when it is staring you in the face?'

'No, I won't, and nor should you! You surprise me, Mado. I thought that you, of all people, would not give way to despair.'

'Fine words!' the girl said sullenly. 'I'd fight if I thought we had the least chance of escape, but there is nothing we can do.'

Emma lost all patience with her. 'We can look to our

menfolk for a start,' she snapped. Then she called aloft to one of the guards.

'Quiet down there!' the man growled. 'Any more noise and you'll feel the butt-end of this musket.'

'I want some water,' Emma told him firmly.

'Wanting and getting are two different things,' he jeered. 'Want all you like, Miss High and Mighty, you'll get naught from me.'

'I can pay for it,' Emma whispered. 'How will a gold coin suit you?'

'Keep your voice down!' There was a long silence as the man glanced about him, but none of his companions were within earshot. 'You'll get me killed,' he muttered. 'They'll want to know why I have come down to you.'

'No one need know if you are quick about it. If you are questioned, you must say I believed that one of the prisoners had died. You came to check my story.'

There was still silence from above and Emma grew impatient. 'Great heavens!' she cried. 'What have you to fear? Our menfolk are unarmed, injured and bound. Are you not brave enough to face a woman? Of course, if you feel that your master has some use for a pile of stinking corpses?' She turned away.

'He said naught about providing you with water...'

'But he did not forbid it, did he? Perhaps you had best ask him. For your own safety he may wish you to be accompanied...'

'Nay, no need for that,' the man said hastily. Greed had overcome his judgment. As Emma had guessed he was unwilling to share the gold with any of his friends. But would he take the bait? His fear of Chavasse might outweigh the chance of gain.

She waited for so long that the boat was well under way before he reappeared. To her relief he carried a brimming pail. He hesitated, then began to descend into the hold. Halfway down the ladder he stopped. 'Let's see your money first,' he growled.

Emma showed him the coin and his eyes glistened.

'There's more if you'll leave the lantern with us,' she told him.

'Nay, you ask too much! Master would break my neck.'

'We'll douse the light if you warn us,' she promised. 'Are you alone on deck?'

'Aye! The master's in his cabin. He ain't the best of sailors. Chabrol is in the wheelhouse with yon captain. The rest of them have left me to it.' Clearly he wasn't pleased to be the only one on duty.

'Then this is your opportunity,' Emma told him. 'Does your master pay you in gold?'

'No, he don't. More than likely 'twill be in *sous*.' He sounded further ill used.

'Well, then, do as I say.' She added another coin to the one in her hand. 'We shall take care, and so must you.'

'I'll do that all right!' He snatched at the money and handed her the pail.

For a moment she thought that he would refuse to leave the lantern, but, perhaps hopeful of adding to his gains, he set it down and climbed aloft once more.

When Emma held it high, the sight that greeted her was not encouraging. In the dim light it was impossible for her to judge the full extent of the injuries to her friends, but the prone figures had not stirred.

Beside her Marcel choked back a sob. 'Are they dead, *mademoiselle*? There is so much blood…'

'Of course not!' she said briskly. 'Now, young man,

I shall need some help. Let us look to Mado first. Then she too can aid us.'

She would need cloths to wash the wounds of the injured men. A handkerchief or two would be of little use, so with a sigh she raised her skirt and began to tear at the fabric of her last remaining petticoat.

The task brought back vivid memories of Simon. It seemed a lifetime since he had chided her for misplaced modesty when he had insisted upon bandaging her arm. Now modesty was the least of her concerns. What was a petticoat, after all? Besides which, none of her companions were in any condition to show an interest in a well-turned ankle. Above all, she must not think of Simon or her fragile hopes for his safety might desert her entirely.

She was about to soak the lengths of fabric in the pail when Mado stopped her.

'May we not drink first?' the girl asked.

Emma looked closely at the contents of the pail. The water seemed clean enough, so she nodded. 'Not too much!' she warned. 'I think it is fresh water, but we can't be sure.'

'I'll take a chance on it.' Mado cupped her hands and drank her fill. Then she smiled. 'It's fine!' she announced. 'Oh, if only we had a cup we could revive the others.'

'Use the cloths,' Emma advised. 'If they are well soaked, we can squeeze sufficient moisture from them. Pierre may use his hands as you did.'

She beckoned the old man forward and waited until he had slaked his thirst. Then she drew him aside. 'Who is the most severely injured?' she asked in a low tone.

'Joseph took the brunt of it, *mademoiselle*. Six of them set about him.'

'And Yves?'

'Much the same, although they found him easier to subdue.'

'But they did not attack Monsieur Piers, I think you said?'

'He was roughly handled, but they did not think him worth a beating.'

'I thank God for that at least. Now, do you and Marcel revive the injured men. Give them water and wash away the blood. The damage may be less than we fear. Mado will care for Monsieur Piers and I shall help her later. First I must look to Jeanne. She has not spoken since we came aboard this vessel.'

Pierre's face was grim. 'The girl is badly shocked,' he said. 'Doubtless she had no idea that men could behave so ill...'

'I would she had not learned of it,' Emma told him sadly. 'Let me see what I can do.'

Gently she smoothed back Jeanne's dishevelled hair. Then, cupping her hands, she offered the girl a sip of water. Jeanne drank obediently and then, as Emma wiped her face with a moistened cloth, she stirred, gazing about her wildly.

'My father!' she cried. 'Where is my father? Have they killed him?'

Emma held her close. 'Of course not! Your father is the most important person aboard this boat. Who else has the skill to handle it? He, above any of us, will not be harmed.'

Jeanne's tears began to flow. 'You do not know!' she cried. 'They beat him cruelly and still he would not tell them where you were. It was only when they tore my gown and threatened to give me to Chabrol—'

'Don't think about it, my dear. Any one of us would

have done the same if those we loved were threatened. Now, do take heart. Your father would not care to see you in this state.'

Jeanne gazed at her with brimming eyes. 'What is to become of us?' she whispered. 'Where are they taking us, *mademoiselle*?'

'I believe we are making for Marseilles, and there, you know, we may find friends to help us.' It was a forlorn hope and she knew it, but she must not allow Jeanne to give way to despair. 'Do you feel well enough to help me now?' she asked. 'Our menfolk need attention. Yves is bleeding still, I see, and his wounds need binding.'

As she had hoped, Jeanne responded at once, and Emma moved to Mado's side. She was filled with apprehension. 'How is Piers?' she asked. The sick man had been roughly handled when he was hauled aboard the vessel and Chavasse had hurt him cruelly with his cane. To her surprise, it was Piers himself who answered her.

'I'm improving by the minute,' he said cheerfully. 'Mado won't have it otherwise and I've promised Marcel that I won't die just yet.' He looked at her anxious face and grinned. 'Time to see to the others, I believe…they are in worse case than me. Tell me, where is Simon? I don't see him here.'

Emma smiled at him. 'Simon has escaped, thank God! He was the last aboard, and realised what was happening—'

'Only when you called out and pushed him into the sea.' Mado sniffed. 'You didn't even know if he could swim…'

Piers laughed aloud. 'Emma, is that true?'

'I'm sorry to say it is,' she replied with dignity. 'But we were not far offshore.' Her lips began to quiver. 'I hoped…I mean, I thought it best at the time. I could not bear to think that Simon would be taken.'

'Don't worry! You did the right thing. Simon swims like a fish, though I don't doubt you'll be in trouble for such ill usage when you see him next.' He was still smiling as she turned away.

To her relief, both Yves and Joseph had recovered consciousness. Now the giant negro was flexing his cramped muscles. Emma winced as she looked at the huge lump upon his head.

'I've had worse!' he assured her. 'Give me a few minutes, ma'am, and I'll be ready to go aloft and take our friends by surprise.'

'You will do no such thing,' she told him warmly. 'They are too many. One man cannot hope to overcome such numbers.'

'A knife at their master's throat might persuade them to surrender, and I shall have Yves here, and Pierre—'

'And not a weapon between you!' Emma would have none of it and Piers supported her.

'Best to wait,' he insisted. 'It will take some time to reach Marseilles. With any luck, Simon may be ahead of us.'

'To rescue us single-handed?' Mado's sarcastic tone was intended to mask her fears, but it fooled no one. She could not control her shaking limbs.

'May we not do as Joseph has suggested?' Yves pleaded. 'It may be easier to fight aboard this vessel.'

There was uncertainty among his companions, as each of them offered an opinion.

Yves looked about him, pleading for the chance to take some action. 'After all,' he continued. 'On one thing we are all agreed. Even if Monsieur Avedon has reached

Marseilles, where is he to find help for us? We could be imprisoned in some dungeon and even shackled.'

'*Monsieur* will think of something,' Marcel insisted. 'He always does. He will have a plan already. I'm sure of it. He will save us.' He took Jeanne's hand. 'You must not worry, you know. No one can possibly outwit him...'

Marcel's fervent support of his idol brought smiles all round, though there was some shaking of heads. Emma beamed at the boy. His sentiments were much the same as her own. It was Joseph who chafed at the inaction.

'Well, *mademoiselle*, I'll go along with you,' he said at last. 'But I don't like it. We should be taking steps to help ourselves. Suppose that Monsieur Avedon—?' He caught sight of Marcel's face and amended what he had been about to say. 'I mean...suppose we find no help ashore? Chavasse can call on even more of his men to guard us when we reach the port.'

'That's true, but money is his god and I still have gold. Possibly I could buy our freedom.'

Piers reached out a hand to her. 'My dear Emma, do take care. Do not mention the gold. Chavasse would take it from you without a second thought and offer nothing in return. Keep your purse concealed. They have stripped the rest of us of all our possessions. You alone have the means to bribe a guard.'

'I have already done so—' Emma doused the lantern quickly. Her sharp ears had already caught the hissed warning from above. Then she heard Chavasse.

'All quiet down there?'

'Aye, master, not a sound. They'll be licking their wounds, I make no doubt.'

'Very good! It will be some time before we dock. By

then our prisoners should be in a more amenable frame of mind.'

'Are they to have water? They asked for it…'

'That would be Miss Lynton, I expect.' Chavasse peered into the hold. 'Can you hear me, Emma? You asked for water and you shall have it. Let me give you some proof of my Christian charity.' There was silence for a time and then the icy contents of a pail were tipped down upon them.

Chavasse shouted with laughter. 'Is that enough, my dear, or would you like some more…?' He waited, but Emma did not reply and at length he walked away.

It was some time before she dared call to the guard again. Badly frightened by the sudden appearance of Chavasse, the man now refused point-blank to relight the lantern. Even Emma's offer of more money could not move him.

'Gold's no use to a dead man,' he whispered. 'I'd like to help you, miss, but there's naught more I can do for you.'

'I understand…' Emma turned to her companions. 'Is everyone all right?' she asked. 'No one is soaked, I hope…'

Marcel chuckled. '*Monsieur* could not see us in the darkness, so his aim was poor. The water fell in the middle of the hold, not in the corners where we lay.'

Emma sighed with relief. On that bitter winter night the cold would have been felt even more keenly through sodden garments. 'Let us huddle together for warmth,' she suggested. 'Otherwise we shall be chilled to the bone by the time we reach Marseilles.'

Marcel's hand stole into hers. 'Shall we be long at sea?' he asked. 'I hate it down here. It's cold and it smells horrible.'

'Try not to think about it,' she advised. She cast about for a more pleasant topic to divert the boy's attention. 'I have been thinking about the new puppies at the farm,' she announced. 'Will their eyes be open yet, I wonder? Which was your favourite, Marcel?'

'The brown one with the white paw,' he told her promptly. 'I'm to have him for my own when we return.'

A silence fell upon the little group. 'If we return' was the unspoken thought, but Emma thrust it away.

'We must think of a name for him,' she cried gaily. 'Has anyone any suggestions?' Tired, beaten and dispirited though they were, the others followed her lead, but Marcel was asleep before he had made his choice.

It was a blessing, Emma decided. For the others, the rest of that night seemed endless.

It was only when the faint grey light of dawn had stolen across the sky above the open hatch that they heard the unmistakable bustle of a busy port.

Chapter Fourteen

As men tramped across the deck above them Emma reminded her companions to retie the bonds about their hands and feet. It could scarcely matter at this stage, she thought wearily, but she had no wish to provoke Chavasse into a further demonstration of brutality. Then she heard the sharp command above her head.

'Fetch them up!'

'Master, we can't carry them if they are bound like hogs,' the guard protested. 'Yon ladder is too steep.'

'Well then, fool, untie them one at a time and send them up the ladder. Remember, if there is any trouble you will be the one to suffer for it.'

The man scrambled down to them in haste. With his knife at the ready, he started on Pierre's bonds but they parted at his touch, causing the man to stare long and hard at Emma. In silence she held up another coin and he shrugged. He'd been told to release the prisoners. What matter if they had already released themselves? Like Emma, he had no wish to incur the further wrath of his brutal master. He glanced about him quickly. If the other men were free, they might decide to attack him on the spot, but he thought it unlikely. They were a sorry-looking bunch. Besides, he could always call for help.

He sent Pierre aloft at once and Marcel followed him. Next came Jeanne and Mado. As they awaited their turn to climb out of the hold Emma moved closer to Yves and Joseph.

'There must be no trouble on deck,' she warned in an undertone. 'Your task is to care for Monsieur Piers. We can do nothing until we get ashore…I want your word on it.'

Both men agreed with evident reluctance, but Piers supported Emma.

'The last thing we need is a blood bath,' he told them quietly. 'There are the women and Marcel to consider.' He glanced across at the guard, but the man was standing by the foot of the ladder, well out of hearing. 'We must be patient,' he insisted. 'Simon may have reached Marseilles ahead of us. He has more chance of reaching us with help when we are ashore.'

Emma did not meet his eyes. She knew, as he did himself, just how faint was any hope of rescue. Even so, they must not give Chavasse the excuse to kill them even before they landed. On reflection, she decided that it was unlikely. There had been opportunity enough to knock the prisoners on the head and throw them overboard in these last few hours. He had other plans for them, she was sure of it. Now she prayed that her courage would not fail her in whatever ordeal lay ahead.

She was left it no doubt as to what it would be. Bound once more and roped together she and her friends were paraded through the city streets through crowds of jeering *sans-culottes*. Emma eyed them with scorn. These people were not imbued with the high ideals of the Revolution. They were here for the sport. Emma refused to bend her head as rotten fruit and vegetables rained down upon them. Ahead of her a woman picked up a heavy stone. Then she caught Emma's eye, reddened and dropped the missile, turning away as if ashamed.

Beside her, Mado was almost speechless with rage. 'Why is Chavasse doing this?' she demanded through gritted teeth. 'Is it not enough for him to have us in his power? Must he humiliate us further? It is pointless.'

'On the contrary, it is all part of his plan to capture Simon. He is making quite sure that we are known to have landed here today, and that our destination will not be a secret. The crowd is following... Do you not see?'

Mado glanced at Emma's face. 'I'm sorry!' she said in an altered tone. 'I have been thoughtless... You must be worried sick.'

Emma struggled for control. 'I don't care to be used as bait,' she admitted. 'If only we could warn him of this plot.'

Mado smiled at last. 'I doubt if that will be necessary, Emma. Monsieur Avedon is no fool. Marcel is right about him, though I will admit that the boy is biased.'

Emma did not answer her. The comforting words were kindly meant, but it was more than likely that the older members of the party were right. What could Simon do alone? Her feelings of apprehension increased as the prisoners were brought to a halt before a dilapidated warehouse.

'Inside!' Chabrol ordered sharply. He thrust the prisoners ahead of him into the barn-like structure. It seemed little used, though a number of large crates had been pushed against the walls. They were covered in dust and spiders' webs.

'Spiders!' Mado gave a little shriek. 'How I hate them! They frighten me to death!'

In spite of her own worries Emma was forced to smile. Fear of spiders seemed oddly out of place when she considered the deadly perils which they faced. 'They cannot harm you,' she comforted. 'After all, they do not bite or sting.'

'I know it!' Mado looked ashamed of her outburst. 'It is all those legs, I think, and then they run so fast!'

'I think we should forget them.' Emma looked up to see that Robert Chavasse was standing in the doorway. She struggled to her feet. 'We are much in need of both water and food,' she said calmly. 'I presume you intend to keep the bait alive until you have captured your prey?'

'Certainly, my dear. That is my intention and I think we shall not have long to wait.'

'And need we stay bound and roped together?'

'Of course not, Emma, though I advise you against the folly of attempting to escape. This place is perfectly secure and extremely well guarded. I shall even provide you with lanterns to illuminate your little group. Monsieur Avedon must be left in no doubt that his prize is here.'

At his signal some of the guards trooped into the barrack-like interior with pitchers of water and sacks of coarse bread. Those with lanterns arranged them close to the prisoners, leaving the corners of the warehouse in darkness.

'Comfortable?' Chavasse beamed upon them. 'Take heart, my friends! I believe we shall not keep you long.' With that he strolled away, withdrawing the guards as he did so.

'Why have they left us alone?' Marcel was puzzled. 'There is no one here to stop us. Could we not just slip away?'

'We should not get far,' Yves assured him. 'You

heard Monsieur Chavasse. This place is surrounded, even though we cannot see our captors.'

Emma felt sick at heart. She knew that he was right. The trap was set. Now all her enemy had to do was to await his prey. Suddenly she longed for Simon with a passion that frightened her. He was their last remaining hope. Yet even in that knowledge she began to pray that he would not attempt their rescue. Better by far to lose her own life than to see him taken by Chavasse. She was in no doubt as to what his fate would be.

Piers looked at her ashen face. Then he took her hand in his. 'You worry too much,' he said. 'Can it be that you don't share Marcel's belief in Simon? I should be sorry to hear it.'

Emma was very close to tears. 'I do believe in him, but, Piers, he cannot work miracles. I love him so, and I cannot bear to think of what awaits him here.'

'Then don't! Simon is no fool. He will have some plan. Meantime, we must do our part. I suggest that we make the most of these provisions. Won't you see to it? We may be here for quite some time, but even that may be in our favour. It will give us the chance to recover our strength.'

Emma nodded. 'You are right, of course. How do you feel yourself?'

He grinned at her. 'I am improving by the minute, though I don't intend to let that fact be known. You must show great concern about my health whenever Chavasse is near.'

Emma managed a faint smile. She felt ashamed of her own weakness. Surely she could show as much courage as those about her. She, at least, had not been roughly handled. Heartened by her friend's words, she began to hand out the bread.

Stale though it was, her companions fell upon it eagerly. They had not eaten since the previous day. Now, as they washed it down with draughts of water, Emma saw with relief that even this meagre fare was having its effect. Heads went up and conversation quickened. As was to be expected, the main topic was the possibility of escape.

Joseph and Yves had both recovered from their beating. Now they were talking out of hearing of the others.

Piers noticed it at once. 'Come!' he said pleasantly. 'We must have no secrets from each other. Will you not tell us what you have in mind?'

Yves hesitated, but Joseph spoke out boldly. 'I won't be led out to be slaughtered like some animal,' he announced. 'Better to die like a man, here in this place if necessary. At least we can put up some semblance of a fight.'

'Have you forgotten Marcel and the women?' Piers enquired.

'No, *monsieur*, but will they be saved if we do nothing? I think not!'

'You may be right, my friend. However, let me make a suggestion. Monsieur Avedon may already be planning our escape. Should we not give him time to do so?'

Joseph pursed his lips. 'With great respect, *monsieur*, we do not know if the gentleman has survived. Must we wait until it is too late and we are led to our death in chains?'

'No, of course not, but I think we can spare a little more time. I know my friend, and I believe that he will make his move without delay. As for ourselves, we are not in any immediate danger, I believe. Chavasse is using us to bait his trap. He will not injure us before the trap is sprung.'

Emma shuddered. She had never felt so helpless in her life. Was this to be the end of all her hopes of happiness with her love? She longed for him and yet she hoped that he would not come.

As that endless day wore on to its close, her spirits lifted in spite of all. Some of her friends might believe that Simon had not survived that perilous fall into the sea, but in her heart she was convinced that he still lived. Now she tried to imagine what could have happened to him.

Perhaps he had been unable to reach Marseilles. Even had he done so and discovered where she was imprisoned, his own good sense might have convinced him that rescue was impossible. Emma was no martyr. She loved life, and had no wish to lose it, but for her love she would lay it down gladly, if need be.

As darkness fell the prisoners were given food and drink once more. Bales of straw were thrown into them that they might construct makeshift beds. As they huddled together for warmth, Emma sensed Piers beside her.

'Try to get some sleep,' he whispered. 'Tomorrow will be the day.'

She wanted to believe him but, try as she might, she could see no possibility of escape. She fell asleep at last, determined that, if all else failed, she would follow Joseph's lead and sell her life dear. Her enemies would be forced to kill her before she would allow herself to be dragged, a helpless captive, to the guillotine.

When she awakened she was stiff and cold. She stretched to ease her limbs.

For a few seconds she felt disorientated. What was it

that had brought her back to consciousness? She opened her eyes and looked into Simon's smiling face.

In an instant she was on her feet. Then she threw herself into his arms. For just a moment she allowed herself to savour the exquisite pleasure of that embrace. Then she pushed him away. 'You must be mad!' she cried. 'Don't you know that this is a trap? You must go before it is too late.'

Simon kissed her gently. 'Are you unharmed?' he asked.

'Yes! Yes! It was the men who were beaten, but go, I beg of you. You can do nothing here.'

There was a twinkle in his eyes as he looked down at her. 'This isn't much of a welcome,' he complained. 'I suspected that you must have changed your mind when you pushed me into the sea. It was quite a drop, you know…'

'Don't joke, I beg of you!' she cried in anguish. 'Chavasse is close by, and every entrance is being watched. I don't know how you came here, but you must leave at once.'

'A timely warning, Emma, if a little late!' Chavasse strolled into the circle of light. 'Welcome, *monsieur*, I am happy to meet you. This pleasure has been long delayed.'

Simon stared at him. 'For my part I should not describe it as a pleasure, *monsieur*. In the ordinary way I do not consort with butchers.'

'Really? Then your acquaintance is likely to be improved within the next day or so—that is, unless you can persuade our clever little English miss to fall in with my wishes.'

'And they are?'

'Why, Mademoiselle Lynton knows them well

enough. I wish to renew my acquaintance with her father.'

Simon laughed. 'You are too late, *monsieur*. Miss Lynton, as you say, is clever. She has already sent a message to her father, warning him not to trust your promises, I understand that you dispatched that message yourself.'

'You lie! I read the message before I sent it. There was no warning.'

'I fear your classical education has been neglected, my friend. You have not read of the warning to beware of Greeks bearing gifts? Mister Lynton will have noticed it, even if you did not.'

'I see! Well, I must confess that I had wondered why there was no reply.' Chavasse was furious at having been tricked so easily, but he gave no sign of it. He shrugged his shoulders. 'It is no matter! There are other methods of persuasion.'

He reached out a caressing hand and smoothed back Emma's hair. 'Such pretty ears!' he murmured. 'And easily recognised by a fond parent, I have no doubt.' In a horrible parody of courtesy he grasped her fingers and raised them to his lips. 'On the other hand, these dainty members might be sent at intervals.'

Simon drew Emma to him. 'Don't be afraid!' he said serenely. 'Monsieur Chavasse does not yet know it, but his days are numbered.'

Chavasse stepped back a pace and eyed him with astonishment. Then he began to shout with laughter. 'You English are truly a race apart!' he gasped. 'Do you consider yourselves invincible? How do you propose to overcome me, Avedon? You are my prisoner and this building is surrounded. You are no magician, *monsieur*;

indeed, I am tempted to see what a flogging will do to that arrogant manner.'

'I don't advise you to try it!'

'But I have not asked for your advice.' Chavasse looked carefully at the other prisoners. 'Let us be done with this!' He snapped his fingers to bring his men to him. 'Just the other Englishman and these two, I believe. One way and another they will give us information. As for the rest, they are just rabble. Lock them up! They will serve to fill the tumbrils in the morning.'

Emma caught at his sleeve. 'Please spare them, Robert! They are here through no fault of their own, and Marcel is but a child—'

'They helped you didn't they, even if it was for gold? And children, in case you had forgot, have a nasty habit of growing up with thoughts of vengeance.'

'Naught was done for gold!' Mado walked up to him and spat into his face with great deliberation.

He felled her with a single blow and was about to strike again when suddenly he stayed his hand. 'To Madame Guillotine? I think not for this one, nor for the other girl! That would be a wicked waste when there are lusty men about. Enjoy your reprieve, my dears! In these next few days it may be that you will both pray for death.'

Emma felt sick with horror. With every word and deed Robert Chavasse was confirming that he was indeed a monster. Now her friends were to die and she could only blame herself for allowing them to help her.

Wildly she cast about for some way to escape his clutches, but she could think of nothing. This, then, must be the end. All her hopes and dreams of a happy future with her beloved Simon would never come to pass. She gripped his hand convulsively. Within minutes they would be separated, never to see each other again.

She felt a reassuring squeeze and glanced at him. To her astonishment he looked untroubled. Had he not realized that Chavasse meant what he said?

Ignoring the men about him, he kissed her brow. 'Wait!' he whispered softly. 'Do nothing yet!'

But there was no time left. The two guards with Chavasse still had their weapons levelled. There could be no chance of rushing them. In a panic she threw herself into Simon's arms. They would have to tear her away from him.

'A touching scene, my dear!' Chavasse was eying her with amusement. 'I had wondered often where your choice would fall. Such a pity that it had to be upon our friend here! A spy! An adventurer! Ah, well, there is no accounting for a woman's taste…' He turned to one of his guards. 'Get the others!' he ordered.

Emma turned to Simon. 'Whatever happens, I shall love you always,' she told him quietly. 'Will you remember that?'

'I will!' He slipped his arms about her and held her close. 'This is not the end, you know.'

'It must be, my love. Please don't try to spare me. I have made up my mind. I shall try to be brave, but it is so hard to lose you.'

He did not answer her, and suddenly she was aware that he had tensed.

'What is it?' she asked. 'What have you heard?'

'Hush!' he said. 'Listen, Emma!'

She paused. 'I hear nothing, Simon…'

'That is the point. Look at Chavasse! He is wondering why his guards have not returned.'

Emma glanced at her enemy. His face was dark with

rage and his expression boded ill for those who were taking so long to obey him.

Then she heard the tramp of marching feet and his manner changed. 'At last!' he said with satisfaction. 'Say your farewells, my friends! I think it unlikely that you two good people will see each other again.'

'A curious notion, Monsieur Chavasse! You have some reason for making such a statement?' The man who walked towards them from the shadows had an extraordinary effect upon their enemy. No longer young, he was not much above the middle height, but Emma recognised him at once. She had never met him, but her father had pointed him out to her on more than one occasion. This was the legendary Paul Lenoir, poet, philosopher and statesman, and possibly the most powerful man in France.

Chavasse bowed low. 'What a pleasure to see you, sir! I am sorry that you should come upon me at such a time. This matter is unworthy of your attention. It is merely a question of disposing of certain enemies of our country. I have made it my business to capture them. These people are scum. They need not engage your interest.'

'Possibly not, Monsieur Chavasse, but my interest lies in you, rather than your prisoners.'

Chavasse preened visibly. Clearly his efforts had come to the notice of the highest in the land. Now he would be well rewarded.

He was about to speak again, but Lenoir held up a hand for silence. Then he addressed Chavasse once more. 'Tell me, sir! Are you under the impression that this change in our country's fortunes has been brought about simply for your own personal benefit?'

Chavasse stared at him and began to stammer. Much

of his swagger left him and beads of sweat appeared upon his brow. Something was wrong. The dark eyes of his inquisitor had never left his face, and they held no kindly light.

'I—I don't understand,' he faltered. 'If there is aught amiss…?'

'Oh, there is much amiss, my friend. Let us begin with your present accommodation in this city. How did you come by that?'

'It was the home of a traitor…an aristocrat…'

'Monsieur Diderot was no aristocrat. He was a wine merchant, albeit a wealthy citizen. One of our supporters, nevertheless, and a man who disliked the excesses of the old regime as much as we do ourselves.'

'I…I did not know…'

'Then you did not question him? He was executed without trial, perhaps?'

Chavasse wilted visibly. 'There was much to do in this city. Perhaps mistakes were made—'

'Indeed, they were! Now let us turn to the matter of his fortune, and that of certain other gentlemen who have met their end just recently. I have a list about my person…' He took a folded sheet of paper from his pocket and began to read.

Emma listened in horror. It was a roll-call of death. Could so many have been murdered for gain? It was impossible to believe, but the cringing man who faced his accuser left her in no doubt that it was true.

Still he tried to justify himself, turning this way and that in an effort to avoid admitting his guilt. 'I had no thought of keeping the money for myself,' he whined. 'I was holding it in trust for the Committee.'

'Strange, then, that it has not been mentioned. No one

is aware of the amount or the whereabouts of such sums.'

'It wouldn't have been safe to tell. This city is in chaos. It is filled with thieves—'

'One of whom is standing before me!' Lenoir snapped his fingers and suddenly the room was filled with guards. 'Take him!' he said briefly.

Chavasse cracked at last. 'I'll pay it back!' he screamed. 'Have mercy on me, Monsieur Lenoir!'

'As you had on your victims? I wonder that you dare to ask it of me. You will indeed pay, my friend. You may be sure of it.'

Chavasse knew then that all was lost. He seemed to shrink into himself. His head went down, but when he lifted it at last, Emma saw murder in his eyes. They were fixed on Simon.

'This is your doing!' he snarled. With a strength born of despair, he wrenched himself from the grip of the guards and threw himself upon his enemy.

Emma screamed. She had seen the gleam of a vicious-looking blade. 'The knife!' she cried. 'Watch out for his knife!'

Simon evaded the initial charge with ease, but then Chavasse turned with lightning speed and slashed savagely at his arm. He laid it open from wrist to elbow, but then Simon threw him to the ground, using his superior strength to hold the man down.

'Give it up, man!' he said. 'You can't escape.'

It was hatred alone that led Chavasse to fight on, half-blinding Simon with a handful of dust scooped up from the ground. Then he clawed at Simon's eyes, trying to gouge them from their sockets.

Emma could not bear to look as he lost all control, biting, kicking and scratching like some trapped animal.

Then Simon's hands were about his throat, closing inexorably upon his windpipe. That iron grip did not relax even when the thrashing figure grew limp.

Emma ran to her lover then, tugging at his sleeve. 'Pray don't kill him, Simon!' she pleaded. 'Will you soil your hands with him? He isn't worth it!'

Lenoir added his voice to hers. 'Miss Lynton is right. The creature shall account for himself at a Tribunal. He will get his just deserts, I promise you.'

Chavasse came round in time to hear this dread pronouncement. He knew it to be a death sentence and he began to scream in terror.

Emma covered her ears, but Lenoir was unmoved. He signed to his guards. 'Get him out of my sight!' he ordered. 'The fellow disgusts me.'

Emma could not bear to watch as Chavasse was dragged away. She turned to his accuser. 'Must you…?' she asked in a low voice. 'I mean…will it be necessary?'

'To execute him?' The dark eyes were grave as they looked into her own. 'Sadly, I fear it will, my dear. Such blackguards sully the ideals of our Revolution both at home and abroad. Don't waste your pity on him! Save it for his victims, one of whom is at this moment much in need of your attention, I believe…'

Emma turned as Simon slipped an arm about her waist. He gave her a reassuring smile. ''Tis but a flesh wound, my love.'

'Perhaps a surgeon, Monsieur Avedon?' Lenoir eyed him with concern.

'Unnecessary, I assure you. If I might have some water and a cloth? It is merely a matter of binding up the wound.'

Lenoir issued the necessary orders. Then he turned to

the other prisoners. 'All French citizens will stand to the left,' he announced.

Emma began to tremble. Would he regard her friends as traitors to their country? If so, they could expect a dreadful fate. She watched in anguish as the little group began to separate. Mado took Marcel firmly by the hand and joined Jeanne and her father, shrugging off the proffered support of Yves and Pierre.

They stood in silence as Lenoir addressed them. He was in no hurry and for some moments he studied each face in turn. 'Hmm!' he said at last. 'You are an unlikely group of counter-revolutionaries. In this case I am prepared to believe that you acted out of pity for your friends, rather than from a desire to harm your country. You may go to your homes and you will not be molested further. However, even though you have prevented a grave injustice on this occasion, I must remind you that we are at war with England. You may not give succour to our enemies. Any further attempts to do so will be treated with great severity.'

The prisoners stared at him in disbelief. Was this a trick or were they really to be freed?

Then Emma ran to them, torn between laughter and tears. 'It is true!' she cried. 'Monsieur Lenoir means what he says. Go quickly now! You have suffered enough on my behalf.'

They clustered about her, still unable to believe their good fortune. Then Jeanne seized her arm. 'But what of you, *mademoiselle*? What is to happen to you? You heard *monsieur*. As English citizens you are enemies of this country.' The girl's eyes filled with tears. 'I could not bear it if harm should come to you.'

'We shall not be harmed,' Emma told her firmly. 'If *monsieur* had wished to injure us, he would have left us to the tender mercies of Chavasse.' She spoke with a confidence she was far from feeling. At best she must face the prospect of a lengthy stay in prison. She did not betray her fears as she embraced her friends and thanked them. Then she watched them walk away.

'You have been more than generous, Monsieur Lenoir,' she told her captor when they had gone. 'I did not expect it.'

'We are not all brutes, Miss Lynton. Why should I demand more lives? It would serve no useful purpose. Those people posed no threat to France.' The dark eyes never left her face. 'Now, however, we must deal with quite another matter.'

Emma reached out for Simon's hand. At last they were to learn their fate. These last few precious moments might be all the time she had left with him. Together they moved closer to Piers and Joseph and the tension in the room was palpable.

Lenoir addressed his remarks to Simon first of all. 'Tell me, *monsieur*, if I should offer you your freedom, will you promise not to return to France before the end of this present emergency?'

Simon shook his head. 'I must serve my country if I am asked to do so, so I must refuse.'

'And you gentlemen?' Lenoir turned to Piers and Joseph.

Piers spoke for both of them. 'With regret, *monsieur*, our answer must be the same.'

'Well, at least you are honest men…' He paused. 'What does Miss Lynton have to say to this?'

Emma swung round upon her friends. 'What fools you are!' she cried. 'Will you refuse the chance of freedom?' Her fears for their safety were increasing by the minute.

Simon ignored her words. 'Your offer will apply to Miss Lynton, I hope? She is no enemy of France.'

'I am not thinking of myself,' she told him proudly. 'Whatever your fate, I will stay and share it.'

'That will not be necessary, my dear. I need no convincing that you are no enemy of France. You love this country, do you not?'

'I do!' She caught at his sleeve. 'I hate the bloodshed, but it will not last for ever. Please allow my friends to go! I will try to persuade them to do as you wish.'

He smiled at that. 'My dear child, you would have thought less of them if they had given me their word. Is that not true?'

'I suppose so,' she admitted miserably.

'And you will never turn them from their duty, as I think you know. Today they have proved themselves to be men of honour and I am deeply in their debt. Without the help of Monsieur Avedon, I might not have discovered the true enemy in our midst until more harm was done.'

'So what is to become of us?' Emma asked sadly. 'Perhaps you don't intend to shed our blood, but are we to be imprisoned?'

'Only within the confines of a closed carriage which is waiting at this moment to take you to the docks. There you will board the *Chanterelle*, a vessel due to leave at once for the Spanish port of Cartagena. From there it is no great distance to the British colony of Gibraltar.'

Emma caught at his hand and kissed it. 'How can we thank you?' she cried fervently.

Lenoir's lips curved. 'You might consider staying out of trouble, my dear. It seems to attract you like a magnet. Meantime, you will present my kind regards to your father. I have the greatest admiration for his writing.'

His expression was not so genial as he looked at the three men. 'Don't cross my path again!' he warned. 'Next time you may not be so lucky.' He watched as they walked towards the doorway. 'Farewell!' he called. 'Remember me!'

It was not until they had been some hours at sea that Emma recalled the strangely chilling effect of Lenoir's final words. She stood on deck with Simon's arm about her, watching as the lights of the French coast receded into the distance.

'You are very quiet, my love!' he said. 'Is something troubling you?'

'You will think me foolish, dearest, but I was thinking of Lenoir. Was there not something odd about that strange farewell?'

'Lenoir is a realist, Emma. As the Terror increases in France, there will be no place for moderates. The fanatics will take over, in spite of all his efforts and he knows it.'

'But what will happen to him?'

Simon did not reply.

'Oh, you cannot mean that they will harm him?'

'I fear so. He is aware of it. It is more than likely that he will follow many another to the guillotine.'

'I can't believe it! He is such a noble creature. Who else would have helped us to escape?'

'Who indeed? Had I not heard of his arrival in Marseilles, it would have been difficult to effect a rescue.'

'You knew him then?'

'Shall we say that our paths have crossed before?' He smiled down at her and she knew better than to question him more closely on that subject.

'So how did you persuade him?'

'I heard that he was enquiring into the activities of Chavasse. He was happy to listen to my information.'

Emma hung her head. 'I'm sorry that I tried to persuade you to give him your word that you would not return to France when it was against your principles. Can you forgive me?'

'On that matter, yes. You spoke from love alone. Yet there was another serious incident which gave me cause to doubt you…'

'Oh, Simon, you can't mean it! What can you be thinking of?'

'Just an occasion when I was pushed into the sea from a great height. I tell you, madam, that it was with some misgiving that I agreed to accompany you aboard this vessel. Even now, I fear for my life…'

'You cruel creature! How can you tease me so? I declare, when we reach England, I may consider finding myself another beau.'

'Then let us hope that he will be a stout warrior. I shall fight for you, I warn you.'

Emma lifted her face to his. Her eyes were misty. 'You have already done so, my beloved…' She sighed with happiness as his lips found her own, whilst ahead of them the full moon laid a silver path across the waters of the Mediterranean, pointing the way to a new life for Emma and her love.

*   *   *   *   *

MILLS & BOON®

Live the emotion

Historical
romance™

A MODEL DEBUTANTE by Louise Allen

Before, Miss Talitha Grey had been penniless. Now she'd
inherited a fortune and, thanks to Lady Parry, was to be
launched into society! But Tallie was harbouring a shameful
secret – one that would ruin both herself and the Parry
household if it were discovered. And Lady Parry's nephew –
the gorgeous, *suspicious* Lord Arndale – knew far too much…

THE BOUGHT BRIDE by Juliet Landon

Lady Rhoese of York was an undoubted prize. A wealthy
landowner, she would fill the King's coffers well if one of his
knights were to marry her. Army captain Judhael de Brionne
accepted the challenge. After all, Rhoese was beautiful enough
– albeit highly resentful. Surely he would be able to warm his
ice-cold bride given time?

RAVEN'S VOW by Gayle Wilson

American merchant John Raven had offered the lovely
Catherine Montfort freedom in exchange for marriage – and she
had accepted, despite her father's assertion that he would rather
see the interloping colonial dead than wed to his daughter.
Catherine had expected nothing from Raven – but found herself
wishing for a wedding night for real!

REGENCY

On sale 6th May 2005

*Available at most branches of WHSmith, Tesco, ASDA, Martins,
Borders, Eason, Sainsbury's and all good paperback bookshops.*

Visit www.millsandboon.co.uk

0305/62/MB123

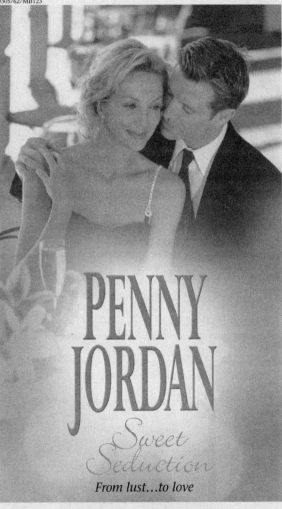

PENNY JORDAN

Sweet Seduction

From lust…to love

On sale 1st April 2005

Available at most branches of WHSmith, Tesco, ASDA, Martins, Borders, Eason, Sainsbury's and all good paperback bookshops.

MILLS & BOON®

**Volume 11
on sale from
7th May
2005**

Lynne
Graham
International Playboys

*A Vengeful
Passion*

2 FREE

BOOKS AND A SURPRISE GIFT!

We would like to take this opportunity to thank you for reading this Mills & Boon® book by offering you the chance to take TWO more specially selected titles from the Historical Romance™ series absolutely FREE! We're also making this offer to introduce you to the benefits of the Reader Service™—

- ★ **FREE home delivery**
- ★ **FREE gifts and competitions**
- ★ **FREE monthly Newsletter**
- ★ **Exclusive Reader Service offers**
- ★ **Books available before they're in the shops**

Accepting these FREE books and gift places you under no obligation to buy, you may cancel at any time, even after receiving your free shipment. Simply complete your details below and return the entire page to the address below. You don't even need a stamp!

YES! Please send me 2 free Historical Romance books and a surprise gift. I understand that unless you hear from me, I will receive 4 superb new titles every month for just £3.65 each, postage and packing free. I am under no obligation to purchase any books and may cancel my subscription at any time. The free books and gift will be mine to keep in any case.

H5ZED

Ms/Mrs/Miss/Mr ....Initials ....

BLOCK CAPITALS PLEASE

Surname ....

Address ....

....

....Postcode..................................

Send this whole page to:
UK: FREEPOST CN81, Croydon, CR9 3WZ